To. Addie

BEST FRIENDS FOREVER

From Mum + Zeva x

Easter 2022.

ALSO BY DAWN GOODWIN

The Accident
The Pupil

BEST FRIENDS FOREVER

DAWN GOODWIN

First published in the United Kingdom in 2019 by Aria, an imprint of
Head of Zeus Ltd

A CIP catalogue record for this book is available from the British Library.

ISBN 9781788549349

Cover design © Charlotte Abrams-Simpson

Aria
c/o Head of Zeus
First Floor East
5–8 Hardwick Street
London EC1R 4RG

www.ariafiction.com

For my best friend

13 May 2012

The rain pelted against Vicky's bedroom window, the storm outside in full voice, moaning and clambering at the glass and bricks.

She sat up in her bed, wincing as her brain thudded against her skull. She hadn't realised she'd fallen asleep. An almost empty bottle of red wine on her bedside table glared at her accusingly. Next to it, teetering close to the edge, sat a half-full glass, the rim stained with lipstick.

She ran a hand through her matted hair. It was still damp from the rain earlier. Her face felt tight, her eyes dry, whether from the tears or the cold outside, she wasn't sure.

She felt wrung out.

Her phone started ringing, the same insistent chime that had pulled her from unconsciousness moments ago.

The ringing stopped, then started up again almost immediately. She scrambled around for the phone. It was here somewhere. She must've had it in her hand when she fell asleep, but where had she dropped it? She felt around under her pillow and pulled out the vibrating mobile.

She expected to see Anna's name on the screen, but it was a voicemail message. 'Vicky, it's David. You need to call me back. It's Anna. There's been—'

His voice sounded like it had cracked wide open.

But Vicky didn't need to hear what he was saying. She knew.

The truth was out.

'Sorry, I don't want to tell you in a message like this. Call me back. It's Anna. It's Anna…' His voice petered out.

Vicky listened to the message again, her body cold, her stomach hollow.

She scrolled through her recent calls. She had called Anna four times tonight, sent her countless WhatsApp messages. None of them had been read. No little blue ticks showing that she was just being aired.

She looked back through the messages. What had she said in them? Her eyes tripped over the typed words and emojis.

She had to call David back. It would look strange if she didn't. Maybe it wasn't as bad as she thought.

She drained the glass of wine, then refilled it with the last of the bottle. Guilt was giving her quite a thirst. A single, red drop of wine ran down the stem of the glass. Vicky watched its progress, then wiped it away with a trembling finger before it reached the bottom.

She hit redial. It rang for a second before David answered. 'Vicky.' He sounded strange, like a deflated balloon, his voice cavernous.

'David, I'm so sorry. I don't know what to say—'

'You know already? Who told you?'

'I – er…'

He cut her off. 'What am I going to do without her? What are the kids going to do?'

'We can work it out, David.'

'I told her not to drive that death trap of a car. I offered to trade it in. But she wouldn't listen. She kept saying it was the one thing her dad had given her in between stepmothers that she couldn't part with. Now look. It's killed her.'

'What?'

'With the rain and the terrible suspension, she must've – I don't want to think about that. I have to explain it to the kids, call her father. Jesus.'

Vicky's brain scrambled to hold onto the words he had said. 'She's dead?'

'I know, I can't believe it either. I keep expecting the police to come back and say it was a mistake. Someone else had been driving. Even that it was a sick joke. Anything but this.'

'She's dead.'

'I have to go. I just… thought you should know. I'm sorry.'

'David, wait! What—' But he was already gone.

Vicky stared at the reflection looking back at her from the mirror across the room.

What had they done?

I

David opened the fridge and stared at the jars and bottles, bags of limp lettuce and neatly stacked Tupperware boxes. Casseroles, lasagnes, cottage pie, all donated with sympathy. Or pity.

He couldn't remember what he was looking for. He stood, his mind blank, his hand clutching the handle and the cold air tickling his face. His eyes fell on a half-eaten jar of lemon curd on the top shelf.

Anna loved lemon curd on sourdough toast. He had always hated the texture of it. Now the jar would never be finished. He grabbed it and flung it hard across the room. It hit the blue mosaic tiles on the kitchen wall and shattered, the yellow gloop sticking like snot.

He sunk to the ground, his back against the fridge, as sobs wrenched from his gut.

The fridge began to beep, outraged at being left open for so long, but David stayed on the floor, his chest heaving, watching the lemon curd ooze down the tiles Anna had chosen.

Minutes passed and he knew he should get up but willing his legs to move was beyond him. His eyes flicked to the clock above the kitchen doorway. The kids would be home any minute. That thought alone propelled him to his feet, a little unsteadily. He swiped at his wet cheeks and sniffed loudly.

Stepping over the mess, he headed into the hallway, then up the stairs, every step laboured. The sun streamed into the corridor at the top of the stairwell, pushing with insistence through the open door of the main bedroom, desperate for him to notice, but he merely walked through it and sat heavily on the bed. He needed to pull himself together, splash water on his face, plaster on a mask that would convince his kids he was in control. Someone needed to be – for them.

His eyes flicked to the bedside table. Anna's belongings were neatly stacked next to her alarm clock. On the day after the accident, her alarm had gone off at 6.30 a.m. as it always did and he had simply lain in the empty bed after a sleepless night, letting the cheerful banter of the radio DJs wash over him, disbelieving, hoping she was already downstairs.

She wasn't.

Now, his eyes ran over the box of tissues, the tiny china bowl where she put her jewellery each night, a couple of hairbands with strands of her dark hair clinging to the elastic, and the pile of books, neatly stacked, spines facing out the way she liked it. A complete contrast to his side where used tissues lay amid a jumble of magazines, pens, spare change and a book he had been trying to get into for months, lying open, face down, the spine cracked.

David picked up the book Anna had been reading and scanned the back of it. A woman with a secret who was trying to put her past behind her and make it as a writer apparently. He remembered Anna saying how good it was, her face a mask of concentration when she was reading. The corner of a page close to the end was turned over. She had almost finished it. Now she would never get the chance to see how it ended, what the big secret actually was. Maybe he should read it instead. He got to his feet and placed it carefully on his own bedside table, then straightened up the magazines, stacked the books, balled up the used tissues and scooped the spare change into his pocket, trying to mirror the other side of the bed where dust was starting to settle.

It had been four weeks since the accident.

Four weeks since he had lost his wife.

Lost was a funny word for death. He knew where she had been, but wasn't sure where she had gone. She certainly wasn't here. So yes, she was lost. And so was he.

He walked into the en suite bathroom and flushed the tissues away, then flushed the evidence of his tears away too, the water like a cold slap on his cheeks.

The doorbell chimed downstairs and he inhaled deeply, exhaled slowly and went to greet his children.

His mother had said it would be less confusing for them if they returned to school as soon as possible. A routine would help them cope, she'd said. He wasn't sure if it was working or not. They were quiet a lot of the time. Understandable, considering the bottom had dropped out of their small world. The one constant, the woman who was their everything, was suddenly gone and, at the ages of five and seven, they were facing a future without her. The thought made him want to weep again, but he was now at the door and it was opening and they were in front of him, their eyes wide and their smiles a ghostly reflection of their mother.

'Hi guys! How was school?'

He hugged them close to him before they dumped their book bags and headed into the kitchen, on the hunt for after-school sustenance. He followed them with his eyes, then turned to his mother. 'How were they today?'

Louisa Price gently placed a warm hand on her son's cheek. 'They were fine, David, they were fine,' she said before following her grandchildren down the hallway.

A moment later, her voice reached him where he was still standing, head down. 'What on earth happened in here?'

David sat at the kitchen table, staring into a cup of coffee while his mother cleaned up the bits of broken jam jar. She was rambling away while she worked, the words a jumble of sounds and syllables without meaning. The kids had plonked down in front of the television in the lounge as soon as they'd shed their coats and the canned TV laughter now added to the white noise in his ears. They weren't joining in the laughter though. Harper and Lewis hadn't laughed in weeks.

'Nanny, I'm hungry,' Lewis whined from the other room.

'I'll be there in a minute,' Louisa called back, wincing as she got to her feet, the wet cloth clenched in her fist. David could feel her eyes on the back of his neck, but carried on staring hypnotised into the coffee.

'Did you hear what I said?' Louisa said gently as she rinsed the cloth at the sink.

He looked up then. 'Hmm?'

'About the Olympics torches they have to make for school?' Her sigh was almost inaudible. 'Let me get them a snack, then we need to talk.' She rummaged in the fridge, pulling out ham, cucumber and carrots.

David watched her for a moment, then got to his feet and headed towards the French doors and out into the lukewarm June air. He breathed deeply, feeling the weight of claustrophobia lift a little. Not for the first time, he felt the urge to run. He didn't know where he would go, but his feet burned to start running and not stop, to keep going until he couldn't breathe, couldn't think, couldn't feel any more. But a faint whisper in his ear told him he couldn't outrun this.

Louisa found him there five minutes later, his hands clenched in tight fists, staring out at the grey sky.

She approached his rigid back carefully. 'David?'

He didn't respond, so she reached out a hand and touched his shoulder lightly. 'Come. Come and sit with me a moment.' She led him over to the patio table, ignoring the streaks of dirt and dead leaves that littered the glass surface, symptomatic of the hangover of winter. She pulled out a chair and dusted a cobweb from the seat before he fell into it, the weight on his shoulders dragging him down.

She paused, then crouched in front of him. 'David, look at me.'

It took a moment before he met her stern gaze.

'It's time to pull yourself together.'

'What?' He moved to get to his feet again.

'No, listen to me. You need to hear this.'

Her voice had that tone from his childhood, when he needed reining in for some misdemeanour or other. Except this time he hadn't done anything wrong.

'David, it's been a month and I know that's not long, but…' She sighed. 'Nothing I say is going to help you right now, but those two beautiful children in there need their father more than ever and you're not here. I've been where you are. When your father died, I wanted to curl into a ball and shut everything out, but I couldn't. I had you and your sister to think about and that helped me through, gave me the strength to carry on.' She smoothed his hair like she used to when he was little. 'I'm not helping you by being here. It's time for you to start healing and getting on with the job of being a parent, scary as that is on your own. So tomorrow I'll return home and you can start creating a new routine with the kids, maybe think about getting back to work, even part-time? Besides, Joyce next door has had enough of looking after Charlie and his smelly litter tray. She's threatening to evict him. What do you say?'

He didn't say anything at first, but a barrage of emotions flittered across his face. Then Lewis burst out of the open door, tears streaming down his face.

'Nanny, Nanny! Harper says I can't watch *Peppa Pig*!'

Louisa got to her feet, her knees creaking as she did, and hugged Lewis to her before heading indoors to resolve yet another situation, exhaustion evident in the wrinkles on her brow. David watched her go, his thoughts whirling.

A vibration in his pocket distracted him and he pulled out his mobile to read the text that had come through. Probably another message of condolence, people offering their empty wishes and shallow promises of 'anything we can do to help'. There were less of them with every passing day.

> Been thinking of you a lot lately and hope you're bearing up ok. Was wondering if I could come and see the kids sometime? I'm always happy to help if you need some time to yourself. Call me? Vicky

He read the text again, then slipped the phone back into his pocket before following his mother indoors. She was sitting on the couch between Harper and Lewis, her arms hugging them close as they stared at an episode of *The Octonauts*, a compromise apparently reached. He watched her for a moment, suddenly realising how much she seemed to have aged in the last few weeks.

Hadn't they all?

He returned to the kitchen, made a cup of Earl Grey tea in a fine bone china cup, added a spoon of sugar and a dash of milk, just the way she liked it, then returned to the lounge and placed the cup on the coffee table in front of her.

She smiled at him, her brow furrowed.

'You're right. It's time. I can't thank you enough for everything, for being here, but I need to start doing this on my own. So, Chinese for your last night?'

Her smile was full of pride, worry and love, and his gut clenched as he walked away to find a takeaway menu.

2

Vicky felt nervous as she rang the doorbell, which was silly because this house had been her second home for so long. But that was when Anna still lived in it. Vicky had known David a long time, but you could count on one hand the occasions they'd spent time alone.

She'd seen him at the funeral, of course. Not that she could remember much about it. She'd self-medicated with vodka in order to get through it. But she had been struck by how broken David had looked and she hadn't known what to do with that. She wasn't entirely sure what she had expected. He'd always been such a physical presence before, so to see him decimated, like an empty husk, had been a shock. Then her focus had shifted to Lewis and Harper, wide-eyed in their sombre, stiff outfits chosen specially for the occasion, and he had fallen out of her consciousness.

After that, it became harder to call him, ask him how he was, take that first step of reconnecting, especially as she was quietly battling with the gaping hole left in her own life. Anna had been her constant companion since they were thirteen years old, their only time apart being the university years when Anna had gone off to make something of herself (and meet David) while Vicky stayed behind and watched, an eyewitness to Anna's much more exciting and privileged life. In those days, she had hoped that Anna would return to her; this time she knew without a doubt that she wouldn't.

The only reason she had texted David last week was because the gnawing ache inside her couldn't be ignored any more. She needed to maintain a connection to Anna somehow because without that, she felt like she was falling into a hole that she couldn't claw her way out of, so she'd sent a tentative text. He hadn't replied straightaway and she had tried not to read too much into it. But of course, she had analysed it endlessly, kicked herself for being too forward. The usual.

His reply came the next day. A simple message:

We're okay. Kids would love to see you. David

She'd replied suggesting the following weekend when she didn't have the dirt of a workday on her skin and they didn't have the weight of school hanging over them.

And here she stood, her shaky knees clad in clean jeans that hung a little looser thanks to the most effective diet there is: grief. Anna would be pleased at that at least. Vicky's hand hesitated over the doorbell, then she squared her shoulders, adjusted the heavy bag in her hand and pressed the buzzer.

The house next door had a Team GB flag attached to the aerial of their car. It flapped and twisted with the rise and fall in the breeze. Olympics fever was starting to grow, even though the opening ceremony was still weeks away. Vicky wasn't all that interested and figured the excitement would peter out before long.

The door was flung open almost immediately by Harper, who rushed at her legs with force.

'Hey, Bug! Wow, I've missed you! You okay?' Vicky dropped the bag to the floor and knelt down to hug her back. As she released her, she felt a smaller body climb onto her back. 'Lou-Lou! There you are!' Lewis hugged her tightly around the neck, threatening to cut off her air supply, but she didn't mind at all. She felt her heart lift a notch for the first time in a month as pure love flooded through her for her godchildren.

'So am I coming in then?' The kids squealed in delight and dragged her inside.

'Daddy, Daddy! Vix is here!' She followed their rushed footsteps into the lounge and pulled up short. David was sitting on the edge of the couch, his hair on end. He looked up at her with a wan smile and got to his feet, looking as though it was a feat of endurance to do so. 'Vicky, lovely to see you.' He approached her with his arms outstretched and she leaned into him briefly, then subtly pulled away before the coarse stubble on his unshaven face made contact.

The David she knew was a man of substance. Anna used to joke that he had more potions and oils in their bathroom cabinet than she did. He was always impeccably groomed and dressed neatly, with a heady scent of aftershave swirling around him that made you want to lean in and breathe deeply.

The man standing in front of her now looked like he hadn't set foot in a shower for days.

'Coffee? Tea?' he asked before retreating in the direction of the kitchen, his bare feet shuffling beneath his tracksuit bottoms. She watched him go, open-mouthed.

The kids jumped around her excitedly, talking at once, wanting to show her stuff, asking if they could play a game.

'Hey, hey, guys, slow down! I'm here for a while, so cool your boots. Now, I may or may not have some stuff in this bag for you.' They launched at the bag in her hand, but she held them back. 'But… let's help Daddy with the tea, then I'll show you, okay?'

The kids charged into the kitchen. Vicky took a breath and looked around her. Every surface seemed littered with mugs, plates, abandoned socks and empty food packets. There were crumpled beer cans lying on the coffee table and a pizza box in the corner of the room, greasy with cheese. The air was musty and stale.

She followed them slowly into the kitchen, noting as she passed the dining room table littered with rice-crusted Indian takeaway containers, some with fat flies the colour of fresh bruises feasting on the remnants.

The kitchen was no better. David had his back to her and was rummaging in the cupboards for a clean mug.

'Why don't I wash us a mug each?' she said cautiously.

He had the good grace to blush as he looked around. 'I've been a bit busy. It's kinda full on around here,' he said in a low voice. He fell into one of the brightly painted wooden chairs at the round kitchen table in the corner of the room and pushed away a used cereal bowl. Milk slopped over the rim.

'I can see that.' She looked around again, then said to the children. 'Right, you two. It's never too early to learn how to load a dishwasher. If you want to see what's in my bag of tricks, then you need to help Daddy by bringing all the dirty dishes you can find and helping me to put them in this dishwasher, okay? Think of it like a little treasure hunt and whoever collects the most gets a special prize from the bag.' They looked at her eagerly and nodded, taking the bait with gusto.

'But carry everything carefully. No prizes for breakages! Start in the lounge. Ready? Go!'

They dashed away. David watched wearily.

'So….' Vicky said as she ran the hot water tap over the sink and grabbed the two mugs nearest to her. 'I won't ask how you're doing.'

'Yeah, best not to.'

'I thought your mum was staying with you?'

'She left last week; told me it was time for me to start getting on with things myself.' He looked around unenthusiastically. 'Doing well, aren't I?'

Lewis returned with his little hands full of plates, the top one threatening to topple from the pile. Vicky grabbed them quickly. 'Keep it up, big guy!' Vicky dumped the dishes on the counter, then high-fived him. He beamed in delight and rushed off again.

She plunged her hands into the hot water and scrubbed the coffee stains from the mugs, unsure what to say next. What came out was, 'I miss her.' She swallowed back the wave of emotion that rushed over her.

'Yeah,' he replied.

She finished rinsing the mugs and grabbed a dishtowel from the counter as Harper appeared with more glasses and cups.

'Right, Bug, Dishwasher Class 101.'

For the next fifteen minutes, Vicky showed the kids how to load the dishwasher, washed more dishes that wouldn't fit, and got Harper and Lewis to collect the takeaway containers into a large rubbish bag. Once everything was cleared and the countertops wiped down, she put the kettle on and called the children over to the table.

'So the results are in… and I can now reveal that the winner of the Chores Challenge is…' She rapped her hands against the table in a mock drumroll. 'Both of you!'

The kids beamed from ear to ear and Vicky noticed out of the corner of her eye that even David cracked a small smile.

'What do we win?' Harper shouted.

Vicky rummaged in the bag at her feet and pulled out two wrapped packages. The one wrapped in Marvel superheroes paper she passed to Lewis and the other, wrapped in bright red watermelon paper, she passed to Harper. They immediately ripped into the parcels, revealing sticker books, colouring pens, modelling clay and craft packs – enough to keep them occupied for a while.

'What do you say, kids?' David said quietly.

'Thank you,' they chorused and rushed at her again for hugs.

'Ah, but there's more…' She reached into the bag again and brought out a bakery box. 'I have afternoon tea for us all! You know how much your Aunty Vix loves cake.

Now, how about you head into the dining room and start on those sticker books and I'll get some plates?'

She watched them go with a smile.

'You're always so good with them,' David said.

'Well, the way things are going, they're the only kids I'm going to have and I love them like my own. Now, how about that cuppa?'

She busied herself with making the tea and putting out plates, feeling the silence stretch and mould heavily around them and wondering how best to fill it once the roil and bubble of the kettle had stilled.

'I had such a funny thing happen to me this morning. I was in New Look trying on a jumpsuit and it had this long zip up the back. Anyway, I should've gone for a size bigger than I did, but I've lost a bit of weight, so I thought I could squeeze into it.' She knew she was babbling, but she couldn't help it. 'It was too small, of course, but when I tried to take it off, the zip was stuck and wouldn't go down. I wrestled with it for a good ten minutes, sweating like mad, and thought I would have to call someone to help me. Mortifying! Luckily, it came open in the end, but if Anna had been there, she'd have killed herself laughing...' Vicky's voice trailed off and she cringed into the mugs she was filling. She put the kettle down and turned back to David. 'Oh god, I am so sorry, bloody insensitive. I just... she would've liked that story.'

David looked tortured for a moment, then a smile ghosted across his lips. 'You're right, she would've laughed. You're not being insensitive. That's the thing. She's still everywhere. Everywhere I look, every cupboard I open.' He looked around the room as though he could see her.

'And will be for a long time, maybe forever. I feel it too. I keep wanting to text her or call her and then I remember and—' She stopped and turned back to the tea. 'Of course, it's harder for you than anyone else.'

'You look good though, Vix.'

The compliment warmed her from her toes. 'From the neck down, maybe,' she replied with a chuckle.

She carried the mugs over to where he was sitting, his eyes vacant. Pulling out a chair, she said, 'How are you really doing?'

He didn't answer, just stared into space, as though he could see Anna standing in front of him, could reach out and touch her.

Vicky went to speak again, but he said, 'It's like I know I should be doing stuff, you know? Like cooking, making sure they're eating right, washing, tidying up, because I know that's what she would've wanted me to do, but I can't. My brain is telling me to get up and do it, but my body is refusing. But I also don't want anyone else doing it. I got rid of the au pair because it felt wrong having her here. It felt *intrusive*. Does that make sense? Or do I just sound like a man who is slowly losing it?'

'No, you sound like a man who has just lost his wife. I know it's hard. I feel like someone has ripped off one of my limbs.' She looked at him closely. 'Maybe you need to talk to someone?'

He sighed and ran his hands through his hair. 'I've been given information on support groups, therapists, all of it, but how is talking about it, about *her*, how I'm feeling, how sad I am, going to bring her back?'

'It won't, but it will help you feel less… lonely, I guess?' She reached out and placed her hand on his arm. 'Look, none of this is easy and I'm no expert, but I do have an inkling of what you're feeling because I feel it too. I've known Anna longer than I've known myself really. She was a constant for me since we were teenagers and …' She swiped at her nose, not wanting to start crying in case it set him off, conscious of the little people in the dining room who didn't need to see the grown-ups in the kitchen falling apart. 'You can talk to me, if it helps? We used to spend hours talking and, well, just because she's gone, it doesn't mean you've lost me too. I think—'

She was interrupted by Harper and Lewis rushing into the kitchen, sticker books flapping.

'Is the cake ready?' they chimed in unison.

She watched David closely for a second, then said, 'Coming right up.'

She placed the bakery boxes in the middle of the kitchen table, along with the plates. The boxes were full of brownies, custard slices, gingerbread men and iced buns – enough sugar to help them momentarily forget the sourness in their lives. 'What do you fancy? A little bit of everything?'

The four of them sat together, the only sounds coming from licking lips and fingers. Vicky noticed that David hardly touched the brownie she had put on his plate. She pushed her own custard slice away, Anna's voice echoing in her ear. *A moment on the lips, Vicky…*

'So how is school going, guys?'

'Fine,' Harper replied. 'Our teacher is reading *Charlotte's Web* to us in class.'

'I used to love that one. What about you, Lewis?'

'Okay.'

'Just okay?'

'Yeah.'

'You must be getting excited for the Olympics. Are you doing lots of stuff about it for school?'

'Yeah, we made torches last week,' he replied unenthusiastically.

'Sounds fun.' Vicky frowned. 'Has something happened that you want to tell me about?'

Lewis prodded at the icing on his bun, making it squish under his finger. Vicky waited, watching him closely. Eventually he said in a mousey voice, 'Connor's mum helped him make his torch. It was really cool, with bright orange flames and gold paint and everything. Mine was rubbish and he laughed at it. Then he asked me why I don't have a mum any more.'

Vicky flicked her eyes at David, but he was glaring at his plate.

'Well, it's not that you don't have a mum. You will always have a mum. It's just that she's not able to be here with us right now, but she's with us in our hearts and our memories and in a million other little ways.' She paused, considering his small, round face. 'Sometimes, I think that I can see her when it's raining and there's a rainbow outside, or when I hear the ice cream van tinkle down the street and it sounds like the way she used to laugh. Or when I hear the *EastEnders* theme tune, because she used to hum it to you when you were a baby. So next time Connor asks something like that, you tell him that your mum is the most special one of all because you carry her with you in your heart.'

David launched to his feet, propelling his chair onto the tiles with a clatter, and stalked from the kitchen.

Vicky watched him go, feeling her cheeks burn. Had she said too much? Gone too far? She should've let David answer. He was probably pissed off at her for stepping on his parenting toes.

She reached out a hand and caressed Lewis's cheek, then said, 'Those buns won't eat themselves.' He smiled, his moment of sadness dissolving into the icing on his lips. She watched the two of them for a moment longer before saying, 'Back in a minute.'

She found David in the lounge, sitting rigidly on the couch, his hands clasped into fists between his knees and his jaw tense.

'I'm so sorry, David. I shouldn't have jumped in there with Lewis.'

He looked up at her with red-rimmed eyes. 'No, no, you said all the right stuff. I'm just... I was supposed to help him with that stupid torch project and I didn't. Harper did it with him on her own. How shit is that?' He stared down at the floor. 'I wish I knew what to say like you do. I don't know what to say to them. I can feel them pulling away from me. Anna would be fucking furious with me.'

'She'd be more furious with me for letting them eat all that sugar and fat in there!'

He smiled a little. 'I've missed having you around, Vix.'

'Me too.' She sat next to him. 'Listen, I've been thinking. I've got loads of leave to take at work – if you need help with the kids, I could take some time off, come and help you, get them off to school, help around the house, that kind of thing. For a little while, anyway.'

'Thanks Vix, but I need to do this, I need to sort myself out. Anna would want me to step up.'

'Okay, well, if you change your mind, you know where I am. Why don't you go and lie down for a bit and I'll entertain the kids? Go on, you look like you need it.'

She watched him as he dragged himself from the room.

Vicky spent the rest of the afternoon doing crafts with the kids, her fingers sticky with playdough and her sleeves dabbed with paint. David reappeared some hours later when she was reheating a casserole she'd found in the freezer.

They had a quiet dinner together, then she bathed Lewis and Harper and put them to bed. David remained in the lounge; his vacant stare fixed unseeing on a football game.

'I'm gonna go, but if you need anything, just shout, yeah?' she said from the lounge doorway as she shrugged into her coat.

'Thanks, Vix, you've been a godsend today. It's done wonders for the kids.'

She came over to him, hesitated, then gave him a light kiss on the cheek. 'Anytime. Anna would expect nothing less of me.'

As she closed the front door behind her, she paused, chewing on her lip. Then she headed off in the direction of the train station.

Dear Anna,

It's weird to write that. We haven't written letters to each other since you went to university. I suppose it's not the done thing any more. We've certainly sent enough texts and emails to each other – lots of emojis, single lines and abbreviated words, which I used and you hated. Always such a stickler for good grammar.

And now we've come full circle, back to letter writing, but only because I really want to talk to you and can't think of another way of doing it. Because you're not here any more. You're at best floating around, looking down on us and probably laughing at how badly we're getting on with things. If you're up there, of course. No guarantees on that.

At worst, you don't know anything about this because you're in a box, feeling nothing.

Who knows? Death is funny that way. We don't know what we should be afraid of, but we are.

I hope you're not afraid any more. I imagine you were that night. The night you died. I imagine you were terrified.

So to make me feel better – less guilty? – I'll write everything down for you, so that you can finally get an inkling of what it was like to be 'Anna's friend' for all these years. Since no one will read these, I can be as brutally honest about Perfect Anna as I want and say all the stuff I wish I'd said to your face all this time. What's the worst that can happen? Are you going to haunt me?

You see, being your best friend was hard. It was the highest of highs and the lowest of lows. You could make me feel a million pounds, then cut me to ribbons with one withering comment.

You knew you could do that. You enjoyed it.

And I let you because there was always the chance of a high. Those chances were few and far between towards the end though, weren't they?

I went to see David today. I left it a while, I know. Four weeks. But I wasn't sure if I should get in touch with him or if it would be weird, seeing him without you. It was awkward to start with, but you'll be pleased to hear the kids are okay. Well, as much as can be expected. He's fired the au pair, so no chance of him shagging her in your absence.

He's not okay. The place was a mess. Takeaway boxes piled up, dishes unwashed – he looks unwashed, to be honest. Smells a bit too. You'd be horrified. I swept through the place as best I could and spent some time with Lewis and Harper. I said I'd go back and see them again because I think you'd want me to keep an eye on them for you. Wouldn't you?

On the way home, I went past your grave and left some carnations for you. I know you hate carnations, but that's why I did it. Because you'd hate it.

Because the truth is, I'm fucking angry at you.

I told you what would happen. I warned you. But you wouldn't listen.

Vix xx

September 1986

Vicky pulled at the fraying sleeves of her jumper, trying to tuck the edges in so that no one would see the damage to her second-hand uniform. Everyone else looked immaculate. It was morning break on the first day of term and she was still trying to find her way around the girls' school without drawing attention to herself. There were students everywhere, chatting, laughing, running, shoving. She stood alone in the corner, watching from beneath her lashes.

How the hell had she ended up here? It was the local comp, but from a different world to what she was used to. She had moved to Twickenham with her dad over the summer to be closer to her nan after her mother had died, but the girls here spoke with rounded vowels and had clean, neat fingernails instead of long, painted talons and a predilection for profanity.

She needed to pee, but couldn't remember where the toilets were. She recognised two girls from her class walking towards her. 'Excuse me, um, can you tell me where the toilets are please?' she asked quietly, red warmth spreading over her cheeks.

They stopped and stared, their eyes drawn to her fraying cuffs. One of them, her hair pulled so tightly into a high ponytail that her eyes looked taut, scowled at her. 'You're that new girl, aren't you?'

'Yeah, that's right.' Vicky stared straight back at them.

The two girls shared a look, then ponytail girl said, 'Sure, you just go along that main corridor through there and all the way to the end, down the stairs and then follow that corridor around to the right. You can't miss it.' Then they walked away, giggling behind their hands.

Vicky frowned, not sure whether they were winding her up or not, but the pressure on her bladder decided the matter for her.

She walked quickly along the corridor against the flow of traffic streaming into the playground. No one took any notice of her. Ahead of her she could see the stairs the girl had mentioned. She clattered down them, ignoring the fact that it was getting darker and quieter the further she descended.

She reached the bottom, trying to remember which way they'd said to turn. She turned right. The corridor was deserted, and smelled damp and musty. Maybe she'd gone the wrong way. It was really dark too, with no windows to break up the cold, bare walls. Just as she was about to turn around and head back, she noticed a small doorway at the end. She pushed it open and peered into the half-light. It was a bathroom, but it looked derelict. The sinks were yellowing, a tap dripped continuously, and the air smelt of mildew and urine.

Wow, they could really do with updating the toilets at this school.

However, she didn't have much of a choice but to rush into one of the cubicles, her bladder now straining to let itself go. She slammed the cubicle door behind her and locked it hastily. There was no toilet seat, but she didn't have time to try the next stall along. She hoisted up her skirt, dropped her knickers and adopted a hovering squat position just in time, sighing audibly with relief.

What she hoped was dirty water pooled around her new school shoes and the base of the toilet. The cubicle walls were covered with the usual graffitied filth about teachers, schoolgirls long since gone and rude suggestions. The obligatory spitting penis drawing; initials in crude hearts; and someone called Sharon taking the bulk of the vitriol in this stall. She was clearly popular with the boys. Vicky wondered where Sharon was now, if she was still a student or if she had been driven out by spiteful tongues.

Vicky finished just as her thighs were beginning to burn. Morning break wasn't long and she could hear the bell ringing for them to return to class. She tugged on the lock, but it was stiff. Putting some muscle into it, she tugged again, but it refused to budge. Using both hands, she pulled and pushed in case she was turning it the wrong way, but it was stuck tight.

Panic started to itch at her throat. She looked around frantically. There was no gap above the door and the gap below was too small to crawl under. No window either.

No way of escape.

She hammered on the door with her fist, pushing and punching as though sheer brute force would make a difference. Sweat soaked into her blouse and she started to cry in frustration.

What felt like a lifetime passed. She couldn't even sit on the toilet lid because there wasn't one. Instead, she rested her forehead on the dirty wooden door, ignoring the splinters of wood pricking her skin as the tears subsided. Crying wouldn't help, but shouting might, mortifying as it would be if someone found her in such a state.

'Help, is anyone there? Help!'

Then she started to scream. Maybe that would bring someone running.

After five minutes, her throat was red raw and she was starting to think she would be here for the rest of the day. Surely someone would need the toilet soon?

Just as she was about to resume shouting, she heard the bathroom door creak open.

'Hello?' she shouted. 'Is anyone there? I'm locked in!'

'Are you Vicky?' a voice replied.

'Yes!'

'There's a trick to the latch. You have to push the door up and back while pulling the lock hard to the left. That should do it. Not that anyone uses these toilets any more because they're so disgusting.' Her voice was lilting with a posh twang.

Vicky did as she was told and yanked on the door as the lock flew open. Standing in front of her was a tall, pretty girl who she recognised from her class. She was smiling sympathetically.

'Thanks,' Vicky mumbled.

'No problem. Mrs Babel sent me to look for you when you didn't turn up for registration. I overheard that bitch

Sophie telling Tracey that she and Maya told you to come down here. They are such cows, those two. They know that no one uses these loos. I'm Anna Maxwell, by the way.'

'God, I'm so embarrassed,' Vicky said as they made their way out of the bathroom and back along the corridor.

'Hey, don't worry about it. We'll get them back. I've been looking forward to getting one over on those two witches for ages. Let them laugh at you today, but revenge is a dish best served cold.'

'Huh?' Vicky stopped in the corridor.

'Meaning we let them have their fun for today, but just when they think we've forgotten all about it, we'll get them back when they least expect it. You've got me on your side now.'

Vicky studied the slim, leggy girl next to her, with her beautifully glossy dark hair and clear skin. 'Why?'

'What?'

'Why would you be on my side? You don't even know me.'

'I may not know you, but I hate them. So I'm gonna side with you on this one. Besides, it'll be fun getting them back. I like a bit of drama.' Her eyes were glinting like steel. 'What do you say, Vicky?'

She held out a tiny hand to Vicky, who hesitated, then smiled and shook it. 'I say you're on.'

Three months later, Sophie and her friend Maya were expelled for putting laxatives in Mrs Babel's coffee during breaktime, resulting in her having a particularly embarrassing toilet accident during afternoon registration. Although they both denied any wrongdoing, empty laxative packets were found in their schoolbags – and the final nail in their coffin was the witness statements from both Vicky and Anna, who apparently saw them stirring something into the teacher's coffee and laughing when it was left unattended on Mrs Babel's desk. No one thought to check Anna's bag for the rest of the box of laxatives or the receipt from the chemist.

Mrs Babel was too traumatised to return to work.

3

'Fuck!' David shouted as he stood on a stray piece of Lego lying abandoned in the middle of the lounge carpet. He threw himself onto the couch, muttering under his breath and waiting for the nausea to subside.

He shouldn't have had all that whiskey last night. The bottle was still sitting on the coffee table, its emptiness taunting him. But once the kids had finally gone to bed, not without a lot of shouting from him and a few tears from them, that was when the silence got to him. The unmoving air of the empty room pressed down and cloyed at him, no matter how loud he turned up the television. So he'd filled a tumbler with whiskey and let the alcohol create the illusion that she was here with him, sitting beside him with her cold feet tucked under his legs, passing scathing criticisms of the reality TV fuckwits on the screen in front of them. It was like a poor CGI imitation of the real thing flickering in front of his eyes, but growing in clarity with every shot of whiskey, until one too many had knocked him into a blissful, unconscious sleep.

Now he was regretting it. He held his throbbing head in one hand and rubbed the sole of his foot absently with the other. He could hear cartoons screaming from the TV in the kitchen, Harper and Lewis quiet for now, their eyes glued to animated characters hitting ten bells out of each other against a background of fake laughter.

He rested back in the seat and caught a whiff of grease that made his stomach lurch. The coffee table was littered once again with empty takeaway boxes. He looked away, disgusted, but couldn't summon the energy to get up and clear them into the bin. He closed his eyes and let the noise lull him into a thin sleep.

He woke with a start. Lewis stood in front of him, poking him with his finger. 'Daddy.'

'Yeah, what is it?'

'I'm hungry.'

'You're always hungry.'

Lewis stared at him with wide eyes.

'Fine. Let's see what I can find.' He struggled to his feet, the nap having done nothing to alleviate the banging behind his eyeballs.

At least he remembered to step over the Lego this time.

He peered into the fridge, found very little that was edible apart from some mouldy cheese, wrinkly apples and bottles of beer, then rummaged in a cupboard.

'Spaghetti shapes on toast do you? What time is it anyway?'

He looked over at the clock above the oven. 12.04 p.m. Bloody hell, where had the day gone? How long was he asleep? The kids had been watching TV since they'd got up at 7am.

He needed to give himself a shake, get to the shops, find some proper food, at least get them out into the fresh air. Maybe he should take them to McDonalds for lunch on the way to the supermarket.

'I know, let's go out for lunch. How about chicken nuggets from McDonalds? I'll even spring for a milkshake.'

Lewis's face lit up. 'Harper! Harper! We're going to McDonalds!!' He rushed from the room.

'Get your shoes and coats on. Chop, chop!' David shouted after him.

He wandered back into the lounge, rubbing the sleep out of his eyes.

'FUCK!' he screamed as he stood on the Lego again. He picked up the offending weapon and threw it hard across the room. It pinged harmlessly off the wall. Anger seethed through him. He grabbed the empty whiskey tumbler and pitched that after the Lego, the glass shattering into tiny fragments.

'Why can't you pick up after yourselves? You lazy little sh—' He stopped as he saw Harper's face cowering in the doorway, her eyes wide and fearful. He took a shaky breath. Then another.

'I'm sorry, Daddy is just a little cross right now because I've stood on that piece of Lego twice. And it hurts. A lot.' He exhaled again, plastered a rictus smile on his face. 'Ready to go?'

'What about the glass, Daddy? Mummy would—'

'Yeah, well, Mummy's not here, is she? Come on, let's go.' *Before I change my mind.*

The kids were quiet in the car. David drove white-knuckled, silently admonishing himself, the look on Harper's face tattooed into his brain. God, he was a mess.

I smell too. Whiskey and sweat. Jesus.

He pulled into the McDonalds car park and waited for a van to vacate a space in front of him. Rummaging in the glove compartment, he found a can of Lynx, gave himself a generous spritz in each armpit, ignoring the coughs from the backseat, then pulled into the now vacated parking space.

Plastering that same smile on his face again – the one he had come to adopt like a permanent mask, a bit like the Joker in the *Batman* films – he got out of the car and opened the door for the kids.

The addictive smell of chips and fried onions made him feel instantly more human as they pushed into the noisy interior of the restaurant. Kids shouted, parents looked glazed and the staff yawned, but there was an underlying energy to the place, probably from all the preservatives in the air. Who said junk food was bad for you?

'Right, what'll it be?' David said, rubbing his hands together.

He recited their order to the disengaged kid working behind the counter. Collecting their tray of boxes, they made their way over to a vacant booth. The kids tucked into their food as though they hadn't eaten in days, as did David, his hangover demanding something salty and greasy. The two Big Macs he'd ordered hardly touched the sides. No one said anything. When every last French fry and nugget was consumed and David had wiped the ketchup from their hands and cheeks, they made their way back to the car and drove over to the supermarket.

David hardly noticed the silence or the tiny voice in his head telling him that it wasn't normal for two small children to be this quiet.

The supermarket was packed with weekend shoppers stocking up on essentials. David had a moment of panic as he realised he had no idea what to get. Anna had sorted all of this before, with her endless grocery and recipe box deliveries. Probably best just to wander the aisles and see what was on offer.

'Hold tight to the trolley and let me know if there's anything you like.'

What did they like? Not only had Anna taken control of the shopping, she'd sorted the cooking too – or had instructed the au pair accordingly.

'Lewis, you don't like tomatoes, do you?'

'I do, especially the little ones.'

'Oh.'

'That's me, Daddy,' Harper replied quietly.

'Okay, well, everyone likes broccoli, right?'

'Neither of us do,' Harper replied. 'Why don't I see what we can get?'

He looked closely at his daughter then, suddenly seeing what she would look like in twenty years' time when she was grocery shopping for her own kids, and felt completely inadequate. He resisted the urge to run from the supermarket, instead saying, 'That would be a huge help, Harps.'

The next half an hour passed quickly as they filled the trolley with fruit, vegetables, cereal and plenty of ready meals and snacking food to get them through an apocalypse. The trolley was overflowing by the time they turned down the last aisle. Most of it was probably stuff Anna would never consider letting them eat. The trolley groaned under the weight of all the additives and preservatives.

A woman was standing at the end of the aisle, studying the back of a bag of frozen tofu intently as David leaned into the ice cream freezer.

'Chocolate, vanilla, strawberry or all three?'

'All three,' Harper and Lewis chorused and the woman turned at the sound of the glee in their voices.

'David!'

He chucked the three tubs into the trolley and turned to look at the woman.

'It's Bea, Anna's friend from book club.'

Who the fuck is this?

'Right, Bea, how are you?'

'More importantly, how are you?' She looked at him beseechingly and rested a hand lightly on his arm.

'We're fine, Bea, thanks.'

'Ah, I do feel for you.' She started to stroke his arm like he was a pet dog in need of affection and he wanted to slap her away. 'Anna was a dear friend and I miss her terribly, so I can't imagine what it must be like for you. Even my husband – you haven't met him, but you should. You'd get on like a house on fire. Anyway, even Tim was distraught when he heard. I didn't think he knew Anna, but apparently they'd done some work stuff together at some point. He couldn't believe it. Distraught, he was. We both said it must be so hard—'

'Yes, I know.' He pulled his arm free. 'Anyway, must crack on.'

Her lips tightened at his ill-disguised snub, then she cast a critical gaze over the trolley.

'Stocking up, I see.'

'Yip.' He started to back away.

'You need to be careful – lots of hidden salts and sugars in that trolley. Anna liked an organic diet for the children.'

'Well, Anna's not here, is she?' he said for the second time that day. He noted Bea's sharp intake of breath and the look of shock on her face with perverse relish, then walked away quickly as guilt pissed all over him.

When they eventually got to a till, David began to unload the trolley onto the conveyor belt on autopilot, keeping his head down for fear of seeing Bea again, with her disapproving glare.

'Do you have any bags?'

'Sorry?'

'Do you have any bags?' the woman manning the till repeated. She was chewing on gum, her teeth gnawing and spittle stringing between her lips.

'Er, no.'

'How many do you want?'

'I don't know. As many as I need.' He could feel anger building again. Stupid bloody question. How should he know?

She stared at him blankly, then handed over a pile of plastic carrier bags.

David rolled his eyes and went back to stacking the groceries.

'Daddy?'

'Yes, Harps?'

'Where's Lewis?'

'What?'

'Lewis? He's not here.'

David looked at her in confusion, then around him. 'Where's he gone?'

'I don't know.'

'But didn't you see him wander off? When last did you see him?'

When last did *he* see him?

'He was there when you were talking to that lady. At the ice cream.' Her lip was quivering.

'Shit. Okay, you carry on doing this. I need you to carefully put all of this onto here so that this lady can add it all up for us, okay?'

Harper looked unsure. The woman behind the till kept chewing, disinterested.

'It's fine, Harps. I'll be back in a minute,' he said, already pushing past the people in the queue behind him, his head swinging from side to side as he headed back to the freezer section. He tried to ignore the hammering in his chest, but panic was making him blind to the faces around him and he couldn't make anything out.

There were no little boys in the freezer aisle, so he weaved into the next aisle, the panic wrapping its fingers around his throat.

He started to shove people, ignoring the shouts of 'hey' and 'watch it!'

Minutes passed as he retraced their steps, his breathing shallow as the panic throttled him.

'Have you seen a little boy anywhere?' he asked a woman examining the back of a chocolate bar.

'Er, no, sorry.'

He didn't wait to thank her, just kept walking.

'Excuse me,' a male voice said behind him.

He turned.

'Are you looking for a boy? Brown trousers and a blue checked shirt?'

Was that what Lewis was wearing? How could David not have noticed what his son was wearing that day?

'Er, yes,' he said.

'I just saw him by the comics in the next aisle.'

'Thanks, thanks.' He sprinted into the next aisle to see Lewis sitting on the floor in front of the comics, his legs folded and his eyes glued to *Spiderman*.

'Lewis!' He grabbed him and hugged him tight, the panic receding a little. 'There you are! What were you thinking? Wandering off like that?'

Lewis looked startled. 'I needed the toilet, so I went to look for it.'

Then David noticed the wet patch on his trousers.

'But you didn't make it, huh?'

Lewis started to cry. 'I'm sorry, Daddy. Please don't shout at me again. I tried to find it on my own.'

David's heart crumbled.

'Hey, little man, it's okay, all forgotten. Hey, tell you what, grab that comic and—' he scanned the shelf in front of him, '—that one there for Harps and we'll forget all about it. Time to go home, I think. Too much excitement for one day.'

Lewis picked up the comics and David scooped him up in his arms, paying no attention to the warm wetness that soaked into his shirt.

He rushed back to the tills, ignoring the disapproving glares from the people in the queue, gave Harper a kiss – 'Proud of you, Harps' – and put Lewis down so that he could start throwing things into the bags. He needed to get out of here. He felt like the walls were closing in on him, as though he couldn't breathe, like every pair of eyes was judging him. He wanted to scream at the lot of them, 'I'm doing my best! Can't you see she's left me and I'm drowning?'

Within minutes they were in the car park, Lewis safe but tightly squeezed into the trolley seat and Harper clinging to the handle with both hands. When they reached the car, he strapped them into their booster seats himself, threw the bags into the boot and climbed behind the wheel. He sat for a moment, feeling his heart hammering and the blood banging in his ears.

He drove home sensibly, not trusting that something else wouldn't happen if he went over the speed limit. Leaving everything in the car, he opened the front door, helped the kids out and took Lewis straight upstairs to change, guilt squirming under his skin like an insect as he dumped the wet clothes in the overflowing laundry basket.

Only half an hour later, with another whiskey in his hand, did he allow himself to think about what had happened. Harper and Lewis were at the dining room table paging through their new comics. He watched them for a moment, then headed into the lounge and closed the door behind him. His hands started to shake and he gulped at the air.

What a fucking disaster. I can't do this.

Tears streamed down his cheeks as he considered all the horrible scenarios that could've come true, each one worse than the last: Lewis running into the car park and getting run over; being taken into care for being allowed to run around a supermarket alone in pee-stained trousers; getting abducted from the ice cream aisle by a lone paedophile, never to be seen again…

The doorbell intruded into his panic attack. He decided not to answer it, his rattled brain immediately jumping to the absurd conclusion that it was Bea coming to berate him for his shocking parenting skills.

The doorbell rang again a few seconds later, then fell silent. He drained his glass, took a few steadying breaths and tried to get himself in check. He had to do better.

The lounge door inched open slowly and Harper's big eyes peered around it.

David swiped at his cheeks. 'Hey, Princess, what's up?'

She came towards him slowly and sat gently on his knee, as though worried she would hurt him. She wrapped her arms around his neck and snuggled into his shoulder.

'Hey, what's up?'

She peered up at him again. 'Where has Mummy gone, Daddy? Since she's not here any more.'

He winced as she repeated his words back at him. 'I'm sorry, Princess, I shouldn't have said that because it's not true.'

'It's not?' Her eyes were wide with expectation.

'No, it's not. Mummy is in heaven, but she's also here—' he put his hand on her heart '—and here—' he put his hand on her forehead '—which means she will always be with us, especially when we need her the most.'

'But I want her here now.' She began to cry.

'I know you do. So do I.' He hugged her tight, not knowing what else to say, not trusting himself to say the right thing.

'Hey, how about we have some of that ice cream we bought?'

Shit, everything is still in the boot of the car, probably defrosting.

'Let me just unpack the shopping and then I'll dish us up some – all three flavours, right?'

She smiled a little and slid from his lap, then curled up in a ball on the cushion next to him.

His heart broke a little more, which surprised him because he thought it was already in a million tiny pieces.

He sloped to the front door, his legs as heavy as his soul, and pulled on the latch. Sitting on the front step was a big bunch of flowers, brightly coloured and fragrant. He looked around, but there was no one there. A card poked out of the top of the arrangement.

David and family,
So sorry for your loss.
Regards,
Sebastian and the team at Tyrion PR

Her boss. David had never liked the smarmy bastard. It was typical of Sebastian to wait until weeks after her death and then hide behind a garish gesture. Better late than never though, he supposed. He picked up the flowers and took them straight over to the rubbish bins at the side of the house, shoving the entire arrangement in as far as it would go.

After unloading the car, packing away the shopping, sweeping up the broken glass from before and clearing the empty takeaway containers from the dining room table, he settled on the couch with Harper and Lewis, bowls of ice cream in their laps and *Finding Nemo* on the TV. While they watched, he pulled his phone from his pocket and scrolled through to Vicky's number.

I need your help. I can't do this alone. David

The answer was almost immediate.

Anna would want me to help as much as I can. I have some leave to take at work, so why don't I come and stay for a few days to help you get back on your feet? For the kids. Vix x

Dear Anna,

David isn't coping, you'll be pleased to hear. We used to have those conversations, do you remember? About how long was a suitable time for your husband to wait before moving on if you died? You used to always say you'd be heartbroken if David got over you too quickly, how you'd haunt him if he replaced you within a year.

Well, no need for any visits from the other side yet, Anna. He's a broken man. You did that to him.

Can you see him from where you are?

I've moved in for a while to help out. Don't worry, I'm not sleeping in your bed or anything. I'm in the spare room, the one done up just in case someone important comes to stay. I don't think anyone else has slept in there since your mother died, have they? Except for me, of course. I've spent a few drunken nights in that bed. I've never known when to stop when it comes to booze. You were the one always in control – of food, drink, men.

The kids are okay though. I think they're enjoying having me around. When I arrived on the doorstep yesterday, it looked like something had exploded in that

house again. Takeaway boxes everywhere, half-empty cups, crusty cereal bowls. I think that's pretty much what they'd been eating since my last visit.

David was in a state. Sounds like he lost Lewis in the supermarket – nothing to worry about, but it shook them all up. He told me a little bit about it over a few glasses of wine last night after I'd put the kids to bed. Lewis was especially clingy, wanting an extra story and an extra hug before he'd let me turn out the light. I said I'd be staying for a bit and that made him feel more secure, I think. He's so much more sensitive than Harper. She's a mini version of you. She has an inner strength and steely determination about her that will help her survive, but Lewis needs some TLC.

That's where I come in. I've said I'll stay for a week and see how it goes. David needs me too. That much is painfully clear.

I may have brought a takeaway with me last night, but I've just been out to buy a recipe book, the basic one by Jamie Oliver, and I'm going to attempt to cook something from scratch for them tonight. It's pretty cold and miserable outside, so a stew or something. I can picture you laughing at me. What could possibly go wrong, right?

Yeah, I know, everything! You were a brilliant cook. I used to hate you for that. The way you could rustle up something out of nothing, cook for a crowd without breaking a sweat, always a domestic goddess.

From the outside, the perfect wife and mother.

I've only ever needed a can of beans and a loaf of bread until now. But I want to do this – for them and for you. To make it up to you. I feel closer to you knowing I'm helping them, knowing I'm filling your shoes in some small way.

I'll let you know how I get on.

Vix x

October 1986

The wind whipped their ponytails as they trudged up Sycamore Road. Vicky was still half asleep and her school bag pressed down on her shoulder right on the spot where a bruise was blossoming. She shifted it to the other shoulder. The mornings were getting darker and colder, but Vicky still preferred autumn to the fake happiness of summer, when everyone put on a smiley face because they felt obliged to if the sun was shining. At least in autumn, everyone could admit everything was shit – and she could keep her jumper on.

Anna was chattering away about some event she had to go to with her parents on the weekend. 'I wish I didn't have to go. My dad's work people are so dull and there's no one else there my age. All he does is flirt with the secretaries and Mother just gets drunk. It's times like these when I wish I had a sister. I wish you could come with me.' She linked her arm through Vicky's.

Since they'd met in what they'd labelled the 'dungeon' bathroom a month ago, the two girls had become firm friends, despite being polar opposites in every way. In fact, the only thing they had in common was that they were both only children. Vicky was surprised to discover that Anna didn't have many friends. Not that she would have pointed that out to Anna, of course. She had also quickly come to realise you didn't want to get on her bad side.

The other Year 7 girls certainly feared Anna, but with a sense of awe and idolisation as they copied her words and style from afar. It was like she was untouchable. She carried herself with an air of quiet confidence that demanded respect and created a force field of power around her that only Vicky had managed to penetrate. Vicky suspected this was because Anna knew not to feel threatened by her, since there was nothing particularly enviable about Vicky. That was fine with her though. She didn't need any other friends. But she did want to impress Anna, so she found herself trying to tone down the crasser side of her personality, cutting out some of the slang she peppered her conversations with, wearing smaller hooped earrings, that kind of thing.

However, Vicky also knew to tread carefully around Anna. Last week, their geography teacher had given Anna detention for not handing in her homework and she'd sneaked into school early the next day and scattered finely ground peanuts all over his desk. The teacher was later seen leaving the school on a stretcher after suffering from anaphylactic shock due to his severe peanut allergy. Anna got out of the detention.

The terraced houses at this end of Twickenham hugged tight to the pavement, most with netted curtains still drawn to the morning and peeling paint betraying front doors that had been slammed more often than not. Two small pint bottles of milk stood to attention on the front step of one of the houses halfway up the hill. The door behind it was painted a garish pillar-box red, one shade too bright to be tasteful.

'Looks like some people are still in bed,' Anna said, indicating the milk.

'Lucky them,' Vicky mumbled.

'I know, right? Not fair.' She'd slowed down as they passed the house.

Vicky tugged on Anna's linked arm. 'Come on, we're going to be late.'

Anna stopped abruptly. 'Vix, sometimes life isn't fair.' Her eyes glinted like ice cubes. 'And I feel it is our duty to act on such imbalances.'

'What are you on about? Come on, I can't get into trouble for being late again. My dad will kill me.'

Anna ignored Vicky's pleas and instead did an about turn to head back towards the red door. Vicky rolled her eyes behind her back.

Anna stopped, looked in both directions, then picked up one of the milk bottles. She pushed her thumb into the foil lid, removed it with a flick of her fingers and casually rolled the full bottle of milk down the street. Milk poured from the neck as the bottle rolled, leaving a white, frothy trail in its wake.

'Anna! What the hell?' Vicky felt brittle beads of anxiety settle in her gut.

'Well, if they're too lazy to get their milk in…' She grinned at Vicky, then held the second bottle aloft.

'Don't! They've paid for that!'

'Stop being a bore, Vix. It's just a joke. I'm trying to make you laugh – you're so grumpy this morning.' Her eyes sparkled as she took the lid off the second bottle. She pulled her arm back to roll it like a bowling ball just as they heard someone pull back the chain on the red door. Anna froze, then flung the bottle hard against the red door. Glass and milk exploded everywhere. Anna took off, grabbing Vicky by the arm and shouting 'Run!' as she fled.

They raced up the hill. Vicky was too scared to turn around. She could hear someone flinging angry words at their backs. Anna flicked a quick glance over her shoulder, then started to laugh loudly and stopped running. Vix stopped too and dared to look back. A tiny, elderly woman in a long floral nightdress and a hairnet was hollering and shaking her fist at them, the rollers in her hair quaking in fury.

Anna merely flicked two fingers at her and took off running again.

Vicky paused, then charged after Anna. She could still hear the woman's rage.

They only slowed once they had put a few streets between themselves and the angry pensioner.

'Wow, she was pissed off!' Anna panted, her eyes fizzing.

'What if she knows who we are? She could tell on us. We're in our bloody school uniforms!' Vicky's heart was still racing, her pulse banging in her throat. The woman had looked vaguely familiar. Vicky swallowed against the sour taste in her mouth.

'She won't! She doesn't have a clue who we are and she's probably half-blind anyway. She was ancient. Woke you up though, didn't it? Should've seen your face! That's what friends are for, Vix.' She grinned. 'Come on, we're going to be late.'

By the time she trudged home later that day, Vicky had forgotten about Anna's stunt that morning. She had a ton of homework, a bag that was sitting too heavily on her bruised shoulder and an empty belly because Anna hadn't felt like eating at lunchtime and didn't want to wait for Vicky while she went to the canteen.

She threw her bag down in the hallway and headed straight into the kitchen. Her dad was sitting at the Formica-topped table, wearing a stained white vest and tracksuit bottoms, a can of beer and a packet of painkillers open in front of him.

'Hey, Dad. How was work?' She opened the fridge and rummaged inside before grabbing a yoghurt pot.

Her dad watched her carefully.

'Everything okay?' she asked.

His eyes narrowed and she felt her stomach drop.

'What is it that I do, Victoria?' He hardly ever called her by her full name, which meant she was in deep shit.

'You drive a taxi,' she replied quietly.

'And when do I do it?'

'Mostly at night.'

'Correct. So when I do get home from the night shift, I like to go to bed and get a good few hours of kip in, don't I?'

'Yes,' she replied, wondering where he was going with this. Her dad had been driving the night shift ever since

Vicky's mum had died unexpectedly the year before. One day she was there and the next she wasn't. She'd been standing in their kitchen, washing up at the sink. When her dad had found her, she was slumped on the floor, her hands still soapy and a pan of soup burning on the stove. A blood clot apparently.

It had taken weeks for Vicky to realise that her mother would never have dinner waiting any more, or give her light kisses on the top of her head as she strolled past, or have her scissors ready whenever Vicky needed her frizzy, unruly hair trimmed. Vicky still found herself thinking about her mum at random moments throughout the day, could feel stray tears prick at her eyes when she heard a song she liked or laughed at something she would've found funny. The smell of gardenia made her catch her breath, a physical reminder of her mother's hand cream.

Now, she and her dad stayed with Vicky's nan, who worked through the day while her dad was home – usually sleeping off the night shift – but was there in the evenings when her dad went to work. A guardian tag team.

'So when I get woken up three hours into my kip by someone banging on the door, I'm not going to be too pleased, am I?'

'No, you aren't.' Vicky suddenly knew where this was going.

Her dad shot out of his chair and grabbed her by her bruised shoulder before shoving her hard into the chair facing him. 'You going to tell me what the hell you were up to this morning?'

'Nothing.'

'Well, an irate Mrs Webster thinks otherwise.'

Vicky frowned. 'How did she know who I was?'

'That's all you're worried about?'

'No, I… er… it was just a joke, a prank, that's all.'

'Mrs Webster is eighty-two years old with a heart condition and a dodgy hip. That milk you broke was for her tea and breakfast. She had to get herself to the shops before she could even have a cuppa this morning, not to mention that she had to pay for more milk out of her pension allowance. And in answer to your question, she recognised you because your mum used to do her hair for free once a week.'

Now Vicky remembered her. She had often been in the salon where her mum had worked when Vicky went there after school.

'I had to pay her for the milk and offer her some free lifts to the bingo for the next few Fridays to calm her down. What the hell were you thinking? And who were you with? They should be paying for this too.' His voice was rising, but Vicky kept her eyes on his hands.

'No one, just someone I was walking with – and they started it,' she mumbled.

Vicky didn't want her dad to have anything to do with Anna. She didn't want her new friendship tainted by his anger, an anger that had multiplied and evolved with every month that had passed since her mum died, as though he blamed her for still being there when his wife wasn't. The anger had started as a small vibration, an undercurrent that she could feel beneath the surface. Then it started to bubble up into his words, like a bilious ulcer. It had been only a matter of time before it reached his hands. Sometimes it fed on alcohol, the number of beers he drank after his shift increasing exponentially, but she usually missed the aftermath of that, saved by him passing out before she saw him. Other days, like last week, his insomnia and constant back pain from an inflamed sciatica meant he would drink more, sleep less and pick apart everything she said and did, usually ending with a bruise somewhere on her body that she would have to hide in PE classes.

Yesterday it was a slap across her bare legs and a punch to her shoulder after she had forgotten to put piccalilli on his ham sandwich.

'That's not good enough!' He shoved her hard now and her chair upended, the legs flipping into the air so that she hit the floor hard. Her head banged against the linoleum in tandem with her right forearm colliding with the edge of the table. The force of the fall took the wind out of her, but she scrambled to her feet as best she could, trying to get out of his reach, her head ringing and her breath catching in shallow gasps. The sharp sting of his backhand slap caught her across her thigh. Tears pricked at her cheeks, each one flavoured with surrender.

'Get out of my sight before I give you something to cry about!' he roared and she took off out of the kitchen. Grabbing her bag, she fled to the safety of her room, closed the door firmly and threw herself onto her bed, sobbing.

When the tears subsided, she sat up and stared out of her bedroom window at the grey sky outside. She knew what Anna had done wasn't right and she felt terrible for Mrs Webster, but she hoped Anna wasn't in as much trouble as she was. She really liked her and needed her as a friend. There was no one else.

And she had to admit that in that moment, as they fled the scene of the crime, Vicky had felt alive. Blood pumping, nerves jangling – a high she'd never reached before.

Still, it had been at the expense of someone else and that wasn't right.

She grabbed some writing paper from her desk and, after a moment of thought, penned a letter of apology to Mrs Webster. Tomorrow morning she would get up early to go and buy Mrs Webster something from the corner shop, maybe some Roses chocolates or something. Anna would probably scoff at the idea, but she needed to do it.

For the rest of the evening she stayed in her room, doing her homework and extra revision. If she was going to get out of this house, she would need to use her brain to do it. When her nan called her down for dinner later, after her dad had left for work, Vicky didn't say anything about the red welt on her leg or the lump on the back of her head where she had hit the floor. She ate her dinner in silence, the food like wood shavings on her tongue, then they snuggled on the couch in front of her nan's favourite soaps.

'Why be nice to that bitch when she dobbed you in it?'

Vicky knew Anna wouldn't get it, but she had forced her to come with her to the shop and then to deliver the chocolates and milk to the red door. 'Because I feel bad and she's just a little old woman who can't afford more milk.'

Anna's lips were pulled down in a sulk.

'I can't believe you got away with it. It was your idea,' Vicky said, tasting the resentment on her lips.

'Sorry! I didn't know she knew you, did I?' Anna kicked at the dirt as they stood outside Mrs Webster's door.

Vicky could feel her pulse rattling as she raised her hand to knock. She rapped three times, then stepped back a polite distance. Anna leaned on the wall, peering at her nails and casually chewing gum.

The lace curtain next to the door twitched and a pale face eyed them before the chain was drawn and the door inched open.

'Vicky Dean. What do you want?'

'Mrs Webster, I – we – just wanted to apologise for yesterday. It was disrespectful and we should've replaced your milk straight away.' She stepped forward and thrust the chocolates and milk at the little woman.

Mrs Webster eyed Vicky suspiciously, then tentatively reached out and took the gifts. 'Did your dad put you up to this?'

'No, he doesn't know I'm here and I'd rather he didn't either,' she replied quietly.

Mrs Webster shot a disapproving glance at Anna, who was still staring at her fingernails disengaged, then went to close the door on them. Before she did, she looked back at Vicky and said, 'You remind me of your mother. You're kind, like she was. Just be careful who your friends are or they'll ruin you.' Her eyes flicked at Anna. 'And don't let me see you hanging around my door again.' Then she closed the door firmly on them.

Anna rolled her eyes. 'Cow! Come on.'

Anna set off up the street towards school. Vicky trailed behind her, not wanting her to see the tears in her eyes.

'What did she mean anyway?'

'About what?'

'About reminding her of your mum? Where is she anyway?'

Vicky took a deep breath. They'd only been friends a few weeks and Vicky hadn't told Anna about her mum. It wasn't the kind of thing that came up in conversation that often.

'She died.'

Anna stopped. 'What? When? You never told me that.'

'Last year. That's the reason we moved here, to live with my nan so that she could help look after me when my dad is working nights.'

'Shit. Why didn't you say anything?'

'I don't like to talk about it,' Vicky mumbled.

'My mother can be the biggest bitch sometimes, but that's still better than not having one at all.' Anna threw her arms around Vicky and squeezed her tightly.

Vicky drew in a sharp breath as Anna touched the fresh bruise on her arm from where she had hit the table.

Anna frowned. 'You okay?'

'Just a bruise, that's all.'

Anna paused, then said, 'Just how angry was your dad?'

'Very.'

She could see Anna's lips forming a question she didn't want to hear.

'Look, it's fine, okay? It's complicated. He gets angry, has done since Mum died – and he drinks a bit. But he's always in pain – his back – so he takes painkillers and stuff. He does his best and I don't see him that much 'cos he works nights. Please don't tell anyone about any of this. Please.' Vicky's eyes were wide and frantic.

'Hey, no way, won't tell a soul.'

They carried on walking.

'God, I feel like such an idiot now. If I'd known, I wouldn't have pulled that stunt, honest,' Anna said after a moment.

'S'okay.'

'No, seriously, let me make it up to you. Come over to mine after school. Mum won't mind. You can stay for tea and we'll just hang out. What do you think?'

Vicky wanted nothing more.

Anna's house was everything Vicky's was not. An imposing, double-fronted, detached house in the smarter end of Twickenham near to the green, that put Vicky's little terraced house to shame. There was a gravel driveway that crunched and shifted beneath their feet as they approached the big wooden door with its shiny brass knocker and polished letterbox. Big ceramic pots housing little, shaped trees framed the front steps. Anna produced a key from her backpack and flung open the door to reveal a wide hallway with a checkerboard-tiled floor, an old-fashioned coat stand, neat wicker baskets for hats and scarves, and a vase of orange roses on a small side table next to the telephone.

Vicky stood in the doorway, feeling like a dirty smudge, as Anna called out, 'Mum! I'm home!'

A tall, thin woman with long, impossibly straight hair appeared from a doorway down the hall, wiping her hands on a tea towel.

'Hi, love. Good day at school? Oh! Who's this?' Her eyes widened.

Vicky tugged at her fraying jumper.

'Mum, this is Vix. She's staying for tea.'

'Er, hi, Mrs Maxwell. Only if that's okay, of course?'

'Oh… yes, of course, of course.' The woman tugged and pulled the tea towel between her hands as her eyes swept over Vicky. 'Make yourself at home. It's nothing special for tea. Just lasagne. I hope that's okay?' Vicky could think of nothing better. She only got to eat lasagne on those rare occasions when she went to a restaurant.

'Sounds lovely, thank you, Mrs Maxwell.'

'Can she call her dad quickly to let him know?' Anna said.

'It's okay, he'll be in bed, so no need,' Vicky interjected.

'Well, the phone is there if you need to make a call. I'll be in the kitchen if you need anything, girls. I'll get some biscuits and lemonade for you, shall I, darling?' She flitted away on her spindly legs as Anna rolled her eyes at her back.

'Ignore my mum, she's so embarrassing. She's a bit highly strung. Come on, let's go up to my room.'

Anna kicked off her shoes in the hallway, leaving them where they fell, and led the way up the stairs. Vicky placed her own shoes together under the hall table and followed Anna, careful not to touch the magnolia painted walls in case she left a mark. Everything looked immaculately clean and dust-free. The photographs on the walls up the stairwell were perfectly aligned, mostly images of Anna in various stages of her childhood, while the intricate glass ornaments all pointed forward, neat and evenly spaced. Cream curtains fell to the floor in perfect folds above a pale carpet that felt as plush as velvet under her feet.

At the top of the landing, a cat sat to attention. Its thick, dark fur framed beady eyes that watched her as she approached. Vicky gave it a wide berth. She hated cats, found them creepy.

At the end of the corridor was a bedroom easily double the size of Vicky's. Dominating the centre of the room was a queen-sized, four-poster bed straight out of a fairytale, with white netted drapes and fairy lights strung from the posts. The walls were decorated in tiny rosebud wallpaper, much of which was covered by posters depicting the smiling faces of Duran Duran, Madonna and A-ha. A large, white desk sat beneath the window, covered with a jumble of stationery and books, and across the room a heart-shaped dressing table was littered with hair accessories, make-up and brightly coloured jewellery, a tiny white stool tucked beneath it, waiting.

Anna flung herself on the bed and reached over to her bedside table to turn on the radio. Pop music belted into the serene space, Kylie wishing she should be so lucky.

'This room is amazing,' Vicky said as she wandered from the desk to the dressing table, her fingers hovering over the minutiae of Anna's life.

'Yeah, it's okay. I'm sick of the cutesy wallpaper and stuff, but my dad won't let me redecorate it just yet.'

Vicky thought of her own room with the bare painted walls showing the cracks in the plaster, her brown carpet and uninspiring bedspread. She made a promise to herself to make it a more inviting space in case Anna ever came over, but also knew she wasn't about to let that happen anytime soon.

For the next few hours, they laughed, listened to music, messed about with make-up and Vicky felt the rods of tension that had been keeping her upright relax a little. Anna's mum made good on her promise and delivered freshly baked chocolate chip cookies and lemonade on a tray, but Anna shooed her out of her room pretty quickly. Vicky ate three cookies in quick succession, then noticed the way Anna was watching her.

'Careful, a minute on the lips but a lifetime on the hips, Vix. That's what my mother says, anyway.' Vicky put her fourth cookie back on the plate.

At six-thirty, Anna's mum called them down for dinner. Vicky hadn't realised the time flying by and knew she should've called her dad by now, but put it out of her head, determined not to let him ruin what was turning into a brilliant day. The sheer scale of Anna's life in this big house was unfathomable to Vicky. Her nan's terraced house felt narrow and claustrophobic in comparison.

As Vicky followed Anna into the dining room, she pulled up short at seeing a tall, handsome man already sitting at the table, dressed in a crisp white shirt. He was serving himself salad but looked up as Anna pulled out a chair and said, 'Hey, Daddy.'

'Hey, princess – and who's this?'

Vicky blushed at his deep, throaty voice. Her eyes flicked over his thick hair, the stubble on his chin and his Adam's apple bobbing above the dark-blue tie that hung loosely at his throat.

'This is my friend, Vix. Come and sit here, Vix.'

'Well, hello Vix. Nice to meet you.' He smiled and Vicky's legs melted as she slid into the chair next to Anna.

The table was neatly set with matching plates, silver cutlery and even a serviette at each place, rolled and fed into a silver serviette ring. Vicky felt like an alien lifeform in this immaculately ordered dining room.

'Here, help yourself to salad,' Mrs Maxwell was saying, but her smile was thin compared to the wide grin Mr Maxwell had treated Vicky to. Mrs Maxwell's eyes kept flicking at her husband like a nervous tic.

Vicky added some salad to her plate, aware that there were ingredients in it that she didn't even recognise, let alone eat on a regular basis. Lettuce made her want to gag and tomatoes were gross, but she didn't want to appear rude.

Mrs Maxwell then went from person to person serving a tidy square of lasagne onto each plate. The smell made Vicky's mouth water and she had to restrain herself from diving face-first into the pasta.

Vicky felt something glide past her leg and gasped. Anna looked under the table. 'Oh, that's Murphy, my mother's stupid cat,' Anna said with a grimace of distaste. 'You love that cat, don't you, Mother?'

The cat jumped up onto Mrs Maxwell's lap and her face lit up as she stroked and purred at it.

'Darling, please, not at the table,' Mr Maxwell replied and shooed it down. Mrs Maxwell looked crestfallen as she watched Murphy saunter away.

Mr Maxwell was asking Anna about her day and Anna responded by complaining about her RE teacher, who to be fair really did seem to dislike Anna. Vicky listened while chewing as politely and quietly as she could. She noticed that Mrs Maxwell had next to no lasagne on her plate, but a large serving of salad. That was how she stayed so slim then.

Vicky forced herself to eat some lettuce.

'And what about you, Vix? What is your favourite subject at school?'

'Lame question, Daddy,' Anna said.

Vicky put down her fork and said quietly, 'Maths. I'm pretty good at it and I enjoy the logic of it.'

'She is amazing at it, actually.' Anna turned to her. 'You should so tutor me! I'm rubbish at maths.'

'Yes, well, if you'd applied yourself more at maths, you would've passed the entrance exams for Ravenscourt and you wouldn't be stuck at that state school you're at now,' Mrs Maxwell said, then a rush of colour flooded her cheeks. 'Not that there's anything wrong with the school you're both at—' her eyes flicked over Vicky, '—but Anna did have the opportunity to go to a private school.'

'And I'm happy where I am, Mother. So just let it go. Besides, I've got Vicky now.'

Mrs Maxwell went back to drinking repetitively from the large glass of white wine clutched in her hand, the food sitting mostly untouched on her plate.

Vicky kept quiet for the rest of the meal, feeling like a stain and painfully aware of the social differences between her family and those sitting around the table with her, discussing their upcoming skiing holiday in the Alps. Once the dinner was over, she made her excuses to Anna about having to get back home before her dad left for work. As it was, she knew he would've left already, but she felt completely out of her depth in this neat, tidy, cavernous house.

She thanked Mrs Maxwell for dinner but received a dismissive glance in return. Mr Maxwell had disappeared behind a door further down the corridor straight after they'd finished eating and Vicky could hear his deep, throaty voice conducting business loudly over the telephone.

She walked home slowly, her feet dragging. How could she possibly have thought she and Anna could be real friends? They came from different worlds. Two worlds that would never be able to co-exist symbiotically. She was the gum on the sole of Anna's patent leather shoes and they would never be in the same league.

Vicky tried to avoid Anna the next day at school, but it was impossible.

'Hey, you avoiding me?'

'No, I... er...'

Anna grabbed her arm and spun her around on her chair and Vicky grimaced as Anna's hand squeezed the bruise on her forearm.

Anna frowned. 'Show me.'

They were sitting in their form room. Vicky pulled her sleeve lower. 'No, not now.'

But Anna wouldn't leave it alone. She made a beeline for Vicky during morning break and finally caught up with her on the field.

'Show me your arm, Vix. Please.'

'It's nothing.'

'It's not nothing.'

Vicky threw her bag down and sat cross-legged on a patch of grass. Anna sat next to her and carefully pulled up Vicky's jumper to show an angry, purpling bruise on the underside of her arm. Just above it were what looked like finger marks, now yellowing rather than the vivid purple of the newer bruise, making her arm look like there was a dark face staring back at her, taunting her.

'Wow,' Anna said.

'Yeah.' Vicky wanted to cry, not just from shame but from frustration at the injustice of her life compared to Anna's, who didn't seem to have anything to worry about or be scared of, had two loving parents and yet still acted like the world owed her something.

'I know what we need to do,' Anna said, then started rummaging in her school bag. She pulled out a black marker pen and pulled Vicky's arm into her lap. 'When I look at this, I don't see a bruise that hurts. I see a face.'

Vicky rolled her eyes at her and went to pull back her arm.

'No, seriously, look closer. Here's the eyes…' She drew black circles around the marks, added long lashes and big pupils. 'And here's the mouth…' This time she drew a wide smile around the welt left by the countertop. 'Now if we add a small nose here—' Vicky watched as the pen dug into her skin, leaving ink marks behind, '—and some little ears, a tuft of hair…' Anna was sticking her tongue out a little as she drew. 'There, that's better. That makes him so much friendlier. We shall call him Bernard.' She gestured at her handiwork.

Vicky looked down on the cute, smiley face of a chubby man and felt herself smile.

'There isn't much I can do about your dad, apart from trying not to get you into trouble again, but I can make you look at this differently. If you make every bruise into a smiley face, maybe it will make you feel better.'

Tears did spring to Vicky's eyes then and she pulled Anna into a tight hug.

Anna pulled away and locked eyes with her. 'I've got your back, Vix, and you've got mine, right?'

'Right. Always.'

4

Vicky moved in on Monday with the intention of staying for one week. David made a plan to go into the office that afternoon, knowing that Vicky would collect the kids from school for him. She'd done it before and he had no concerns whatsoever that there would be any problems. He met her at the house after dropping the kids at school, once more looking like the business-sharpened, well-groomed man he used to be. The whiff of stale alcohol and body odour had been replaced by his signature fragrance of sandalwood and he'd felt more himself as soon as he shed the tracksuit bottoms, ran a razor over his cheeks and knotted the tie at his throat once more.

He told her to make herself at home and headed into the office, the drive there feeling both strange and familiar after over a month away. But the one emotion overriding everything else was relief. He felt a sense of release the further he drove away from the house, knowing he was putting some distance between himself and the weight of responsibility that had been pinning him down since he'd unwittingly become a single parent.

This felt more natural. This was something he knew he could do.

However, the office proved a more substantial hurdle than he'd anticipated, with everyone offering empty condolences and not daring to meet his eye in case he broke down in front of them or something equally as awkward. He could count on one hand the number of colleagues who had attended Anna's funeral, the hypocritical bastards. Sympathy is fine at arm's length, but don't get too close in case it's contagious.

He felt like everyone was watching him, looking for signs that he was cracking up. Anna's car accident had been all over the local news the day after it had happened, with the police appealing for witnesses and every known detail discussed and analysed as rumours buzzed like flies over her corpse. Had she been drinking? Was someone else involved? Where had she been that night? He knew his colleagues had formed their own opinions of what had happened, the whiff of scandal as addictive as the caffeine in the coffee room, but David was still waiting for some sort of explanation from the police and made regular calls to the DI in charge of the case, only to be told they had no further information to share.

His boss had said to take as much time off as he needed and David had been reluctant to return to work, but once the awkwardness of the first few hours back in the office had passed, he began to see the benefits of being distracted by his job. A backlog of calls to make, emails to wade through and meetings to schedule meant that time ticked over quicker than it had in a long while.

In fact, by the time he pulled into the driveway later that evening, he heard himself actually singing along to the New Radical's song 'You Get What You Give' on the radio. He stopped short, guilt making him turn the volume button down. Anna had hated that song. Then the unwelcome thought that she would never sing along to another song again made him snap the radio off altogether.

He pushed through the front door to be greeted by the foreign sound of laughter. He frowned and stepped over the schoolbags and coats lying abandoned in the hallway like a jumble sale. Anna had always made sure the au pair packed the kids' bags away and that their coats were hung up nicely as soon as they came in. He pushed the comparison to one side along with a duffel coat.

The kids were sitting on the couch, one on either side of Vicky. They were laughing at an episode of *The Simpsons* on the television. Anna had hated them watching that programme.

'Hey guys.'

'Daddy!' Both kids leapt up and hugged him, before returning their bums to their seats and their eyes to the screen.

'Hi, how was your day?' Vicky said with a smile.

'Okay, thanks. Everything fine here?'

'Yes, perfect. Everyone seems to have had a good day.' She wriggled out from under the children and got to her feet. 'Fancy a beer?'

He followed her into the kitchen.

'Um, you know Anna wouldn't let the kids watch *The Simpsons*. Just saying…'

Vicky paused in front of the fridge. 'Oh, sorry, they said they watch it all the time, little fibbers. I won't let them again then.'

She handed him a cold beer as he loosened his tie. He looked at the bottle, an artisan beer from the local organic brewery he liked. Vicky must've got them in while he was at work.

The comforting smell of fresh laundry hovered in the air. 'You've been doing laundry.'

She took a slug from her own beer. 'Yeah, I was filling time, getting on top of the housework and stuff, you know, and thought I'd change all the sheets while they were at school. Oh, then I found a whole pile of Anna's clothes in your bedroom on her chair and I figured I'd throw those in as well, in case, you know, you wanted to think about a charity donation or something...' Her voice trailed off at the stricken look on his face.

'The clothes on her chair? You washed them?' He slammed down his beer and raced into the utility room where the basket of clean washing was waiting to be sorted and put away. He started rummaging through the basket, pulling jumpers, jeans and tops from the pile.

'What's wrong? Did I do something wrong?' Vicky stood behind him, her arms crossed tightly and her eyes gaping.

He turned on her, grasping a midnight blue chiffon blouse to his face. He looked wounded, his skin a deepening shade of red. 'I was keeping them as they were because they still smelled like her. Her perfume, her skin...' His voice was strangled, as though every word was a barb catching in his throat. He breathed in deeply, inhaling the fabric. 'Now it just smells like softener.' He dropped the blouse and it fluttered to the floor. His foot crushed it as he pushed past her violently. Vicky felt her shoulder hit the doorframe, but she didn't cry out.

He stormed upstairs and she heard a door slam. She rubbed her shoulder and started folding the ransacked clothes back into the basket.

He emerged an hour later when Vicky sent Lewis up to tell him dinner was ready. She had gone to a lot of effort to make a beef stew in Anna's slow cooker, but she could already tell without tasting it that the meat was tough and bland, like chewing on a sock.

David came into the dining room looking calmer, but with reddened eyes. He settled into a seat at the dining room table and began to serve himself some of the stew.

'David, I'm so—'

'Don't. We'll talk about it later, but I overreacted. It's been a strange day.'

Vicky looked down at her plate, covered with congealing gravy and undercooked carrots. 'Well, this sad stew won't make you feel any better.'

'It's a bit chewy, Vix,' Harper said. 'But it still tastes nice,' she added hastily.

'Thanks Harps. Maybe I should cut some slices of bread and you can eat as much as you like and mop the gravy up with it. Would that help?'

She didn't wait for an answer, but got to her feet and busied herself with slicing big doorstops of bread from a crusty loaf she'd picked up from the bakery earlier. She spread thick layers of butter on each one.

The other three watched her curiously, the air in the room intense and heavy. 'So how was school, guys?' David asked into the silence.

As Harper and Lewis regaled him with their stories, Vicky sat back down and pushed her food around her plate, her teeth chewing on her lip. She felt something brush her hand and looked down to see David's palm resting on hers. She looked up at him and he smiled reassuringly and winked.

After dinner was rinsed away, the kids went up to get ready for bed. David found Vicky in the utility room sorting the laundry into neat piles ready to be put away.

'I'm sorry I overreacted earlier. It just came as a bit of a shock, you know? I mean, it's not like I could smell her much any more or anything, but...'

She stopped, one of Anna's T-shirts in her hands. He fought the urge to tell her to put it down. 'No, it's my fault. I took a liberty by even going into your room. I was just trying to help, make myself useful, you know? But I overstepped and I apologise.'

'No, no, while you're here, I want you to feel as though this is your home. It's what Anna would want. And god knows I'm not getting to the jobs that I'm supposed to do, that Anna did – or got the cleaner to do, anyway. So ignore me. I'm a dick.' He held out his arms and she moved into them, hugging him back awkwardly, feeling the strangely intimate sensation of his chin on her head and his hands warm on her back.

'Now, let's get those monsters into bed and maybe we can open a bottle of wine or something,' he said into her hair. 'God knows, I need it.'

Vicky stepped quickly out of his arms and coughed self-consciously. 'Oh, before I forget, a bouquet of flowers was delivered today. I put them on the side table in the lounge. There's a card.'

'Really? Another one? Bloody hell, how long do people carry on sending them? I got one from Anna's boss last week.'

'Oh?' Vicky frowned and looked away.

David headed into the lounge where a large display of lilies was scenting the air. At least this one was more understated. He pulled the card from the vibrant green stems.

David,
Sorry for your loss. You don't deserve what you got. We should talk sometime.
Rachel Woods.

Vicky came up behind him.

'Rachel Woods? That's her boss Sebastian's wife, isn't it?' David asked as he reread the card. 'Not sure what she means by that.' He handed the card to Vicky, who read it and shrugged.

'I guess sometimes people don't know what to write. She obviously didn't know he'd already sent a bunch – and maybe she's just trying to be supportive or something. I think you should just ignore it. I'm here if you need to talk.' She scrunched up the card in her fist and pocketed it. 'Speaking of which, where's that wine?'

The rest of the week was both awkward and enjoyable. David's initial feelings of relief grew as the days passed.

He could see the kids starting to enjoy themselves more, the sounds of laughing, bickering and talking filling the hollowed-out rooms as they responded to the attention Vicky was lavishing on them.

She made them lunch boxes every day with sandwiches cut into shapes and little notes to make them smile. She played board games with them after school and David would come home to the image of Vicky on her hands and knees tied in knots on the Twister mat or counting out Monopoly money with her banker's hat on.

Their dinnertimes were filled with happy chattering about three things they did well during the day and one thing they could've done better. It made up for some of the frankly inedible meals Vicky attempted to cook every evening.

With each day, David could see glimmers of the children coming back to life again, flashes of Lewis's sense of humour and Harper's flamboyant imagination, and he could feel some of the broken pieces rattling around inside him start to fit together again, the edges knitting together like a healing wound.

For most of the time that the kids had been going to school, Anna had relied on an au pair to collect them and entertain them until she got home, often later than him. He'd gone along with it because she had always been a reluctant homemaker, more comfortable organising an event in her role as co-ordinator at a PR company than doing jigsaw puzzles and finger painting. He knew how important her job had been to her, but it was refreshing to see the kids blossoming from some dedicated attention from Vicky.

David had dismissed the au pair after the accident as he couldn't bear to see anyone in the first few weeks, then had toyed with the idea of hiring her back, but seeing how well the kids were responding to Vicky now made him wonder whether he should consider trying to negotiate his working hours so that he could be home in time for them finishing school himself. Vicky made it look so easy.

However, as Sunday evening loomed, David could feel a sense of impending doom hovering over him at the thought that he would once more have to take on the responsibility of the children from tomorrow.

While Vicky was busy making dinner and the kids were entertaining themselves on their iPads, David distracted himself by running his eyes over his social media accounts for the first time since Anna had left them. It was like a wormhole. Five minutes could easily stretch into an hour of flicking through banal comments on Twitter and random brag posts on Facebook. Without considering what he was doing, he clicked on Anna's Facebook page and felt his breath catch as her profile picture filled his screen. He took a moment to drink in the familiar sharp lines of her face before he scrolled down and saw a number of posts from friends saying how much they missed her. Most of the posts were from Vicky. Photos she'd tagged and comments she'd posted since the funeral, as though Anna would reply at some point.

His grief was so encompassing that sometimes he forgot how much Vicky must miss her too. He set his phone aside and went into the kitchen.

He watched from the doorway as she peered at a recipe book, her tongue sticking out and a frown folding her forehead. She was trying to turn a pile of ingredients into an edible fish pie. He took a sip from his bottle of beer, then came up behind her.

'Can I help?'

She jumped a little, so deep had her level of concentration been. 'No, no, I think I've got it. I'm not sure if the white sauce should be lumpy though.' She chewed on her lip.

'Just keep whisking it, I think. That's what Anna…' He felt heat and cold rush over him simultaneously. The sound of her name still had a physical effect on him.

'That's why I'm making it tonight. Anna made a wicked fish pie, I remember. I can't see mine being anywhere near as good as hers, but I'd like to give it a try. And if it's dreadful, I'll just pop down to the chippy since it's my last night here. Oh, and I've promised the kids that we'd watch a movie all together. I've got popcorn and sweets and stuff.'

David sighed. He had to admit it had been brilliant having her with them, not just for the kids but for him too. Just having someone in the room with him in the evenings after she'd wrestled the kids into bed was like someone throwing a warm blanket over him. He hadn't needed to turn to a bottle of whiskey for companionship. Hearing her laugh at a comedian on the television or listening to her chat about some of the stuff the kids had done after school made him feel less alone, less disconnected. The quiet in the evenings was certainly one of the hardest things to get used to. Vicky had a laugh that came from her belly, rotund and throaty, and you couldn't help but join in when it filled the room.

He didn't want to think about how he would cope when she was no longer there.

Not tonight though. Tonight he wanted to enjoy hanging out with her and the kids. They'd done that with Anna on occasional Sunday evenings, usually when she'd worked all weekend and hadn't seen them much, but David would invariably fall asleep during the film, only to be woken by Harper loudly telling him off for snoring and Lewis telling Anna off for looking at her phone instead of the film.

He handed Vicky his bottle of beer and she took a sip gratefully before passing it back. 'I've really appreciated you being here, you know, Vix. More than you realise,' he said.

Vicky smiled at him. 'I've loved being here. It's made me feel closer to her, you know?'

'I was just looking at Facebook. First time I've looked since...'

'Yeah. I've been posting quite a bit, I know, but it helps me somehow. It's like I'm still having a conversation with her. You should try it – put some posts up or some Instagram stories about how you're doing, how you're coping with the kids and stuff. People relate to that. And it might help you too – it's like you're talking to someone but without the awkward eye contact. You'll probably find loads of other dads in a similar boat who will reach out to you too.'

'Maybe.' He looked away. 'Here, let me pour you some wine.'

'Hmm, will it help my cooking abilities?'

'It might.' He laughed, then went to grab a glass from the cupboard. Opening a cold bottle of white wine, he glugged a substantial amount into the glass and handed it to her. 'You'll be pleased to get back to work yourself tomorrow. No more running around after us.'

She turned back to the sauce bubbling on the stove. 'Not really, I've actually enjoyed myself – and the company. It's shown me what I'm missing, being single and all that. It can get lonely. But no chance of kids for me, really. Not now. Anna never knew how lucky she was.' She looked across at him quickly. 'But less washing of your pants will be nice.'

He smiled and pulled on his beer. 'You know you didn't need to do all of that, the laundry, ironing and everything. I feel like we've exploited you somewhat.'

'Seriously, I haven't minded at all. Like I say, it's my only chance to play house with a family I care a lot about. Now, are you going to set that table or what? I think I might have salvaged this white sauce. Just need to get this in the oven and whip up a salad.'

Lewis came in then, kicking his football aimlessly. 'Hey, little guy. You okay?' Vicky asked.

'I'm bored.'

'Well, I could shove my shoes on and we could head out into the back garden, kick that ball about for a bit before dinner if you like?'

His face lit up. 'Really?'

'Yeah, at least for half an hour while it cooks. Fancy it?'

He didn't answer but ran off, and they soon heard the shoe cupboard in the hallway creaking open. 'Guess that's a yes then.'

The look of delight on Lewis's face hadn't gone unnoticed and David felt his heart squeeze.

'I'll join in too. I could do with a run-around,' he said, patting his non-existent belly.

'Great, go and see if Harper is up for it and we can do girls versus boys.' As he left, he peered back at her as she licked her fingers after pouring the white sauce over the fish. He smiled to himself.

David pulled on the trainers he found lying abandoned by the back door, feeling both lighter and weighted with guilt. Anna had never joined in when he was playing with the kids. She didn't like to get dirty or wet. She would stay inside, watching through the window, or would take herself off on the weekends, leaving him to entertain them, saying she needed 'me time' or volunteering to work on a PR project at work. In comparison, Vicky was happy to get her hands dirty with paint, her nails painted in messy, lurid colours, her hair pulled and knotted into a myriad of weird styles and grass stains on her jeans from diving to save one of Lewis's goals.

David didn't want to compare them, but hadn't been able to help himself all week, when the world was quiet around him and the beer buzz let his thoughts run unhindered. He didn't have time to analyse the conflicting feelings swirling through him now though because Harper and Lewis were running at him, their shoes and coats on, with Vicky chasing them, shouting and cheering. He smiled again and followed them into the sunny back garden.

It turned out that the girls were quite good at football. David and Lewis battled hard, but the game was tied 3-3 after twenty-five minutes. David pulled Lewis aside for a team chat. 'Right, little man. We need to focus. This is ours for the taking. I'll distract Vicky and you cut through and score, *capisce*?'

'What does "capisce" mean?'

'Never mind. You know the plan, right? Give me five.'

David went for a high-five, which Lewis missed. He aimed again and this time hit David's hand so hard that it stung. 'Good lad.'

They got into position and David winked at Lewis. He took off with the ball, with Harper coming straight at him as he suspected she would. Just as she reached him, he dribbled around her, then shot the ball square to Lewis before throwing himself at Vicky and clasping his arms around her before she could tackle Lewis. He held her tightly as she squirmed and squealed.

'Foul! Foul! Obstruction!'

They fell onto the grass in a pile, with Vicky pressed up against David, still held tight in his arms. Lewis ran through with the ball and scored, cheering loudly.

'Yeah!' shouted David.

'No fair!' Harper wailed. 'Vix, tell them they cheated!'

'It's the age-old tactic of distraction,' David said into Vicky's ear as he held onto her. She squirmed some more and managed to twist in his arms to come face to face with him.

'That's a cheap trick, David, just so that you can beat a pair of girls who were wiping the floor with you. Not something we'll see in the Olympics in August!'

'Well, I had to do something.' He smiled at her and everything around them seemed to hold still for a moment, like a caught breath.

A frantic beeping interrupted, and Vicky shoved him away. 'The fish pie!'

She shot into the kitchen, leaving David to compose himself and get to his feet.

That evening, he sat on the couch with his arms draped around Harper and Lewis on either side of him and Vicky squeezed in at the end. Occasionally, his hand would accidentally brush against her shoulder and she would look over and smile distractedly. A bowl of popcorn was propped up in his lap and she would reach over and grab a handful every few minutes, the bowl leaning into him when she did.

He wasn't interested in the film, but the kids were engrossed, the only sounds from them the rattle of chocolate wrappers and the crunch of popcorn. He felt content, which surprised and saddened him in equal measure.

Every now and then, Vicky would bray with laughter, which would set the kids off too, and he'd find himself smiling, happy in the moment.

Then he'd catch himself. What would Anna be thinking right now if she could see this? Would she be angry at how easy it had been to let Vicky in this week? Or pleased since she was her oldest friend?

He had never fully understood their friendship. Vicky and Anna were poles apart in every way and yet they had been inseparable for years. Despite having known Vicky for so long, it was only this week that David felt like he had actually begun to see her for who she was. His eyes had always been on Anna, his attention completely monopolised by her, to the point where he had considered Vicky a distraction, an intruder in that Anna's attention had never fully been on him in return. Vicky had been like a skulking shadow over them, always there even when she wasn't. He had been painfully aware that the only person who truly knew Anna, who she let in enough to know her, was Vicky. David only knew a version of Anna, the version she created for him, and he had spent the early years of their marriage trying to convince her to let him see the other side of her. In later years, he had grown tired of the battle and accepted that she might wear one mask with him, but another with Vicky. As a result, he had been unfair to Vicky, had made callous assumptions about her, snap judgements, not let her get as close to him as she could've been.

Now he was seeing her for the lovely, kind, generous friend she was.

And it was killing him.

He shuffled in his seat, suddenly feeling hot and uncomfortable in his skin. Maybe it was just that he wanted anyone to be there, to try and take Anna's place. And Vicky just happened to be the one who had shown up at his door first.

Maybe.

Next week would be different. He would get into a routine, start putting the kids first, figure out how to make it work on his own.

This was too complicated and confusing, like finding a wine gum in your packet of jelly babies.

That's all Vicky was. A nice distraction, but not his reality.

Vicky's phone intruded into his thoughts, the notification chirping like a baby bird. It was sitting on the side table next to him and, as he reached out to pass it to her, he saw the name 'Rachel Woods' above the text alert. He frowned and looked closer, but Vicky snatched the phone from him.

'Why is Rachel Woods texting you?'

'Um, I dunno…' She opened the text, the screen angled away. 'Oh,' she said quickly, 'basically just saying what she'd said to you, you know, with the flowers? That if I need to talk or whatever…'

'I didn't even know you knew her.'

'I don't really. I met her at that work thing I went to with Anna once and we got chatting, swapped numbers, you know. Haven't heard from her since. She knows I'm Anna's best friend though.' Vicky turned her phone over and clasped it tightly to her chest before turning her attention back to the screen.

'Was,' he replied curtly.

'What?'

'Never mind.' He turned back to the TV too, but couldn't quite feel the smile on his face any longer.

Dear Anna,

The week has flown past and I'm in bed in your spare room for one last sleep before I return to my shithole of a flat.

I'm not going to lie. I had hoped David would ask me to stay longer. It's been fun cooking, looking after them, hearing them laugh. We had a good time today running around in the garden, playing football, the sun warming our cheeks. God, I sound like a probiotic yoghurt advert.

Then David got all weird when we sat down to watch the movie. He hardly said two words to me and was very quick to go up to bed afterwards. I guess he's still adjusting to a different female presence being around.

Some days he seems thrilled to have me around, his eyes crinkling at the corners like they do. Other times

I catch him looking disappointed when I walk into a room, like he was expecting someone else.

You.

I know how he feels. I still expect you to come in here, climb into the bed with me with your thick woolly socks on because your feet were always cold and your hair pulled into a short ponytail that always looked amazing, while mine always looks thin and like I have a growth coming out of the top of my head. You used to curl up next to me and we'd laugh about the stupid things I'd done the night before or the depth of my hangover. Or you'd let me cry about yet another failed attempt at a relationship or one-night stand, knowing that you were safe from all that as long as David sat patiently waiting for you downstairs.

But he never saw the real you, did he?

You were applying Instagram filters to yourself long before the technology was introduced. David saw you through sepia tones. I saw you clear as day though, with all your flaws and imperfections, no filter.

When we were kids, I used to watch you and then later try and imitate you in front of my mirror. I was in awe of how you seemed to cast a spell over everyone, trick them into seeing what you wanted them to see, while I felt naked, stripped bare all the time. I would try and adopt your little mannerisms, the way you'd twirl your hair around your finger when you were concentrating or tilt your head when someone was talking to you. They'd think you were listening intently, but I could tell by your eyes that most of the time you were just asking the right questions to be polite and not actually listening to their answers. The person you were talking to went away thinking you had shared a moment with them while you'd turn to me and yawn dramatically or roll your eyes, call them pathetic behind their back.

I was just as pathetic as them though, wasn't I?

I wanted your approval just as much as they did. In fact, I wanted to be you – to live your life, wear your clothes, live in your skin, with your perfect family and your perfect face. You knew that and you liked it. You fed off it.

Now I have had a taste of this life of yours and I don't want it to end.

I would do anything to make sure it doesn't end.

Vix x

November 1988

'Vix! You've got to help me!' Anna launched herself at Vicky, her eyes frantic, as they met at their usual spot to walk to school.

'What's wrong?'

'You know that maths test today?'

'Yeah?' Vicky burrowed her chin further into her coat, the wind cold on her cheeks. Anna didn't appear to be feeling the cold today. Her coat was unbuttoned and hanging loosely off one shoulder, her tie knotted in a perfect Windsor knot but hanging short, dangling a long way above her exposed belly button like an arrow, above which her blouse was knotted, showing off her tiny waist. The teachers would make her fix it all when she got to school, but for now she knew she would get more than a few admiring glances on her way there.

'I haven't revised. I meant to last night, but then Mike – you know the guy from that party last week? He called and I was on the phone to him for ages chatting. He's so lovely… anyway, I just totally forgot about the test.'

'So blag it, like you usually do.'

Anna's bottom lip protruded and her eyes were downcast as she kicked at a stone in the street. 'I can't. My dad says I have to start getting better marks or he's going to send me to boarding school.' She grabbed onto Vicky's hand. 'Seriously, my life will end if that happens. I want to stay here with you. I can't think of anything worse than being shipped off.'

Vicky's pulse jumped at the news. She didn't want Anna to leave either. She was the only good thing in her life at the moment. Things with her dad were getting worse, his hands getting heavier and his tongue sharper every day.

'So what do you want me to do?'

'Help me to cheat. You sit in front of me, so all you have to do is shuffle over a little bit, write a bit bigger and I can then make sure I'm getting the same answers as you. We can move the desks closer. No one will notice.'

'I don't know. If we get caught and my dad gets called…' She went cold at the thought of what he would do.

'It won't happen. We have that new supply teacher in again this week and he's clueless. I also think he has a bit of a crush on me, so if he does catch us, I'm sure I can find a way of … distracting him.'

Vicky rolled her eyes. Anna seemed to think no one was immune to her charms.

'Please, Vix! I can't bear the thought of not seeing you every day.'

Vicky thought about it for a millisecond, then agreed.

'Excellent! Knew you would!' Anna hooked her arm through Vicky's and they headed towards the school gates.

'Vicky Dean and Anna Maxwell, can I see you both after school please?'

When their names were called during their maths lesson the next day, Vicky knew their scheme had failed. Anna was less concerned. She claimed to have a plan ready to diffuse the situation, but Vicky began to concoct a survival strategy in her head for when she got home, just in case.

As they approached the classroom after the final bell had tolled, they found the supply teacher, Mr Surtees, standing behind his desk, attempting to appear stern as he held their two tests in his hand.

'Ladies, take a seat.'

They sat on command, Vicky peering nervously from beneath her heavy fringe while Anna sat confidently, a small smile on her lip-glossed mouth, her legs crossed so that her skirt sat high up her milky white thigh.

Mr Surtees came around the front of his desk and leaned against it, crossing his long, corduroy-clad legs at the ankles. Vicky kept her eyes averted from Anna, knowing that if she looked at her, she would start giggling nervously, which would not help their case.

Instead, she sat on her hands and swung her feet under the chair.

'Ladies, your tests from yesterday.' He put a test in front of each of them. Vicky was thrilled to see she'd scored 97% and a quick glance at the test in front of Anna showed she had exactly the same score. Vicky chewed on her lip. She hadn't expected Anna to copy *every* question; just enough to get her a solid mark.

'As you can see, you both scored 97%. Vicky, that's not unusual for you from what I hear. Well done. But Anna, this is most unusual for you, it would seem.' He folded his arms and stared at them. Vicky figured he was aiming to be intimidating, but he had quite a baby face with eyebrows that sat high on his forehead, giving him a permanently startled look.

The girls remained mute.

'Well? Don't you have anything to say?' The eyebrows rode even higher.

'I revised a lot for this one, sir,' Anna replied. 'I'm pleased to see my hard work has paid off.'

He sighed and ran a hand over his face. 'Anna, you got *exactly* the same as Vicky, even the few she got wrong. How do you explain that?'

'Vix has been tutoring me, so I guess she just taught me the mistakes she makes too.' Anna smiled lightly at him, unfazed.

Vicky kept quiet, not wanting to make things worse, but Mr Surtees had other ideas.

'Vicky, is this true?'

'Er, I have been tutoring her, yes.'

'And the two of you didn't cheat on the test?'

Anna raised her hand to her chest in mock indignation. 'Sir! What an accusation!'

He frowned at her, then looked back at Vicky. 'Vicky, I'm disappointed in you most of all. I've heard you're a good student, I believe you are expected to go places with your maths ability, but I can't let this lie. I know you two are best friends, thick as thieves by all accounts, and I can only assume that this was planned. I will have to let the headmaster know, call your parents in and you will be disciplined.'

'No! Sir!' Vicky leapt to her feet. 'You can't! My—'

Before she could carry on, Anna calmly interrupted her. 'Sir, it was all my fault. Vix didn't know I was copying her test. I was sitting behind her and she didn't know I could see her work. It's me you should be disciplining, not her.'

Vicky swept her wide eyes from him to Anna and back again, fear making her tongue stick to the top of her mouth. The idea that the headmaster would call in her dad filled her with concrete dread. A few days ago, he had pressed the end of the hot iron onto her thigh after she had left a minor burn mark on one of his shirts. The blister had only just started to heal over.

Mr Surtees looked at Anna closely, considering her for a moment. Vicky saw her glide her tongue slowly across her bottom lip. Mr Surtees looked away quickly.

'Okay, Vicky, you can go. Next time, make sure you cover your work more carefully. Anna, stay where you are. I want you to sit here now and redo the test so that we can ascertain just how much you do know. Then I will have a conversation with the headmaster.'

'But, sir!' Anna replied, irked.

'No buts. Sit.'

He moved back around his desk and began to rummage in one of the drawers.

Vicky raised her eyebrows questioningly at Anna, who replied with a shrug of her head, indicating for Vicky to go. 'Wait outside for me. I won't be long. Close the door behind you,' she whispered, then she turned her back on the teacher, loosened her tie a notch and undid a few buttons on her blouse so that a tiny slice of pale pink lace from her bra peeked through.

Vicky frowned, but grabbed her bag, muttered, 'Thanks, sir,' and shuffled from the room, trying to get her panicked breathing back under control.

Closing the door behind her, she rose up onto her tiptoes to see through the small glass window at the top of the door.

Anna approached the desk where Mr Surtees was still leaning into the drawer. Vicky saw her reach over and put her hand on his, could see her mouth moving as she leaned in and spoke close to his ear in quiet tones, twirling her hair as she did. Mr Surtees stiffened, but made no move to pull away.

Vicky dropped down off her tiptoes, not wanting to see any more.

Minutes passed before the classroom door was flung open and Anna marched from the room, fury etched all over her face.

'What happened?' Vicky asked as she scrambled to keep up with Anna.

'That fucker!' she growled. 'He's determined to call my parents. Couldn't persuade him out of it.'

'Shit.'

'Yeah, which means they'll definitely ship me off to boarding school when they find out.'

'God, Anna, why couldn't you just revise like you're supposed to?'

Anna turned and glared at her, her expression feral. 'Some of us aren't as smart as you, Vicky. Some of us actually have a life instead of hiding our faces in books every day. And don't forget, I just covered for you in there. You were a part of it, so be careful.'

Vicky stepped back at the vehemence in her voice.

'And that little turd of a man,' Anna continued with venom, pointing her finger like a dart in the direction of the classroom, 'is not going to ruin my life. Come on.' She stalked up the corridor.

Vicky paused, but only for a second before following her.

Anna came to a stop outside the headmaster's office. His name, Mr Dewberry, stencilled on the door in thick, black lettering, was intended to make students quake in their sensible shoes, but Vicky didn't have time to worry as Anna grabbed her arm tightly. She inhaled sharply at the strength in Anna's tiny hand. 'You need to back me up on whatever I'm about to say, okay?'

'Okay.'

'Swear?'

'Yes, I swear.' Anna dropped her arm and Vicky rubbed at the heat left behind by Anna's fingers.

Anna knocked hard on the door and a muffled 'Come in' came in response.

She stormed into the room, indignation pulling her back straight and her shoulders down. Vicky followed more cautiously.

'Miss Maxwell, Miss Dean, what can I do for you?' the bespectacled man behind the wide desk said. He pushed his glasses up onto his bald pate and smiled calmly.

'Sir, I need to make a complaint about one of the supply teachers.'

Mr Dewberry, a rotund man with a bushy moustache that more than compensated for his lack of hair and a propensity to sweat through his suit jacket, placed his hands on his desk and frowned. 'Oh dear, that is unfortunate. Have a seat and tell me what your concern is.'

'My concern is that Mr Surtees has just sexually assaulted me,' Anna replied without taking the seat on offer.

Vicky whipped her eyes at Anna.

'I see.' He paused, then said, 'That is a very serious allegation, Anna.'

'I'm not lying! Vicky saw it. She was outside the classroom and saw him through the window. He grabbed my boob through my shirt and said that if I told anyone, he would say that I cheated on my maths test. And I didn't! I worked really hard on it. Vicky has been tutoring me.' Anna started to cry, the tears dripping one by one from her indignant eyes. 'My parents want me to transfer to a boarding school in Yorkshire and I think they're right. I can't stay at a school where there are pervert teachers. And I'm sure my dad will want to let the police know too.'

'Now, now, let's not be too hasty.' Mr Dewberry got to his feet and rushed around the desk, then led Anna into a chair. He passed her a box of tissues from his desk before turning his panicked eyes on Vicky. 'Is this true, Vicky?'

Vicky had a second to decide if she was going to back up her friend or ruin a young teacher's career.

'Yes, it's true. I saw him touch her up and whisper in her ear. Anna was really upset and pale when she came out of the classroom.'

'So there was no cheating going on?'

'Not at all, sir! Anna has been working really hard at her maths.'

'Right, okay, thank you Vicky.' He returned to his own chair, his brow creased with worry.

Behind his back, Anna winked at Vicky.

Vicky could imagine the cogs turning in Mr Dewberry's brain. His moustache quivered as he ruminated over the situation.

Anna had mentioned a few times how her dad had donated money to the school over the years to improve their facilities since Anna was hell bent on staying there. He'd funded their new minibus, as well as the improvements to the netball courts when Anna had decided she wanted to be on the team, and she knew that Mr Maxwell's ongoing generosity would be sorely missed if Anna were to leave the school.

'Okay, I need to talk to Mr Surtees and get his side of the story, but I think it's best if you both keep this to yourself for now until I have all the facts. Then we can decide if it needs to be taken further or not. For now, I think you should both go home, take your minds off what has happened and we can talk again tomorrow. Is that fair?'

Anna sniffed melodramatically. 'Yes, sir, that's fair. My maths mark will stand though, won't it? I did work really hard.'

'Yes, Anna, the score will stand and well done for putting in the extra work. And to you, Vicky, you're a true friend.'

'Thank you, sir,' Vicky mumbled.

'Off you go then. I have an uncomfortable conversation ahead with a certain maths teacher now.' He shuffled them from the room and closed the door firmly behind them.

Anna pulled Vicky down the corridor and out of earshot. 'Thanks, Vix, I think he bought it.'

'Bloody hell, Anna, what have you done?'

'What? He was looking down my shirt, you know!'

'Only because you were making it very difficult for him to look anywhere else!'

'Oh please, he'll be fine. He'll get a slap on the wrist and that's it.'

'He might not! You may have ruined his career, all because of a poxy maths test!'

'Wow, Vicky, I thought you were my friend.'

'I am!'

'Well, you're not acting like it. Whose side are you on? I don't think we can be friends any more if you're going to be like this. You know, I can change my story and say you were in on it very easily. What would your dad think of that? Huh? I'm going home.' And she stormed off, leaving Vicky gaping at her rigid back.

Vicky took a slow walk home, mulling everything over in her head. By the time she'd opened her front door, she'd come to the conclusion that her friendship with Anna was far more important than some stupid teacher's career. Anna was right, he'd be fine. Men only got a slap on the wrist for these things. Mr Dewberry was probably patting him on the back right now, asking him what it had felt like and high-fiving him.

She dropped her bag, made sure the house was still empty and that her dad wasn't home early, before picking up the phone and calling Anna's house.

It rang for a while before a quiet, thin voice said, 'Hello?'

'Hi, Mrs Maxwell. It's Vicky. Can I speak to Anna please?'

'Hi, Vicky, of course, let me call her for you.'

Moments later, Anna picked up the phone and said, 'What?'

'I'm sorry, Anna. I was just taken by surprise, that's all. I didn't know you were going to say that. You're right, he's just a stupid teacher, but you're my best friend. I'm really sorry. You know you can always count on me. I'd do anything for you.'

There was silence for a moment, before Anna said, 'I stitched him up good and proper, didn't I?' She giggled, then said, 'So are you coming over or what?'

When their next maths class came around, there was a new teacher behind the desk, a stern, older woman called Mrs Russell, with greying hair, a pussy bow blouse and a tweed skirt over sensible shoes. Mr Surtees had been unceremoniously dispatched and the incident was never mentioned again, apart from a brief conversation with Mr Dewberry, who expressed to the girls his apologies that the incident had occurred and said that he hoped that the teacher in question's removal was sufficient an outcome that the authorities need not get involved.

5

David used to love Sundays. Lazy mornings, pyjamas until lunchtime, roast dinners and cuddling together under blankets watching television before sleepy eyes were put to bed. Even Anna had been more relaxed on Sundays. He'd usually insist on it being just them and if others intruded, he'd get annoyed and irritable. Usually that irritation came in the form of Vicky turning up for the afternoon, intruding on their dinnertime, calling for long telephone chats during the movie and distracting Anna with her latest drama.

But now he found himself wishing Vicky would intrude. It had been a week since she'd left and the house was quiet again. Too quiet. His mother had come over on Wednesday to see the kids and do 'a bit of a tidy up', in her words, but she'd left expressing her surprise at how everything looked in order.

In fact, he'd been coping okay. He'd cooked a few things out of the recipe book Vicky had left, had organised a shopping delivery before he went to work earlier in the week (mostly just reordering whatever Vicky had ordered on his account the week before) and had been organised enough at work to carry on some projects at home so that he could be there to pick them up from their after-school clubs.

But he was exhausted. All that scheduling, compartmentalising, ticking off lists and prepping. Not to mention Harper and Lewis's scrapes and bumps that needed salving, the petty arguments that needed refereeing and the cajoling necessary for everything from getting their shoes on to doing their spelling homework. It was constant and thankless.

But he'd done it and got through the week. And now it was Sunday and he was dreading it all starting up again tomorrow.

Now he knew why Anna had loved Sunday nights – because it meant she could return to work the next day. Especially before she died. She'd been spending a lot of time working on a new project, which had meant they'd seen less and less of her on the weekends. She had looked forward to the working week while he'd had a quiet sense of foreboding. Groundhog Day blues. She'd loved her job; his was tedious, just done to pay the bills.

Things had changed now though.

After the kids were in bed, he sat on the couch in his dressing gown and socks and turned on the television. The channels flicked past his eyes without him settling on anything. It was only 9 p.m. but he was seriously considering going to bed. That or pouring a drink – and he knew what the safer option would be.

His head snapped up at the sound of the home telephone ringing.

The last time he remembered taking a call on their otherwise quiet landline was on the evening of Anna's accident.

It had also been at about 9 p.m., the night sky dark and ominous outside the bay window where he'd stood to hear the words that had changed everything.

Your wife has been in an accident.

He could still remember the feeling of confusion that had washed over him initially, followed swiftly by fear, shock and then overwhelming physical pain as the voice on the phone elaborated on what had happened.

David got to his feet slowly now, the memory of that night constricting him like a straitjacket. The only reason he considered answering the call was because he didn't want the phone to wake the kids. He stumbled over to the handset sitting on the coffee table and answered it.

'Hello?'

Silence replied to him.

'Hello?' he repeated.

More silence, but then he thought he could hear the inhalation and exhalation of breath on the line, a faint sniff.

'Hello? Is anyone there?'

This time there was an audible click as the caller hung up.

David stood staring at the handset for a moment, trying to convince himself it was just a wrong number, but he felt cold and shivery.

He sat down abruptly as a fresh wave of grief and loneliness washed over him, like an unexpected splash from a puddle in the street.

Just thinking about her made him feel trembly and he laced his fingers in his hair, pulling at the roots, feeling the tiny stabs of pain grounding him as the strands resisted against his tugs.

The ring of the doorbell brought him a moment of pause.

What the hell?

It rang again and he shot to his feet.

He opened the door but kept the chain on, peering around it like a nervous geriatric.

Vicky stood in front of him. 'Hi,' was all she said.

'Vix! What are you… just a sec.' He closed the door again long enough to unhook the chain, then opened it fully and gestured for her to come in. 'It's late. Are you okay?' He suddenly felt very exposed in his gown and socks, with his hair on end. He pulled tightly on the cord at his waist. 'Um, sorry, I was just… you know, going to bed.' It sounded pathetic in his ears.

'I know, I'm sorry, it's late, but I didn't want to come earlier and interrupt your evening with the kids. I left something here last weekend and I need it, so I… er …'

Her words were awkward and stilted, nothing like the camaraderie and banter they'd shared only a few days ago.

'Oh. Okay. I could've brought it to you, saved you a trip or… did you just call me? On the home phone?'

'Me? No.' She shuffled from foot to foot, avoiding his eyes.

'Well, feel free to go up and have a look in the spare room. I haven't actually been in there since you left, so it'll still be there.' He stepped back from the door.

'Thanks.' She dropped her bag in the doorway, slipped off her filthy trainers and tiptoed up the stairs.

David returned to the lounge, then fluffed the cushions and straightened the blanket on the couch unnecessarily.

He tried to flatten down his hair. Maybe he should take his socks off.

Before he could, Vicky was back. She looked dreadful: twitchy, like she'd had too much caffeine, her eyes wide and a tiny bit manic, and her skin sallow. 'Got it, thanks. Right, well, I'd better let you get off to bed. I'll see you soon, I guess. Love to Harper and Lewis, yeah?'

'Hey, Vix, you okay?'

'Yeah, yep, just great.' Her stiff smile told a different story.

'Listen, stay for a quick drink. Please? I'm only going to bed because I can't stand the silence, so you'd be doing me a favour. I'll even put some pants on.' He smiled thinly.

She didn't smile back. 'Um, yeah, okay. Thanks.'

'Pour some whiskey for us. I'll be down in a minute.'

When he returned wearing his tracksuit bottoms, she was perched on the edge of the couch, a tumbler clutched in a visibly trembling hand.

'You want to tell me what's up?'

She sighed and put her glass down on the coffee table. 'You know, Anna and I had different opinions about Sunday evenings when we were at school. I used to talk endlessly about the Sunday stone in the stomach, that feeling of dread knowing that the next day was Monday and it would all start again. But it never bothered her. Tonight, I have that stone in my stomach again.'

She was mirroring his own thoughts and just knowing that made his own stone of dread erode a little bit. 'I know what you mean. I was just thinking about that. Great minds, eh?' He sipped at his whiskey, feeling the numbing burn scald his throat. 'But I thought you enjoyed your job?'

'It's… complicated.'

'Isn't everything? Wanna talk about it?'

She took a large gulp and he was embarrassed to see tears welling up in her eyes.

Oh god, please don't get tearful. I don't think I could bear it. Not tonight.

She took a deep breath and rushed out, 'It's my boss. He's been acting… inappropriately.'

David paused, thrown momentarily, then said, 'What do you mean by inappropriately?'

'He's been getting… handsy with me. You know, touching me and then claiming it's accidental, rubbing my arm, giving me looks, cornering me in the corridor and making innuendos. I just… it's making me hate going to work, but I really need this job. I'm trying to save up to get out of that shithole of a flat. Everything smells like curry because of the takeaway downstairs, which is dreadful when I'm trying to diet.' She stretched her lips thinly until they all but disappeared from her face.

'Can you report him to HR or something? You'll probably find he's done this before and they'll have to do something about it.'

'His wife is head of HR. Besides, I think that's why Barbara was fired last year.' She swiped at a stray tear that rolled down her cheek, glistening and clear.

'Hey, hey, come here.' He leaned towards her and she folded into his arms, pressing her face into his shoulder. 'We'll sort this out, okay?' His brain fired in five different directions at once as she filled the space between them, but darted back to form one clear thought. He heard himself saying the words before he'd even conceptualised them. 'I think I have an idea. Why don't you move in here? As the kids' nanny?'

She pushed away from him, frowning. 'What?'

'Well, you were so good with them when you were here and although I've been okay this last week, it has been hard trying to juggle everything. You hate your flat, we have a perfectly acceptable spare room here and the kids adore you. Why not? You could put the flat on the market and live here while you sell it.'

He was finding it difficult to read her expression. She was either horrified, confused or both.

'Never mind, silly idea...' He turned away and picked up his glass.

'No, no, I... it kinda makes sense.'

He turned back to her. 'It would be a business arrangement, of course. I'd pay you,' he clarified quickly. 'And we could do it for a trial period, say six months or something, but I want you to think of this as home.'

She got to her feet and moved over to the wide bay window with her back to him, twirling her glass in her hand, the dark sky staring back at her.

'What would your family think?' she said eventually.

He frowned. 'Who cares?'

'They've never really liked me and I don't want them to think I'm taking advantage...'

'Of what? Me in my vulnerable state? Pathetic as I am, unable to cope alone?' His voice rose a little and he felt an incredulous heat spread up his neck.

She turned at the tone in his voice. 'I don't think that! I just... I think people will automatically think that of me. People always seem to think the worst of me first.'

He got to his feet and approached her; his arms outstretched. In a softer tone, he said, 'I don't care what they think. All I care about is what's best for Harper and Lewis, and at this stage the best person for them is you because I can only be half a parent to them right now. The other half still needs fixing.'

She sighed. 'Okay, let's do it then.'

'Great. Tomorrow you'll tell that boss of yours to shove his job and you can start moving your stuff in whenever you're ready.' He smiled. 'It'll be fun.'

Dear Anna,

I'm not sure why I did it. Maybe all those years watching you use the truth like a weapon has rubbed off on me.

After I'd left him and the kids last week, I felt adrift. I stayed in bed, not eating, not sleeping, just thinking about you, them, us. Craving the way things used to be, like an itch I couldn't scratch without opening up a wound, but wanting to pick at it anyway. I found my box of photos and stared at them for hours, burning them into my retinas: me and you on school trips; laughing in random shops; pulling faces over glasses of vodka and coke. You always alert and in control, but why had I never noticed before that I was always looking away from the camera and over at you, imitating, checking that I was doing the right thing, desperate to please you?

I could feel the numbness creeping over me until by the end of the week I felt nothing at all. Just empty. Like a rinsed-out milk bottle left on the step, ready to be collected.

Then I found myself at David's door telling him some lie about my boss getting a bit too hands-on. Even as I heard the words coming out of my mouth, I knew it was wrong, but I couldn't stop myself.

He looked so relieved when I accepted his offer to move in. I could feel myself filling up again, the numbness receding instantly.

Okay, so lying about my boss was not cool. Especially the number of times I've been in those situations for real. The truth is I got retrenched from my job weeks ago because the company needed to cut staff and I hadn't been able to turn up to work after you died. No need for me to resign after all.

Maybe it's not lying; it's just telling a version of the truth to benefit my situation.

See, I am just like you after all.

I'll look after them, Anna. I promise. It'll be like you never left.

Vix xx

December 1989

It was bitterly cold and the rain lashed at Vicky's face as she stood at the side of the gaping hole in the ground. Her nan gripped her arm tightly, her thin fingers skeletal against the black sleeve of Vicky's coat.

Vicky peered down into the hole, the wet soil and thin roots like veins threading through the ground, the smell of the damp earth clinging to her nostrils. The rain pounded the coffin lying snugly in the hole. It sounded like someone knocking from the inside. Knocking to get out. Vicky shuddered.

'You cold, love? Come on, let's go,' her nan said.

Vicky took one last look into the hole and turned her back on it with relief. Her feet squelched in the wet grass as they walked away. She had to resist the urge to run, convinced that her dad had been knocking to get out, that he wasn't dead after all and was coming after her.

The wake was in full swing by the time Vicky and her nan arrived at the Traveller's Rest. Not many had come to the service, but all of his colleagues and friends were keen to take advantage of the free booze and sausage rolls on offer at the pub. Her nan shepherded her into a booth in the far corner of the room and Vicky sat, feeling numb, watching the merriment around her. He'd been well liked by all accounts. The life and soul of any party. He'd saved his drunken fury just for her, it would seem.

His slaps, pushes and punishments had intensified in the last year, but only Anna knew the full extent of what Vicky had had to endure during his numerous drunken outbursts. Vicky had learnt to tiptoe around the house, fade into the background, keeping out of sight, but every now and then he'd notice her. She'd started hanging out at Anna's house even more, using the excuse that she was tutoring Anna in maths. Mrs Maxwell looked at her with permanently tight lips, but said nothing about her constant presence. Anna had sat with Vicky while she cried, listened when she needed to rant and provided a safe haven. She knew she could never repay Anna for that.

But it was all over now. He'd never swing for her again. He'd never leave his hand on her knee for a bit too long. He'd never stare at her with that unsettling look in his eye when she came out of the bathroom.

Even so, it was hard to shed the skin of fear she'd grown over the last few years.

Her nan brought her over a plate of food and a coke. 'Hey, I know you miss him and it was a horrible way for him to go in the end, but he's with your mum now. And you've still got me. We'll be alright, won't we?' her nan said, mistaking Vicky's glazed stare for grief. 'Maybe we can do up your room finally, make it a bit more girly for you. What do you say? Us girls have to stick together now.'

Vicky just nodded.

Her nan wandered off to talk to Brian, her dad's closest friend, who was propping up the bar with his substantial frame. A fellow cabbie, Brian had a squashed face like a fat troll, all folds and furrows. His gut hung over his well-worn belt and his shirt strained at the buttonholes. Vicky had never liked him. He was another one who had a way of sweeping his eyes over her that made her feel naked and exposed. She looked away in disgust as he began to hand-roll a cigarette with his chubby, yellowing fingers.

The air in the pub was suffocating, heady with smoke, banter and warm beer. Vicky felt like the wallpapered walls were closing in on her, pushing the smoke towards her in toxic clouds, reaching into her mouth and vaping through her hair. Her breath was coming in thin gasps and she reached for the coke with a trembling hand. Playing on a newsreel behind her eyes was the image of the coffin in the ground, set against the soundtrack of the rain pelting the wood. She picked at the skin around her cuticles, pulling and tearing until specks of blood began to form as she peeled the skin away.

'Hey, you okay? You look like shit.'

Vicky felt a sob catch in her throat at the sound of Anna's voice. 'I thought you weren't allowed to come?'

'Yeah, well, what my mother doesn't know...' Anna threw down her bag and coat and shuffled her bum onto the seat next to Vicky.

When Vicky had shrugged out of her coat when she'd arrived, the sleeve of her dark green jumper had ridden up her forearm to reveal another one of Anna's bruise tattoos, this one transforming the three cigarette burns into a spider, an octopus and a hedgehog. She caught Anna looking at it now and pulled her sleeve down.

'You can't be sad that he's dead?'

'It's not that.' Vicky lowered her voice. 'It's just… finding him like that, on the floor, the vomit—'

'Stop it. We are not talking about it. Put it out of your head and move on. He was a shithead of a dad, a complete twat of a man, and you are so much better off without him. The *world* is better off without him. He had no right to use you as a punching bag all these years, okay? Karma.'

Vicky bit her lip and nodded.

'I've got something for you.' Anna dug in her backpack and pulled out a small, velvet box. She handed it to Vicky with a grin.

'What is it?'

'Open it and see.'

Vicky opened the box to see a thin gold chain nesting inside with a delicate hummingbird charm hanging from it.

She gasped. 'It's so pretty, but what's it for?' Vicky had never owned anything so delicate.

'It's for you, silly. It's instead of the drawings—' she pointed to Vicky's forearm '—because you're free of him now. Free as a bird, get it? And when you wear it, I want you to think of me.'

Vicky looked down at the hummingbird again and felt like her chest was going to burst. All she could say was, 'Thanks.'

Anna shrugged, but Vicky could tell she was proud of herself. Anna scanned the room, then got up and disappeared into the bodies milling about. Vicky looked at the beautiful necklace one more time, then shut the little box with a snap and tucked it into her coat pocket with a smile.

Within minutes, Anna was back with two glasses of coke.

'Thanks, but I've already got one,' Vicky said.

Anna smiled slyly. 'This isn't just coke. Have some. It'll make you feel better. Steady your nerves.'

Vicky took a gulp of the drink and almost spat it straight out at Anna. It burned all the way into the pit of her stomach, then lay there bubbling and roiling like lava.

'What is that?' Vicky wiped her mouth with the back of her hand.

Anna was happily sipping on her own drink. 'I don't know. I just collected up a few stray drinks lying around and mixed them together. There's definitely whiskey and I think that man over there may have mislaid his rum and coke.' She pointed at Brian, who was frowning and looking around him in confusion.

Vicky felt herself smile. 'Jeez, Anna, you're a liability.' She took another drink, a longer one this time, and found it didn't taste as poisonous the second time around.

'Yes, but where would you be without me? Come on, drink up and I'll find us some more.'

6

David wanted to weep with relief when he heard Vicky's voice down the phone line.

'Hi David.'

'Vicky, hi.' He gripped his mobile tightly in his fist, could feel the screen hot against his cheek. His left hand was clasped in a tight fist.

'You okay?'

'No, not...' A sob wrenched from his throat, unbidden, choked. He swallowed against it. He could hear someone washing their hands beyond the toilet cubicle door, so he lowered his voice. 'It's stupid. I don't know why it's affecting me so much.'

'What's happened?'

He took a deep breath and opened his fist to reveal the ticket stub crushed into his palm. 'I brought a coat with me to work today. Haven't worn it in a while, but Lewis spilled something on my other one.' He knew he was rambling, but he couldn't stop himself. 'I put my hand in the pocket and there was a ticket stub inside. From when I took Anna to see Robbie Williams – the last gig we went to…' He laughed bitterly. 'She hated it. I thought I was being romantic.' Sobs took over then, wracking his body. Sweat was making the coat stick to his arms, but he couldn't bring himself to take it off.

'Jesus.' She paused. 'Where are you? Do you want me to come over?'

'Yes, please, well, I… I'm at work, but I have to leave to get the kids from school. I know you're only supposed to move in next week, but I really don't want to be alone tonight. And I don't want the kids to see me like this. I'm a mess.'

'Don't worry, I'll get them from school, then once they're off to bed, we can talk properly. I'll bring a bottle. Sounds like we'll need it.'

'Can you get out of work okay? I don't want to cause more trouble for you with your boss.'

'Oh, no, er… he's not in today, so it'll be fine. Besides, I don't work here any more after Friday, do I?'

'Thanks Vicky, you're a good friend.'

'I've got your back, David. It's what Anna would've wanted. See you later.'

David poured generous glasses of red wine and collapsed back onto the couch cushions, still in the suit trousers he had worn to work, but with his tie loose at his neck and his shirtsleeves rolled up. The weight of the day pushed down on his shoulders. He could hear Vicky moving about upstairs, supervising the bedroom routine like a pro, her animated voice so different from Anna's, who had always insisted on a quiet, regimented bedtime. In contrast, Vicky was singing as the kids brushed their teeth, some inane song about the tooth fairy.

He necked half the glass in one go, then topped it up and rested his head back against the cushion.

He was onto his second glass when Vicky finally made it downstairs.

'Leave some for me!'

He smiled thinly and passed a glass over to her. She sat next to him and tucked her feet up under her long skirt.

'You okay?' she asked.

'I've been better.' David sighed and sat forward, resting his elbows on his knees and propping his heavy head in his hands. 'I called the police again, just before I found the ticket stub. I wanted an update. I haven't heard anything from them for a while.'

'And?' Vicky looked into her glass.

'Nothing new. Still leaning towards an accident with no new evidence to the contrary.'

'But I thought they… didn't they say someone else may have been involved?' She swirled her wine, watching the liquid motion intently.

'Yes, they had witnesses saying they saw another car speeding in the area, but that's as far as it went. They were making it sound like it could be ruled as accidental death.' He chuckled bitterly. 'They even mentioned that the body of a fox was found near to the car. That maybe she swerved to miss it.'

Vicky got up and walked over to the bay window, her back to him. 'You must be relieved then?'

'I don't know what to think or feel, to be honest.' David took a large gulp of his wine. 'I think I really need someone to blame, you know? But to think that a stupid, fucking fox could've killed my wife just feels so… inadequate. So wasteful.'

Vicky was quiet. After a moment, she turned back to David. 'I think I'd rather that than knowing someone hated her enough to hurt her.'

David frowned. 'That was the thing though. No one hated Anna.'

Vicky looked away. 'I know that, but…'

'Yeah, you're right, I suppose. When the police were questioning everyone and looking at me, you, I felt angry and wanted to blame someone – and it felt like they were right. That Anna was trying to tell me something, telling me someone had hurt her. She was acting so strangely that week and you two weren't talking, which was the longest I'd ever known you to fall out. I just…' He sighed. 'I know it sounds stupid, but knowing that there may be no one to blame, I can't be angry any more, so what am I supposed to feel? It just doesn't sit right with me. Anger is better than feeling nothing at all.'

He drained the glass again, then refilled it.

'It's funny. That night when you called me to tell me about the accident, I actually thought you might have done something,' Vicky said.

'Me? Why?'

'I don't know. You sounded so flat and… emotionless, I guess, but it's easy to scout around for a culprit when you're angry and in shock. Everyone looks suspicious.' Vicky returned to sit next to him and put her hand on his.

'And it's okay to be angry. It's still a waste of her life. But you need to find comfort in knowing that maybe no one was to blame. If they do say it was an accident, then it's better for you and the kids to let it go. Accept that it was an accident. A tragic, horrible accident.'

'But what if they're wrong and we never find out what really happened that night?'

'It won't change anything. She will still be gone. You're just searching for a way to fix this and you can't. It is what it is.'

His eyes scanned her reddened cheeks and wide eyes before he looked away. He wanted to rage at her, tell her to take back what she said, but he knew she was right.

Vicky pulled her hand away.

He sighed. 'You're right, I'm sorry. It was just calling them and then finding the ticket, I lost it for a bit.' He shook his head. 'A fucking fox. She hated foxes. Was terrified one would come into the house and attack the kids or something.'

He drank deeply again. Vicky watched him from the corner of her eyes as she took a drink from her own glass.

'You never did say what it was about,' he said.

'It?'

'What you two were fighting about before she…' He swallowed. 'Before the accident. She never said either. Didn't want to talk about it.'

'It was nothing.'

'Really? Considering you were such close friends, for you two to refuse to speak to each other for a week, it must've been something bad. You never went a day without speaking to each other.'

'It was a silly misunderstanding, that's all. I can't even remember exactly what it was about, but we'd made up anyway, that evening.' She got to her feet quickly. 'Listen, have you eaten? I'm starving.'

'No, I… er, I'm not hungry.' He stared into his glass, feeling the melancholy on his skin like a cobweb. He wanted to talk about Anna, but also didn't, like an addiction he knew would hurt him. 'I used to get jealous of how close you two were sometimes, used to wonder what you had that I didn't. It was like you were bound together by some weird girl pact or something that excluded everyone else.'

'Oh, it was nothing like that, we were just… close, like old friends are.' She chewed on the inside of her lip, which made her mouth pull down into a grimace. 'Come on, I'll go grab us a pizza or something. It's probably better that you eat if you're going to finish that bottle.'

'Yeah, you're probably right, but just phone it in and they'll deliver.'

'I don't mind going to pick it up,' she said hurriedly. 'It's quicker and you're running low on milk anyway. I gave Lewis some before bed.'

She rushed from the room and moments later David heard the front door close. He got up and moved to the bay window. Vicky was standing outside on the front step, immobile, staring at nothing, still chewing on her lip. Then she slowly walked away.

July 1990

'Vicky, I need you to come over.' Anna's voice was high-pitched and nasal.

'Why? What's happened?' Vicky had been home from school for about half an hour and was sitting with a cup of tea in the tiny slice of sunshine that had pierced their pathetic excuse for a back garden. It was more like a patch of dying grass with cracked paving stones providing scaffolding for a few flourishing weeds than a garden, but Vicky liked to sit in their one plastic patio chair and breathe in the sunshine, letting it fill her lungs and clear her head.

She felt better out here than she did inside the house, where every room still seemed to smell like her father. It was as though the walls had breathed him in as he lay dying and were now slowly exhaling him all over her like a putrid breath she couldn't avoid.

Sometimes she was sure the house was colder than usual, like ice creeping over her skin. She would avoid looking at his chair in the lounge, the shape of him still indented in the cushion. Her nan hadn't wanted to get rid of it, but Vicky felt like if she sat in it, the upholstery would mould around her and slowly suffocate her, squeezing the air from her lungs until she was inhaled into the very fabric just as he had been.

She knew she was being ridiculous, but as a precaution she stayed at Anna's as much as her nan would let her and sat outside on even the most frigid of days where she could breathe freely.

'I'll tell you when you get here.' Anna put the phone down, giving Vicky no chance to respond.

As she walked up to Anna's front door, the gravel crunching familiarly under her Doc Martens, she wondered what was going on. Probably something to do with the guy Anna had been flirting with at that party last week, or her mother, who seemed to annoy Anna just by sharing the same air as her. She sucked on the hummingbird necklace, the gold pendant cold against her lips. She had worn it every day since the funeral.

Mrs Maxwell's big 4x4 wasn't parked in the driveway, which was unusual.

As Vicky raised her hand to ring the doorbell, the door flew open. Anna stood in front of her, pale but with two patches of redness high on each of her sharp cheekbones. Her eyes were feverish.

She grabbed Vicky by the arm and dragged her inside. 'What took you so long?'

'Sorry, I had to wait for the bus. What's happened?'

Anna took off into the lounge. Vicky followed to find Anna swigging from a bottle of vodka. 'What the hell, Anna? It's only four-thirty!'

Anna swallowed with a grimace and wiped her mouth with the back of her hand.

'That bitch!' Her mother after all then.

Vicky looked around, half expecting to see Mrs Maxwell's corpse propped up in the corner, the way Anna was reacting.

'Where is she?'

'She's gone to a yoga class – to clear her head apparently. She'll be lucky not to fall over in her downward dog considering how much she's had of this already.' Anna waved the half-full bottle, sneering.

'And she drove?'

'Of course, you don't think she would walk, do you? She always drives. Hasn't been caught yet. An expert drunk, that one. Years of practice.'

'Is that why you're pissed off at her? Because she's driving around drunk?'

'No, Vicky, it's not that. I couldn't care less about that – she can kill herself any way she likes for all I care.' Anna's voice dripped bitterness.

Vicky ignored the comment. She knew when Anna was angry that she needed to tread carefully in case Anna took some of that fury out on her.

Anna exhaled loudly. 'It's both of them, actually.' She took another gulp from the bottle, then slammed it on the side table. She flung herself into the nearest armchair. 'So my dad was supposed to meet me after school. We were going to have ice cream and stuff because he's been away so much lately.' Suddenly she looked and sounded like the child she was. 'So I went to his office after school and…'

Vicky waited. Anna looked like she'd swallowed something nasty.

'Let's just say he wouldn't have been hungry for ice cream since he was eating out his secretary on his desk.' Anna burst into tears.

'Fuck!' Vicky said, horrified. 'What did you do?'

'He didn't see me. I was about to open his office door when I saw them through the blinds.' She swiped at her eyes. 'I left, obviously, felt properly sick. In fact, I was sick – rushed straight to the toilet and threw up everywhere, left it for them to clean it up. I came home, figured my mother should know, you know? But when I told her, she just looked at me blankly, like I'd told her we were out of milk or something. Then she said she didn't believe me, calmly called me a liar. Like, why would I lie about that?'

Vicky didn't think it was the right time to mention that Anna had a tendency to twist the truth when she was after something. Although she'd never lie about something like this.

Would she?

'Then what happened?'

'I screamed at her, told her she was a drunk doormat and that it was no wonder Dad had to look elsewhere because she was such a fucking waste of air. Then she said she was going to yoga and left.' Anna leapt to her feet, fury straightening her back and tensing her shoulders. 'I mean, seriously, what the fuck?'

'Maybe she's just in shock or something?'

'Or maybe she knows and is just ignoring it. I mean, she's got everything she needs, right? A cushy life, lots of money that she doesn't have to work for. A divorce would jeopardise all that, so let's just drink it out, pretend nothing is going on.' Anna reached for the bottle again.

'That won't help, Anna.'

For a moment Vicky thought Anna was going to hit her. Her eyes flashed cold in the sudden silence.

Then Anna put the bottle down and said calmly, 'You're right, getting drunk isn't the answer. I'm better than her. That's how she deals with it, not me. I get revenge.' She stomped from the room.

Vicky scurried after her. 'Wait! What are you going to do?'

'I don't know yet,' she shouted over her shoulder. 'I just know I have to do something or I'll explode because I am so fucking angry!' The lounge door slammed against the paintwork as she flung it away from her, the glass rattling with the force. Vicky saw a chunk of plaster dislodge as the handle punctured the wall.

Then she heard Anna say from between clenched teeth, 'What the fuck are you looking at?'

Mrs Maxwell's beloved cat, Murphy, sat in the hallway, eyeing Anna calmly. Anna snarled, 'Get out of my way! I swear she loves this damn cat more than me!' Her foot shot out and connected with Murphy, who yowled in pain and lifted into the air before landing with a sickening thud on his side. Anna kicked at the cat again and Vicky was sure she heard a crunch as Anna's brogue thudded into Murphy's side.

Vicky felt herself freeze in position while Anna kicked and screamed, taking all of her rage out on the defenceless animal howling at her feet.

Then, as if all the air was rushing at her at once, Vicky found her voice and her legs and rushed at Anna. 'Stop!

Stop! You'll kill him! Anna!' She grabbed at Anna's flailing arms and spun her around to face her.

'Hey, Anna! Look at me! Stop, breathe. It's not the cat's fault. It's your dad's fault. Breathe, please.'

Anna was sweaty, her breath coming in gulps, tears and snot all over her red cheeks. They stared at each other, then Vicky pulled her into a tight hug. But Anna remained stiff and rigid in her arms. Vicky released her and crouched down, her hand outstretched towards Murphy. She touched his fur but felt no movement. Her hand came away sticky and warm. Vicky felt her stomach lurch.

'I think you've killed him,' she said in a tiny voice.

Anna said nothing, just remained unmoving, her back to Vicky.

Vicky fought the urge to vomit as she gently picked the cat up in her hands. His head flopped over her wrist, the tongue lolling, the body lifeless. Vicky stood, unsure what to do.

'Get rid of it,' Anna said.

'Um, right...' Vicky looked around, confused.

Think, Vicky, think.

She hurried into the kitchen towards the back of the house. The connecting utility room had a back door leading into the garden. She gently placed Murphy in the sink and turned the key to unlock the door.

Vicky looked around in panic, completely out of her comfort zone when faced with disposing of a dead body. Her eyes fell on the herb garden running along the side of the house by the fence. Sticking up from the soil at the end was a trowel.

She grabbed the trowel and began to dig down behind a rosemary bush, the scent of the leaves heady and overpowering.

The hole dug, she went back to where she had left the cat. Blood had started to seep into the sink and pool around the cat's fur. She retched as she picked him up, her fingers sinking into the wet fur. She needed to wrap him in something or the blood would drip as she carried him outside. A tea towel lay on the countertop, which she grabbed and folded around the body.

Five minutes later, the hole was filled in, the soil smoothed over the broken cat and Vicky knew she would never eat anything flavoured with rosemary again.

As she washed her hands and the blood from the sink, she felt more than heard Anna come up behind her.

'What have I done?' Anna said in a throttled voice. 'Vix, what have I done?'

'Hey, listen, I've sorted it. Murphy is gone and we'll make something up to tell your mother.'

'Oh god, if they find out about this, they'll send me away, probably not even boarding school. Only psychopaths kill animals. They'll lock me up in an institution or something!'

'Take a breath, Anna. It'll be okay. We'll just say Murphy ran away.'

'She'll never believe me – Murphy never leaves the house.'

'She will. You can be very persuasive when you want to be. Or I'll take the rap for you, say I left the front door open when I left today and he followed me down the driveway or something.'

'You'd do that for me? Take the rap for me?'

'Of course I would! You're my best friend. You keep my secrets; I keep yours. That's how it works, right? Now we're even.'

Anna breathed out, reached up a hand to smooth down her hair and closed her eyes for a moment.

When she opened them again, it was as though nothing had happened.

Dear Anna,

I was thinking about Murphy the cat last night.

David said something about how he had sometimes felt jealous of us and the bond we had, like we had a secret pact between us. And I guess we did, didn't we?

You had your secret and I had mine.

I never told you how frightened I was of you that day. The look on your face as your foot kicked out again and again and again. There was nothing behind your eyes. After that, there was an element of fear to our friendship – fear that if I ever stepped out of line, you'd lash out at me like you had at Murphy.

Your mother hated me after that too. Once she heard that it was apparently my fault Murphy 'ran away', I ceased to exist for her. She would look straight through me when I was at your house.

Her alcoholism ratcheted up a notch too, didn't it? To the point where even your dad couldn't ignore it any more. Then he left and you went off to university, and your mother was left alone with just her dead cat's corpse to keep her company. Not that she knew it, of course.

Looking back, Murphy's death affected me a lot more than you. It was just one more thing to add to my list, but you seemed to take it in your stride. You acted as though it had never happened and the affair

was never mentioned again until your dad announced
he was moving out.

But I will never forget it.

Secrets and lies. That's what friends are for.

Vix xx

August 1992

'You're really gonna do this?'

They sat on Anna's double bed drinking tea, with Vicky dunking biscuit after biscuit into her mug so that soggy crumbs now floated on the surface. The biscuits had no recognisable taste to her, but the mechanics of it were comforting.

She could feel tears of frustration welling up in her eyes, but didn't want to give Anna the pleasure of seeing how upset she really was.

'Oh, come on, it'll be fine. You'll be fine. You'll find a great job somewhere and, in a few years, when I'm back from uni, it'll be like we were never apart,' Anna replied.

But Vicky couldn't shake the feeling that Anna would never be fully back with her. She would go and find herself an amazing life away from here, with new friends who weren't as needy – or, worse, Anna would realise how Vicky had been cramping her style all these years. But Anna was all Vicky had.

It felt as though everything was dissolving around her, like the sagging biscuit in her fingers.

Anna leaned over the bed and hugged Vicky tight to her. 'It's just Durham, not the end of the world,' she said into Vicky's shoulder. 'I'll be back every few weeks and we'll do all the stuff we usually do. You can call me anytime as well. There's bound to be a payphone at the residences.'

Vicky inhaled the scent of Anna, a mix of apple shampoo and freshly laundered cotton, before pulling away. 'You're right. I guess I'm just jealous. I wish I had a swish university to go to.'

Vicky had messed it all up. Despite being the smart one of the two of them, she'd let her dad's death worm inside her head until there was no room for anything else. And while she'd been distracted by that and helping Anna get through her exams, Vicky's grades had slipped and she had barely passed her own. Now she was paying the price by facing an uncertain future without any prospects while her best friend had the world at her feet.

Vicky was clearly growing into her father's daughter. He always said she'd come to nothing.

Wouldn't Mum be proud if she could see me now?

'Vix, you'll be earning millions while I'm still stuck with my face in a book. And anyway, how am I supposed to pass without you helping me out? You spent more time on my homework than you did on your own!'

Vicky didn't respond.

'We have loads of time to party before I go though, starting tonight!' Anna pushed off from the bed and flung open her wardrobe. Clothes hung askew on hangers or were bundled into piles; shoes were tossed in any old way;

and jeans lay on the shelves with their legs turned inside out. Vicky yearned to have such choice and knew that if she did, she'd certainly look after it all better than Anna did.

'Dan says he's going to that new club in Kingston tonight and he can get us in. What do you think? You in?'

Vicky wasn't in the mood for playing third wheel to Anna and her new boyfriend, Dan. It was nauseating to watch them together. But with no boyfriend of her own, she had no choice if she wanted to go out tonight.

'Ugh, nothing to wear as usual.' Anna slammed the wardrobe doors shut. 'Come on, let's go shopping.'

'I've got no money.'

'Me neither! But where there's a will, there's a way…'

Vicky followed Anna downstairs. Mrs Maxwell sat in the lounge, her skinny legs crossed at the knee, absently flicking through the pages of a fashion magazine. A highball glass sat sweating on the side table, ice cubes swirling gently around a slice of lemon.

'Mum, we're going into town.' Mrs Maxwell jumped as Anna burst into the room.

'Oh!' She clasped a skeletal hand to her chest. 'Okay, but will you be back for dinner?'

'No, we're going out afterwards.'

'But I've made your favourite, lasagne.' She smiled but it didn't reach her eyes.

'Mother, that's all you really know how to make.' Anna rolled her eyes.

'But I—'

'What exactly is it you do all day?' Anna stared at her coldly.

'I'm sorry?' Her mother looked aghast.

'You don't work, you have a cleaner, you have a gardener and you can't cook. What is it that you do? What is your function exactly? Jeez Mum, you're an embarrassment. I can't wait to get out of here and go off to university.'

'Anna!'

'Whatever. We're going.' She stalked from the room, leaving Vicky standing awkwardly in the doorway.

Vicky was used to hearing the way Anna spoke to her mother after all these years, but the vitriol had ramped up a notch in the last two years.

'Mrs Maxwell, I can take some of the lasagne home with me later if that helps? It's my favourite too.' She smiled warmly.

Mrs Maxwell looked back at her magazine, as though Vicky wasn't even there.

'Vix! Come on!' Anna shouted from the front door.

As Vicky turned to go, Mrs Maxwell leaned over and took a long draw from her drink, her eyes glassy.

Anna was standing over her mother's handbag in the front hall, one hand rummaging through her purse. She pulled out a number of twenty-pound notes and shoved the purse back inside. 'Let's go.'

Vicky grabbed her own bag from the banister and followed her out of the front door.

As they sat on the bus, Vicky could feel her blood hot in her veins. 'You shouldn't have done that.' Her fingers fiddled with the necklace at her throat, twisting it until she felt sure it would break before loosening it again.

'What?' Anna's eyes were pools of innocence.

'Spoken to her like that. Or taken her money.'

'Oh, she won't notice it's gone. My dad is always throwing money at her. Alleviating his guilt, I think. Not that I see him much now that he's moved in with his tart.'

'Still, she is your mother.' Vicky stared resolutely out of the bus window as the streets rushed past in a haze of condensation.

'Woah, hold up! What's got into you?'

'I just… if she was my mum, I'd be a bit nicer, that's all,' Vicky replied quietly.

'Oh, boo hoo, are you playing the "I'm an orphan" card? Is this just because you're still angry at me for getting into uni when you screwed it up? If you're going to be like this, I'll go into Kingston on my own. Besides, you've never had a problem spending my money on yourself in the past.'

Vicky could feel her teeth grinding together, like bone on bone, making her jaw ache.

Anna leaned into her ear. 'Let's not forget why you're an orphan either.'

Vicky had to sit on her hand to stop herself from reaching out and slapping Anna hard. Anna glared at her, challenging her to react.

'Meow, Anna,' Vicky muttered.

'What did you say?'

The silence stretched out between them, filling the air like a toxic cloud.

'So should we head to Dorothy Perkins first? There was a cute little miniskirt in there last week.' And with that, the toxic air diffused as Anna flicked back into normal mode with dizzying speed, like a switch had been tripped.

The store was quiet, with only a few people rifling through the racks of clothes. Anna held an intricate glass bottle aloft and sprayed perfume into the air between them, leaving a sweet and spicy cloud that tickled Vicky's nose and made her sneeze.

'Ugh, that perfume smells awful, like Murphy's pee,' Anna said pointedly, a smirk on her lips, then shoved the bottle back on the shelf. Her arms were full of clothes and she kept poking Vicky with the hangers every time she turned to look at something else.

Vicky carried a skirt and a top in her arms.

'Let's go try these on. I'm psyched about that skirt you've got. I wish I'd seen it first,' Anna said.

Vicky had spotted the plum-coloured leather skirt at the back of a rack and fell in love with it straight away. She didn't have any money to pay for it though. She just wanted something to try on so that it wasn't all about Anna – and a small part of her relished the fact that she had found something that Anna wanted.

They wormed through the store to the fitting rooms at the back.

Vicky pulled the curtain across the cubicle next to Anna, kicked off her sandals and squirmed out of her tight jeans. She pulled on the skirt and reached behind to pull up the zip.

It was perfect. She twisted and turned in front of the mirror, admiring herself from every angle. The skirt skimmed her hips at just the right angle and made her look and feel smaller than she was, no bulges, no muffin top for a change.

The curtain fluttered and Anna shoved her head through the gap.

'Anna, don't you just love this! It's perfect!'

Anna was standing in her bra, her skinny frame highlighted by the outline of her ribs under her pale skin. She screwed up her face and tilted her head to the side. 'Nah, I don't think that's very flattering at all. And totally the wrong colour for you.'

'Really?' Vicky looked back at herself. She smoothed the skirt down over her hips.

'Yeah, it's just a bit... bulky on you. Makes you look big in the hips.'

Vicky took a closer look and could now see how the skirt angled out to make her look wide and triangular. Why hadn't she noticed that earlier?

'Now, what do you think of these jeans?' Anna continued.

Vicky looked over at Anna's long legs clad in black skin-tight denim that skimmed over her non-existent hips. 'You look amazing,' she said in a faint voice.

'Yeah, not bad, eh? I'm definitely getting these. Do me a favour. Go and see if you can find me one of those skirts in a smaller size, would you? I think it'll look better on me. You don't mind, do you? You can just borrow something from my wardrobe later, if there's something in there that fits. Unless you see something else, of course.' She swished from the cubicle.

Vicky bit back tears as she got dressed. Emerging from the cubicle, she flung the skirt onto the pile of rejected clothes and headed back into the store.

Ten minutes later, Anna preened in front of the changing room mirror wearing the skirt Vicky had seen, but two sizes smaller. Typically, it looked amazing on her. 'I am so getting this.' She looked at Vicky over her shoulder. 'You don't mind, do you? I know you saw it first.'

'Sure, go ahead.' Vicky shrugged.

Anna beamed. 'Now, I also want this top because I think it will go perfectly with it, but I don't have enough money for it.' Her voice dropped to a conspiratorial mutter. 'Come in here and put this on under your T-shirt. They'll never know you have it.'

'Why me?'

'Because you have a baggier top on. They'll be able to see it under mine.' Anna's T-shirt was so tight that it was like a second skin. 'Besides, you're better at this than I am.'

'Only because you always make me lift the stuff.'

'At least you know if you don't get a job soon, you can do this for a living.' Vicky knew Anna meant it as a joke, but it stung nonetheless.

'Is that all I'm good for? Nicking stuff?'

'God, you're in a fucking mood today.' Anna sighed dramatically and turned back to the mirror. 'I actually don't want you to come out with us tonight if you're going to be like this. It's a shame though. We don't have many nights left.'

Vicky felt panic twist into a knot of guilt in her stomach. 'Okay, fine, hand it over.'

She shuffled into the cubicle with Anna and wormed into the tight T-shirt, then threw her own T-shirt over the top. The security guard would have to look really closely to notice she was wearing two shirts.

Anna got herself dressed and they headed over to the tills where Anna handed over the money she'd lifted from her mother's purse. Vicky could feel sweat sticking the stolen T-shirt to her back, the extra layer acting as unnecessary insulation in the warm store. She felt a rush of smug satisfaction as she thought about Anna wearing it later, not knowing how much she had sweated in it. That would teach her to make her do her dirty work.

As they headed to the doors, she could see the security guard sweep his eyes over them one by one, then come back to her again. Her cheeks flushed and she knew he would reach out at any minute and haul her in for stealing the shirt.

He watched them closely as they walked past, but before he could say anything, Anna turned to him and said loudly, 'Hey pervert! Keep your eyes to yourself! We're not even sixteen!'

The guard flushed bright red and looked away hurriedly as a middle-aged woman scowled and tutted at him on her way into the shop.

Anna smirked at him, then tugged on Vicky's arm and they legged it.

'Did you see his face? He was mortified that I'd practically called him a paedophile!'

'Fuck, Anna! It's been a long time since you've tried to pass us off as sixteen!'

'It worked, didn't it? Right, let's head to the toilets and get you out of that T-shirt before you stretch it.'

The night started off alright. Vicky told her nan she was staying at Anna's and headed over there early to get ready. She would need to borrow Anna's clothes anyway, since she had nothing of her own that she hadn't already worn a million times.

She wore her own jeans, but borrowed a draped top that Anna had only worn once because she thought it made her look too fat. For Vicky, it hid the muffin top that hung over her waistband as a result of her nan's dinners of sausages and mash, cottage pie, and chops, followed up with steamed puddings and jam roly-polies. Anna's mother seemed to exist on rather exotic food, like stir fries and lentils, always accompanied by salad, whereas Vicky's meals were generally served with a side order of potato cooked in a variety of ways.

Still, Vicky would take her nan's stodgy cooking over her dad's heavy hand any day.

Just thinking about her dad made her stomach clench and her hand reach for the biscuit tin. He still hung over her like a spectral cloud, following her everywhere she went. She doubted he would ever leave her alone. Now, when the thoughts bombarding her bruised brain became too much, she found solace in food, binging on whatever she could find or sneaking out to the corner shop and buying bags of junk – chocolate, cakes, crisps – and eating until her stomach hurt so much that she forgot about everything else.

While they got ready to go out, Anna sneaked a bottle of vodka from the cupboard downstairs, declaring that her mother would just assume she'd drunk it herself. They had a few tugs on the bottle, then Anna set it aside. Her drinking was always half-hearted, as though she wanted someone to tell her not to do it. Vicky was more committed and had drunk half the bottle before they left to head out to the club. She shoved the rest of it in her handbag on her way out. Anna was right. Mrs Maxwell wouldn't miss it.

Anna never discussed her mother's drinking, even when it was painfully apparent that Mrs Maxwell was slurring her words most days. All she seemed to do was sit in the lounge staring into space or flicking through magazines, a glass permanently in place beside her. She wasn't a nasty drunk like

Vicky's dad had been; rather, a vacant, placid one. The classiest functioning alcoholic Vicky had ever seen. Even in a state of permanent mild inebriation, she exuded calm class. There was always dinner ready for Anna, the food left sitting under sweating clingfilm, and the house was always immaculate, but Mrs Maxwell herself floated through the house like a ghost.

This common denominator of a dysfunctional upbringing at the hands of an alcoholic only drew Vicky and Anna closer together. They were victims of the same deficiencies; the result of a toss of the same coin.

But they also handled things in very different ways. Vicky chose to close off that part of her life and not talk about it, while Anna lashed out in different ways, taunting her mother, acting out for her father's attention and often lashing Vicky with her sharp tongue if Vicky dared to challenge her. But Vicky understood why she did it and ignored Anna's jibes about her weight, her dad's death, her lack of a boyfriend. Vicky almost welcomed Anna's vitriol as a replacement for the verbal and physical abuse she had suffered at the hands of her father. It meant she cared, surely? It was only what she deserved and without Anna, Vicky would have no one she could be herself with.

Anna had arranged to meet Dan at the club. She and Vicky got on the bus and sat at the back, passing loud criticism of other passengers and swearing just to get a rise. They were rewarded with raised eyebrows and much tutting, making them snigger behind their hands. But then Dan sidled up to Anna as soon as they arrived and Vicky was shoved aside. At not quite eighteen, Vicky wasn't old enough to buy drinks, so she had to rely on Anna and Dan. At least she had her bottle of vodka in her bag to keep her company.

The evening was relatively dull on the whole and Vicky almost wished she hadn't come. As the clock neared midnight, Anna leaned over to Vicky and said that she was leaving with Dan and that she needed Vicky to cover for her if her mother asked where she was.

'Say I slept at your house, please.'

'Wait, how am I gonna get home?'

'You'll be fine on the night bus. It's not far. Please, Vix! I've decided I want to do this – you know, sleep with him – before I leave for uni. I'd do the same for you.' Dan had his arms clasped around her and his face attached to her neck and suddenly Vicky wanted to be as far away from the two of them as she could.

'Fine, if that's what you want to do. I think you're stupid, but what do I know?'

'Thanks Vix, I love you.' And with that, they melded into the crowd of people on the dancefloor, leaving Vicky standing alone.

Vicky found a seat at the very back of the night bus and ducked down, her legs pulled up and the mostly empty bottle of vodka tucked between her knees. This was what it was going to be like from now on. Vicky alone on a bus with a bottle of vodka while Anna was off making new friends and sleeping her way around Durham.

She felt tears slide glacially through the make-up on her face.

Vicky spent the first week that Anna was away trying to call her on the number she had given her, but no one ever answered the phone. So she ate junk, made herself sick and then repeated it all again in a cycle of bingeing and purging, hoping to making herself feel better. It worked while the food was going in, but then made her feel dirty and ashamed as it came back out.

She had nowhere to go now, since she couldn't hang out at Anna's house any more. It felt like she was slowly suffocating.

She found a job as a receptionist at a local stationery wholesaler in Feltham, but spent most of her time waiting for a letter or a phone call from Anna. Surely she hadn't forgotten her already? As the first week dissolved into the second, Vicky could feel panic building in her stomach like reflux at the thought that she had indeed been displaced – and quicker than expected.

At the end of the second week with still no word from Anna, Vicky decided that a night out would lift her spirits, even if she had no one to go out with. She berated herself for not staying in touch with other girls from school, but then she'd never really had any friends other than Anna – and now she was paying the price for her loyalty. Anna certainly wasn't staying loyal to her.

She sat on the bus into town, her fingers pinching at her forearm under the sleeve of her thin blouse, leaving red welts in a similar pattern to those her dad used to leave on her skin all those years ago. The memory brought tears to her eyes and she wished she'd brought something to drink with her. She sucked on the hummingbird necklace as the bus wound through the dark streets.

When it reached her stop, she clambered off, tick-tacking in her thin heels, the warm breeze flushing her cheeks.

What she hadn't considered was that she didn't have Dan or Anna with her to get her into the club like last time and her birthday was still a few weeks away. Tall, skinny Anna was always mistaken as being older than she was, but Vicky's childish, chubby cheeks and shorter stature made lying about her age more difficult, no matter how much make-up she used. The tall, broad man on the door, with his sharp suit and close-cropped hair, took one look at her and stuck an arm out, blocking her way.

'ID please.'

'But I was here a few weeks ago and you let me in.'

'Sorry love, I need to see ID or you're not getting in.'

'I… I don't have it with me.'

'Then you'll have to go home. It's past your bedtime.'

'Vicky? Is that you?' a deep voice said behind her.

Vicky turned her flaming face to see Dan.

Great, that's not embarrassing at all, is it?

'You coming in?' he asked, pushing his blonde hair from his eyes. Two other guys hovered behind him impatiently.

'I can't, don't have ID with me,' she mumbled.

'Shit, that sucks.' He turned back to his friends and muttered something to them that she couldn't hear.

'Yeah.' Vicky turned to go, her cheeks flaming, feeling ridiculous in her dolled-up outfit, like a child caught playing dress-up.

'Actually, Vicky,' Dan said then, grabbing onto her arm, 'if you're up for a party, why don't you come back to mine with us? We don't mind moving the party there instead. This place can be lame sometimes anyway.'

'I don't know.' She peered at the two guys behind Dan. 'I don't know your mates.' They looked harmless enough, as though they didn't quite fit in with the crowd heading into the club either. One stood in loose-fitting jeans and had sprinkles of dandruff in his red hair and a rash of pimples around his mouth; his shorter friend was bordering on podgy with a bouffant mop of dark hair and a shirt buttoned all the way up to his bulging Adam's apple.

'This is Ross and Stevo,' Dan replied. 'Anna knows them.' Vicky nodded at each of them. 'Come on, what else are you gonna do, anyway? Go home and make some cocoa? Come party with us. My parents aren't home.'

She knew his house wasn't far from where Vicky lived with her nan, according to what Anna had told her, so she felt a little easier knowing she could walk a few streets home if she needed to. But the idea of spending an evening without her wingman keeping an eye on her made her feel nervous and on edge. Then she started thinking about all the fun Anna was probably having and how she clearly wasn't pining for Vicky and she suddenly wanted to go with Dan more than anything else. Besides, Anna had dumped him just before she left. Vicky could imagine herself dropping into conversation with Anna when they did eventually speak again that she had seen Dan, partied with him and his mates, could already hear the anger and jealousy in Anna's voice. The thought made her smirk.

After a quick pitstop at an off-licence, they all climbed back on the bus, taking up the back row and necking bottles of Smirnoff Ice. Vicky could feel herself start to relax as the alcohol distilled into her blood.

At Dan's, glasses of vodka and coke flowed steadily and before long her nerves had eased and she was enjoying herself. Stevo, the chubby one, had a quick sense of humour and twinkly eyes, and the banter between the three lads made her giggle. She felt free for the first time in ages, not hiding behind Anna's cool confidence or dancing around her shadow for her place in the sun, but allowed to be herself and say what she wanted without fear of Anna talking over her, scoffing at her or putting her down.

She hadn't realised until Anna was gone how much she'd hidden behind her.

Dan sat next to Vicky on the couch as they chatted and he made no attempt to disguise the fact that he was coming on to her. But rather than feeling awkward, she was enjoying the attention.

'Have you heard from Anna?' Vicky asked him, the chain from the necklace lacing through her fingers.

He ran his fingers through his blonde hair, then seamlessly flung his arm across her shoulder in a well-practised move. Ross and Stevo were sitting on the carpet at her feet, CDs scattered in front of them. They were pouring the drinks while shoving their hands into packets of crisps as they argued about whether Oasis was better than Blur, whoever they were. Some new bands apparently. The music was loud, but they could just about hold a conversation over the bass.

'No, nothing. But she made it clear that we were over once she left for uni.' He looked sad about that, then took a long drink and pulled Vicky closer in to him. 'But that's okay. Whatever, you know? What about you? Hear much from her?'

'Not much. I've phoned her and sent her letters and stuff, but not had anything back.' Vicky sighed.

'So we both got dumped then, eh? Well, cheers to us.' He clinked his glass to hers. 'Who needs her? Stuck-up bitch. She was never up for much partying anyway. Not like you.'

'Yeah, right, who needs her?' Vicky smiled, then she felt the air close between them as he leaned in to kiss her. He tasted of sugary coke and cigarette smoke, and she hoped she didn't taste like the cheese and onion crisps she'd just eaten.

The music argument was resolved, the volume was turned up a notch on what Ross proclaimed to be 'the best album ever' and the vodka was replaced by shots of sambuca that Dan nicked from his parent's liquor cabinet. Vicky hated the taste of liquorice, but didn't want to be a killjoy, not after what Dan had said about Anna, so she swallowed down the shudders with the shots.

Dan's hands kept her close, his breath hot in her ear as he nibbled on her neck. Vicky wasn't entirely sure she liked it, the sensation leaving her mildly repulsed rather than excited, but the sambuca was making her head cloudy as the room tilted at odd angles. She didn't object when Dan took her by the hand and led her down the corridor to his bedroom. She tripped over her feet and fell into him, suddenly aware of how drunk she was. It was as though she was watching herself from afar, unable to stop herself from following him like a clumsy puppy. She tried to remain in the moment when he pushed her on the bed and started kissing her, his hands roaming over her blouse, then under her blouse, but she could feel the heat of the alcohol pulling her in and out of herself like a kaleidoscope.

Vicky woke with a jerk. She had no idea how long she had been unconscious. She felt sick, her body heavy and immovable. A deadweight was pinning her down, pressing on her stomach and ribs. She was struggling to breathe. The air was being pushed from her lungs, like something was compressing her chest. A face came into focus, millimetres from hers.

Dan. He was on top of her, his eyes squeezed shut and his face twisted into a mask of concentration. His breath was hot and sour in her face. The material of his shirt was pressed up close to her nose and smelled faintly of body odour and Lynx. She tried to pull her arms free from under her so that she could shove at him, but she was trapped. Reality tugged at her, but she felt herself slipping away again, along with an overwhelming relief at the idea of passing out once more.

She came to again and this time the weight pinning her down had lifted. Nausea roiled through her stomach and her head was pounding. Her tongue felt swollen in her mouth and her legs, hips and groin throbbed with a dull pain.

She felt the bed shift and opened her eyes to see Dan get to his feet and shrug into a pair of jeans that had been discarded on the floor. He didn't look at her as he flicked a used condom into a dustbin on the other side of the room. Her eyes focused for a moment on the condom dangling obscenely over the rim of the bin as he left the room.

She was lying on her back, her legs splayed open and her arms at her sides. Her thighs felt sticky. Her brain tried to connect the dots of what had just happened, but she stopped herself, emptied her mind completely. Her jeans were pooled around her ankles, along with her underwear, which felt twisted and stretched, cutting off the circulation, but she couldn't muster the energy to pull them back up, so she wriggled her feet free instead and shuffled under the blanket. Then she turned her back to the room and closed her eyes again, letting herself slip out of consciousness one more time, hoping it was all a bad dream.

When she woke up, it felt like Groundhog Day, but this time the weight was against her back and a strong arm was wrapped around her waist, pinning her against the body pushing into her from behind. A hairy thigh was wedged underneath her leg, twisting her hip at an unnatural angle. This time her head felt clearer, less foggy, as though someone had wiped some of the cobwebs from her eyes. She tried to pull herself away, but the arm was strong. Hot breath grunted in her ear, pungent with alcohol, and the hand clamped to her stomach kept forcing the air from her diaphragm.

'Please, stop…' she whispered, but the panting in her ear was louder. She could hear the insistent rebellion of Paul Weller's 'A Town Called Malice' blaring down the corridor.

She tried to see over her shoulder, but all she could make out was a mop of dark hair.

Oh god. Dan has blonde hair.

She thought she could see movement and shapes in the light coming through the open bedroom door, but she couldn't turn her head enough to make out if someone was actually there. Then she heard laughing and a voice said, 'Wey hey, you lad, Stevo! Sloppy seconds. Get in there!'

The body pressing into her back shuddered and the arm pushed hard once more into her stomach. The pressure, along with the realisation of what was happening, made her heave and she vomited onto the bed next to her. The room filled with the acrid stench of puke and alcohol. She heaved again.

'Fuck! That's disgusting, dirty bitch!' a voice exploded over her shoulder.

She felt the bed shift again as the arm released her. She lifted her hand to wipe the trail of spit from her mouth and flung a glance over her shoulder to see Stevo flicking another used condom into the dustbin. His aim was better and this one disappeared out of sight.

Out of sight, out of mind.

He pulled on his jeans, threw her a disgusted glare and left. She heard a door close down the corridor and the unmistakable sound of someone peeing.

Vicky started to shake. She pushed herself away from the vomit and sat up, feeling woozy from the sudden movement. She took a deep breath, but fear and panic clutched at her throat, making her gag again.

She had to get out of here.

Now.

Before anyone else decided to have a go.

That thought alone propelled her to her feet. Her teeth chattered as she rummaged in the bed clothes for her underwear. She winced as she pulled up her jeans, aware of the pain throbbing between her legs. She thought she saw blood, but looked away.

How do I get out?

Her breath was coming in gasps. She didn't want to go back into the lounge, but her bag was in there. She peered slowly around the door, but couldn't see anyone. The bathroom door down the corridor was still closed and whoever was in there – Stevo, she presumed – was still peeing like a racehorse.

In the other direction she could hear laughter as the song ended and another one began, but it sounded further away than before. They must be in the kitchen. She stretched her brain to remember if she could get out the front door without going past the kitchen. She seemed to think it was through a door off the back of the lounge, so if she moved quickly, she could get into the lounge, grab her bag and get out through the front door before they saw her. But she needed to move fast before Stevo came out of the bathroom.

Holding her breath, she crept along the corridor and into the lounge. A CD played away to an audience of empty crisp packets and bottles, discarded where they had been sitting. She could see the kitchen door, could hear the voices behind it and the tinkle of bottles, but the door was pulled to, blocking them from sight. Her bag sat on the floor by the couch, with her heels lying abandoned next to it. As she tiptoed further into the room, she heard the toilet flush. She grabbed the shoes, her bag and her coat from the back of the chair and charged for the front door.

She fully expected the chain to be on or the door to be locked, like it always was in the horror movies Anna made her watch, but it wasn't. She pulled it open with force, almost knocking herself off balance, then lurched through it and slammed it behind her before tearing down the stairs in her bare feet.

She didn't stop running until she was streets away.

It was fully dark, with few stars in the sky. Just thick cloud overhead, pressing down on her. She took cover in a bus shelter while she pulled on her coat, but her teeth were chattering uncontrollably and her body trembled right into the pit of her stomach.

Her hand reached up to the necklace at her throat, like a comfort blanket, but it wasn't there.

Her throat was bare.

'No, no, no…' she moaned.

She felt inside her clothes, but there was no necklace. It must've come off at Dan's.

In the bed.

Her chest burned with acid at the realisation and it felt like yet another body blow.

She got up and staggered the rest of the way home, her arms pulled tightly around her, numb to her core, her head swivelling around, fear putting her on high alert.

It took a few attempts before her shuddering fingers could hold the key steady enough to get it in the lock. The house was still and quiet. Her nan would be asleep upstairs, snoring nasally into her pillow. Vicky didn't want to see her. She felt sure she would know what had happened just by looking at her. She closed the door quietly behind her and tiptoed past the telephone table in the hallway.

Her eye fell on the chair in the lounge, taunting her silently. She looked away.

The lamp on the table was on and a note sat propped against the telephone.

Anna called for you. Says she gave you wrong number.
New no is 8755381.
Call her tomorrow morning. She'll wait by the phone.

Hot tears streamed down Vicky's cheeks and snot pooled in her nose as she read the note a second time. She set it back on the table and climbed the stairs to the bathroom. Closing the door tightly, she ran the shower until it was as hot as it would go. Her skin felt like hundreds of tiny black beetles were crawling across her, their tiny little feet pricking and nipping. She stood under the steaming spray, her face turned up and her eyes squeezed shut, not thinking, barely breathing, just scrubbing the beetles away.

Vicky didn't call Anna the next morning. She couldn't face telling her what had happened or the shame of hearing Anna tell her what a slut she was.

Instead, she stayed in bed, the covers pulled over her head. Her nan poked her head in at around 10 a.m. to offer her a cup of tea, but she muttered that she wasn't feeling well and was staying in bed.

She couldn't sleep though. Snatches of memory kept peppering her brain. Had she said yes to Dan? They were flirting and kissing at one point, before they headed into the bedroom. But she hadn't actually said yes. But then she hadn't said no. She had passed out for most of it.

And she certainly hadn't said yes to Stevo.

Again, though, she hadn't said no either.

She had been mortal drunk, out of it completely and unaware of what was going on. It was her own fault. For getting so drunk, wearing that stupid tight top, agreeing to go back to their place in the first place. Definitely her own fault. Just another way of punishing herself.

At least they had used condoms – they did both use them, didn't they? A fresh wave of ice crackled over her skin at the thought of now being pregnant. Wait, yes, she remembered seeing them tossing their used condoms in the bin like dirty tissues.

Used and forgotten. Just like Vicky.

If Anna ever found out she had slept with Dan, consensually or not, she would never want to speak to Vicky again. And the necklace…

No, Vicky had to keep this to herself. She couldn't let anyone find out about it.

A week later, Vicky finally felt in control enough to call Anna back. She had hibernated all week, barely leaving the house, calling in sick at work and avoiding everyone for fear they would be able to tell what had happened.

She could still sometimes feel the beetles on her skin, which made her scratch at her arms until red welts stood out in relief.

When Anna finally came to the phone, she exclaimed, 'Oh my god! Where have you been? I'm so sorry, I gave you the wrong number and then I realised I didn't have the right address for you to write back and you didn't put a return address on your envelopes. I mean, how many years have we been friends and I think I've been to your house, like, once? What is that about? Oh my god, you would love it here. There are some seriously smart people. Everything feels sophisticated and classy. Even in the pub we have these deep discussions about philosophy and politics. I'm way out of my depth, but loving it at the same time. Isn't that mad?' She rattled on and on, filling Vicky in on the people she'd met and the classes she'd signed up to. 'Oh, and there are seriously hot guys here and so clever – I realise now how thick Dan was! What was I thinking hooking up with him before I left? How pathetic and desperate was I!'

Vicky let her ramble on, contributing little other than the occasional grunt of acknowledgement.

'Anyway, what have you been up to? Your nan says you have a job? That's great! I'm thinking of getting a job on the student paper.' And she was off again, barely noticing that Vicky had said very little.

Before they said goodbye, Vicky confirmed her address with Anna and promised to stay in touch.

Vicky didn't tell her how much she missed her. She didn't tell her how she felt dead inside. She didn't even tell her how she found herself ruminating day in and day out about how many of her nan's sleeping pills it would take to stop herself waking up again, how high the fall needed to be before her body splattered on the pavement, taking all of the pain and disgust with it, how much gas she needed to breathe in before she fell into a blissful permanent sleep.

Instead, she hung up the phone, went to her room and crawled under the covers before letting the tears flow silently into the pillow beneath her head.

The next day she went up the High Street to the tattoo parlour and asked for a tiny hummingbird to be tattooed on her ankle, followed by a cartoon face on her forearm in exactly the place where Anna had drawn her caricatures when she'd been bruised and battered at school. The sharp stabbing of the needle felt delicious as it pierced her skin over and over, leaving her with physical reminders of who she had been and who she had now become.

7

Vicky tore through the lounge, flung open the door and launched into the hallway. Her red cape flew out behind her as she drew the plastic sword from her belt.

'You're mine, Blackbeard!'

A bloodcurdling scream erupted from halfway up the stairs where Harper lay immobile, tied to the banister with a dressing gown cord. 'Help me!'

'You'll never get your hands on her!' Lewis cackled from the top of the stairs, his face obscured by a homemade Day of the Dead mask. 'She will be sacrificed at midnight.'

'Not if I have anything to do with it.' Vicky swept her cape over her face and stalked towards the stairs, but the material snagged on the handle of the hallway cupboard and tugged Vicky back as the tie tightened around her neck.

'Aaaggghh,' she choked out.

Lewis and Harper started to shriek with laughter at the strained expression on Vicky's face.

'This is why real superheroes shouldn't wear capes, Vix,' Harper said in between giggles.

The thin material ripped as the handle pierced through it and Vicky had to backtrack to free herself.

The doorbell chimed loudly, sounding like the sonorous toll of Big Ben now that Vicky had figured out how to change its original, less dramatic ringtone.

'Harps, can you get that, please? I'm still attached here…' she said as she fiddled.

The door opened behind her and she heard Harper squeal, 'Aunty Chloe!'

Lewis ripped the mask from his face and flew down the stairs in response and Vicky felt her heart sink.

'Hello Vicky. Nice cape,' said a wintry voice behind her.

'Chloe, how nice.' Finally free of the door handle, Vicky turned and took in the image of David's older sister standing inside the doorway, with Harper and Lewis attached to each of her long legs. Her curly hair framed a face devoid of warmth, the lips pinched in thinly veiled dislike.

'We were playing Baddies, Aunty Clo, and I was the baddie this time. Vix was trying to save Harper from where I tied her to the stairs,' Lewis babbled at her and Vicky couldn't help feeling a sense of pride at how much fun they had been having.

'The stairs? That sounds dangerous to me. You need to be careful you don't fall when you're playing.'

Vicky narrowed her eyes.

'Where's David?'

'He's on his way home from work. He didn't mention you were coming over. Can I get you a coffee or something?

I think there's some lemon drizzle cake left. The kids made it with me yesterday.'

'Thanks, but I'm gluten-free and eliminating all processed sugar from my diet. You can go and do... whatever it is you do.' She waved a hand dismissively in her direction. 'I'll hang out with the kids while we wait for David.'

Vicky began to loosen the ties holding the cape tight to her throat. 'Okay, I'll go and get dinner started then. Will you be staying?'

'Thank you, but I thought I'd treat David and the kids to dinner out tonight. You can have the night off.'

'Lucky me,' Vicky said with a tight smile, then walked away into the kitchen, feeling the ice-cold eyes on her back the whole way.

Vicky stood with her hands clasped to the edge of the countertop, anger seething through her. Chloe had always hated her, inexplicably as far as Vicky was concerned, since you could count on one hand the number of times they had met over the years.

Okay, so the night they had met, Vicky had been legless and falling all over David, but it was a long time ago – and Anna had found it funny at the time, just pleased that her best friend and David were getting along, so who knew why Chloe's pointy nose was still out of joint about it?

Vicky took some deep gulps of air. Let them have dinner together. It wouldn't be fun for her anyway. But she hated feeling like the paid help, dismissed to her room for the evening.

But that's what you are. You're not their real mother.

The snide voice in her head brought tears to her eyes and she swiped at them, refusing to let Chloe see any sign of weakness from her.

Instead, she made herself a cup of tea and sat at the kitchen table, the hot mug clasped between her hands, listening to the peals of laughter and animated voices filtering through from the lounge.

The kids like you more, Vicky. Remember that.

Half an hour passed and Vicky's tea was long gone before she heard David's key in the lock.

She stayed where she was, listening as the kids rushed at him and excitedly told him about their surprise visitor.

After a few minutes, she heard footsteps approaching and quickly flung herself at the sink, grabbed a mug and began to scrub it enthusiastically under the running tap.

'Hey, Vix, good day?'

'Yes, thanks,' she said without looking at him. 'So Chloe's here.'

'Yeah, I see that. Sorry, she didn't tell me she was coming. She wants to take me and the kids out for dinner, if that's okay?'

'Of course it is. No need for my permission! Gives me a night of peace and quiet. You go, have fun catching up.'

'Well, we haven't really spoken much since Anna... since the funeral, so would be good to catch up.'

'Of course.' She finally turned to him. 'The kids have done their homework and everything, so I'll just go upstairs, give you guys some space.'

'Oh! You don't have to – disappear, I mean. This is your home too.'

'It's fine. I'm reading this really good book and I want to see how it ends.' She nodded at him awkwardly. 'It's the one Anna was reading actually, the one on your bedside table? I thought I would give it a go.'

'Oh, right.' He frowned. 'I was reading that.'

'Oh, I'm sorry, I just saw it and picked it up. I didn't realise. You can have it back.'

'No, no, you finish it first. It takes me ages to read anything.'

'Okay, well, I'll let you know what it's like.' The air around them fizzed awkwardly. Vicky plastered a fake smile on her lips and walked from the room.

The smile was still there when she closed her bedroom door, her cheeks aching with the force of keeping it in place.

They left in an excited bubble of voices, but returned subdued at 9 p.m., with two tired children and a box containing leftover pizza. Vicky hadn't been able to concentrate on anything since they'd gone, convinced that David would return home and tell her to pack her bags after listening to Chloe slag her off all night. She had sat unseeing in front of the small TV in her room with one hand in a big bag of crisps and surrounded by chocolate wrappers and an empty ice cream tub. Her stomach ached from overindulgence.

These days she tried to keep her bingeing in check, but there were times when she had to give in to it, let the lack of self-control take over and eat until her stomach felt stretched, her throat hurt and her head pounded with the effects of too much sugar. Tonight was like that – just like it had been during the dark period between the argument with Anna before she died and moving in here two weeks ago. A cycle of bingeing, purging, then starving herself. A constant round of punishment and reward. Living here had curbed her bad behaviour, mostly because she was happy and felt settled and secure for the first time in months, possibly even forever.

Clearly, just the idea of Chloe's toxic intrusion was enough to set her off again though and was a reminder that this was not a permanent situation.

Yet.

If she played it right though, David would realise that she was irreplaceable.

She heard the door shut downstairs and shoved all the litter into the supermarket plastic bag that lay discarded on the carpet, like it had blown in accidentally on a strong breeze.

She debated going downstairs and helping David with the kids, but then heard Chloe's clipped, posh voice filtering up the stairs.

Let Chloe do it. She is their aunt after all. And they can be right little shits when they're tired, so good luck to her.

Instead, she switched off the TV, turned on her bedside lamp and got into bed, as though she'd been there all evening reading as she'd said she would.

She could hear Lewis whining and David negotiating. Then a clatter as something was knocked over.

'Shit, David! Why is there so much clutter in this hallway? Anna never let it pile up like this!'

Vicky couldn't make out David's mumbled response, but did hear footsteps up the stairs shortly afterwards and the distinct sound of a child crying.

She strained to hear more, but it was all too muffled for her to make out how much of a fight the kids were putting up about going to bed.

She desperately wanted to hear shouts of frustration and wailing. She knew David was grateful that he didn't have to deal with all of it every night. He came home to dinner made, happy and clean children, and calm bedtimes where all he had to do was stick his head in the room and give them a kiss. Vicky was actually good at all of this, better than Anna had been. Vicky had experienced a few bedtimes when Anna was in charge and there was usually a slammed door, a raised voice and the threat of no story because the kids were acting up. Anna had always hated bedtimes. She'd wanted to rush through it so that she could get back to her own life. But rushing through it made for anxious children, which meant they would push at their boundaries and Anna's patience. She'd told Vicky once that she had had to post David at the top of the stairs like a policeman to stop Lewis and Harper fighting with each other every night.

Things were calmer now though, bedtimes less frantic. Surely David could see that?

The footsteps retreated back down the stairs fifteen minutes later and Vicky fully expected to hear Chloe leave shortly afterwards, but she didn't.

Considering that Chloe drank in extreme moderation, it was highly unlikely they were having a nightcap.

Vicky crept from her room and stopped at the top of the stairs.

Everything was quiet. The kids' rooms were dark and still, a soporific cloud of slumber thrown over each one.

Curiosity burned through her like a craving that was too strong to ignore.

She pulled her gown tightly around her and crept onto the top step. The lounge door was slightly ajar and soft lamplight spilled from it. The sound of muttering filtered up to her along with a whiff of coffee beans.

She crept down two more stairs, consciously choosing to step on the outside where they wouldn't creak or groan and give her away.

She stopped halfway down the stairs where the acoustics were better. It was a trick she'd learned from Harper. Once or twice in the last two weeks, Vicky had come out of the lounge to find her crouched halfway up the stairs with her head pressed to the banister, listening in on what David and Vicky were talking about. She'd asked Harper about it once and she had said that sometimes when she had a bad dream, she liked to sit and listen to their voices. She was quick to say she wasn't eavesdropping, but that it was because she didn't feel lonely if she could hear them talking and laughing. Then she'd go back to bed, able to put the bad thoughts aside.

Vicky had asked her why she never came and told them she had had a bad dream and she replied that Anna used to get cross if they interrupted her evenings.

Now, sitting on Harper's stair, Vicky could understand why she liked it here. The glow of the lamplight, coupled with the muted sounds of talking, was hypnotic and calming. She pressed her ear to the wooden slats of the banister.

'I still don't know why she's here, David. What is she after?' Chloe was saying.

'She's helping me out. She had some problems at work and needed a job. I needed someone to look after the kids while I went back to work. It was the perfect arrangement.'

'And you're paying her?' Chloe continued.

'Yes, I'm paying her.'

'Is she paying rent or for food?'

'No, the room is empty anyway and we all eat together.'

'Sounds like quite a cushy setup to me. Free food, free rent and money in her pocket. Someone's made a smart move.'

'You make it sound so calculating, Chlo. I'm sure it's not like that – and it was my idea, anyway.'

'She's always looked like she was minutes away from being homeless to me, so quite fitting that a wealthy Prince Charming has come along to save her.' Chloe was spitting the words at him. 'What would Anna think if she knew what was going on?'

'Nothing is going on, as you put it. The kids have always adored Vix, as did Anna. And she'd be pleased I was helping Vicky out.'

'Well, before their falling out maybe, but they weren't even speaking when…'

'We don't know what that was about. Just leave it Chlo, you've never liked Vicky.'

Vicky felt warmth in her chest as she listened to David defend her.

'For good reason, David. She was always so… over the top, melodramatic, chavvy. Vulgar is the word. I can't imagine she's a good influence on the kids. The amount of times Anna would tell me that she had had to save her from various situations with men, one-night stands, drunk, out of control… there was always something. Someone that volatile and unstable can't be good for the children after what they've been through.'

'She is not unstable. In fact, she's calmed down since Anna died, like a spark has gone out.' His voice sounded almost wistful.

'And I still say I would've made a much better bridesmaid – you remember what she was like!'

'Really, Chlo? After all this time?'

Chloe humphed audibly. 'Just look at this place, David. It's not like Anna used to keep it. There's stuff piled up; the ironing hasn't been done. For god's sake, her knickers and tights are hanging in the kitchen!'

Vicky's cheeks flamed. She'd meant to do the ironing and put her smalls away this afternoon, but then got distracted by the game with the kids.

'And you should've heard the racket when I got to the door this afternoon. I could hear the screams from down the street!' Chloe continued.

'Screams?'

'Yes. Apparently they were playing some game on the stairs. Harper was actually tied to the banister.'

The heat in Vicky's cheeks flooded down her neck. Chloe was making it sound like it had been dangerous. She resisted the urge to storm into the lounge and set her straight.

'They were playing, Chlo. Lewis told me all about it. In fact, they've been happy lately. I hate to say that because it feels disrespectful to Anna, but this house has had a vibrancy in the last two weeks that was missing even before Anna—'

'Don't you dare! Anna was a wonderful mother. She raised them to be considerate and well-behaved, not noisy hoodlums.'

'Yes, she did, but she didn't foster loud or messy play of any kind. It all had to be clean, tidy and quiet. Sometimes it's nice to hear laughter and chaos.'

'I just want you to be careful. I don't trust her. I never have. The police were awfully interested in her after Anna's accident, don't forget.'

'Because she was her best friend! They spent more time together than we did.'

The conversation paused and Vicky smiled to herself.

Then David continued. 'Look, it's what I need at the moment. It's not perfect, but it's not permanent. The truth is I would like my own space sometimes, but it's not like I can send Vicky to her room or anything when I want to watch TV on my own, like I could with a real nanny. She sits with me every night, which I'm not used to, eats with us, does everything with us really, and I feel bad suggesting that she gives us some space. Anna used to watch her TV and I'd watch on mine in two separate rooms. It was like our own wind-down time and I miss that a bit. Or she'd let me go off with the kids on the weekend and I used to enjoy that time with them while she enjoyed being on her own. Anna was also impeccably tidy, but Vicky leaves her shoes and all sorts lying around so that I trip over everything, which is annoying. And she's a terrible cook.' He paused in what sounded like a character assassination to Vicky. 'I guess I wish she was more like Anna sometimes...'

Vicky didn't wait to hear any more. She rushed back up the stairs, the burning now filling her torso and flooding down the back of her legs like a fever, bringing hot tears to her eyes.

She wasn't enough.

He wished she was more like Anna.

She flung herself on her bed and pushed her face into the pillow to stop herself from screaming.

All this time she had thought David was enjoying her company, relishing the differences between her and Anna, and in actual fact he was wishing she wasn't so different after all. All these years spent trying to be more like Anna and, now that she was dead, Vicky was still living in her shadow. A poor imitation.

If only he knew. If only he could've seen what she was really like.

She sat up and grabbed the last of the chocolate sitting on the bedside table. As she bit into it, a shard fell onto the white pillow case next to her and she took her thumb and smeared it into the immaculate cotton. She contemplated the dark mark, like mud in snow.

So he wanted her to be more like Anna, did he?

Well, after years of practice, that wouldn't be so hard to do.

And if that's what it would take for her to stay here with him, then that's what she would do.

Disappointed, Vicky. Must try harder, Vicky. Isn't that what they've always said?

She wasn't about to let this slip from her fingers.

July 1995

The bar was cramped with sweaty bodies and loud voices. Cigarette smoke swirled through the air, leaving an indelible imprint on their hair, clothes and lungs. Vicky added to it as she puffed on her Benson & Hedges, watching the smoke curl from the end hypnotically.

She sat on a stool at the bar, a pint of cider in front of her alongside an open packet of salt and vinegar crisps. At times, someone would sidle up next to her to order a drink, throw her a glance and a smile and she'd smile back, her head tilted and her eyes curious under her fake eyelashes.

Occasionally, she glanced at her watch, impatiently aware of the time passing. She considered ordering another pint as she drained the last of this one. How much longer should she wait? They were already half an hour late and she was running out of money rapidly.

She shifted on the stool, feeling the waistband of her jeans sitting tightly underneath her ribs. She'd worn the high-waisted ones in the hope that they'd hold her in more, but instead they were cutting into her and heightening the claustrophobic atmosphere of the bar, making her lungs feel constricted.

She stubbed out the cigarette.

'Those things will kill you,' a voice said over her shoulder. She swivelled on the stool to see Anna standing behind her, smiling widely.

Vicky got to her feet as Anna leaned in for a hug. Vicky felt stiff in her arms, uncomfortable with the physical contact after all this time. They'd talked on the phone and written letters to each other over the last few years while Anna was at uni, but now that she was finally seeing her in the flesh, Vicky felt awkward in her own skin, sure that Anna was looking at her and noticing how much she had changed, not necessarily for the better.

Anna hadn't changed at all. She was still tall and lean, with sharp cheekbones and straight dark hair that now framed her face in a shorter bob rather than the long curtain of hair she had grown while they were at school.

'How've you been, Vix? You look good.' Anna's eyes swept over her briefly. She carried on before Vicky could answer. 'This is David. I told you about him?'

Vicky looked over at the man standing behind Anna. Tall, athletic-looking, with his sharply ironed white shirt neatly tucked into beige chinos. He was certainly handsome, but in a contrived way with his short back and sides dark hair, like he'd walked straight out of a teen girl magazine. He had a slight twist to his jaw, as though there was a permanent smirk on his face.

'Hi,' Vicky said.

'Hey.'

'So, what are we drinking? David, get us a round in, would you?' Anna said.

'Another pint of cider for me, please.'

'Cider drinker these days, huh? I'll have a vodka tonic, babe.'

David shuffled in next to Vicky and she caught a whiff of sandalwood and spice from his aftershave as he leaned over the bar.

'So pleased to see you again! It's been ages,' Anna gushed. 'Such a shame we couldn't get together when I was back in the uni hols.'

Anna had requested a few times that they meet up, but Vicky had swerved her every time, not ready to see her in case she could read in the tight lines on Vicky's face what had happened all those years ago. It had taken a long time for her to put it behind her and she was sure seeing Anna would bring it all rushing to the surface again. Instead, she had emerged from a self-induced hibernation a month after it had happened, slapped on make-up and a tight skirt, and had hit the town – and various men – pretty much every weekend since. No strings, no connections. Her way of dealing with it. As long as she knew it was happening, she would never feel that level of fear again.

'How's your nan?'

'She's okay, but getting frail now.'

'I bet she is. Still, cheap rent for you though, still living with her. David and I are looking at getting a place together ourselves.' She reached over and took hold of David's hand as he waited patiently for the barman. 'My dad is looking to invest in a small flat and it makes sense that we move in together since we spend so much time together anyway. We'll just pay rent to my dad instead.'

'Lucky you.' David handed around the drinks and Vicky took a big gulp straight away. 'How are your parents?'

'The same as always. My dad's wife tries really hard, but I don't think I'll ever like her. She's not that much older than me and is painfully stupid. Their kid is cute though. Mum's okay, still rattling around our old house on her own. Oh, I didn't tell you. I got a job with an agency in London! Can't wait to start. David's new job is close by, so we can travel in together every day. Oh, and Dad bought me a car. He's obviously trying to buy me off because of the baby and everything, but it's a cute car. It's a dark blue VW Beetle, but the old shape. Very retro. Remember how we used to love them years ago? A connection of his had one that has been completely reconditioned, so it's brand new really.'

Vicky had never had anything handed to her on a platter in her life. She bit back the resentful snipe that had jumped into her mouth and said instead, 'Cool, can't wait to see it. What do you do, David?'

'I've just finished doing a business degree and I've got a job with an investment bank, starting next month.'

'Sounds… great.'

'What about you?' he returned politely.

'Oh, I'm an office manager for a stationery supplier in Feltham. Nothing exciting. Answer the phones, handle the orders, that kind of thing.'

'Well, a job is a job, isn't it?'

'Yeah.'

They fell silent and Vicky filled it by drinking deeply from her pint glass as she scanned the room. A man across the bar let his gaze settle on her low cleavage, then winked at her. She smiled and looked away.

'So what else is new?' Anna asked.

'Oh, not much.'

'Seen anyone around lately? Anyone we used to hang out with?'

'We didn't hang out with anyone, Anna.'

Anna's eyes flicked over to David. 'Yeah, well, we did, kind of.'

'No, it was pretty much just us.'

'Not that we weren't popular or anything,' Anna said hurriedly. 'We just kept to ourselves, didn't want to get caught up in that whole popular girl culture, you know?' Vicky wondered why Anna felt she had to explain this to David.

'What about you, David? Were you one of the popular ones at school?' Vicky asked with a smirk.

'The sporty one mostly. Rugby, cricket, you know.' He shrugged. 'I still see a lot of my old mates actually.'

'Where did you grow up?'

'Esher. Haven't really left there except for my little sojourn to uni in Durham. I wanted to get away, see what the rest of the country was like. Happy to be back though. The weather is shit up there sometimes.'

Vicky had never heard anyone use the word 'sojourn' before. She raised her eyebrows, then looked back into her pint glass.

The speakers were loudly belting out an Ace of Base song that Vicky despised.

'God, I love this song!' Anna said.

Vicky grimaced. 'No way! I'm more into the Prodigy than this.'

Anna raised her eyebrows. 'Your music taste has changed. So has your taste in clothes, I see.' Anna pointedly swept her eyes over Vicky's outfit again.

'Yeah, well, we all grow up eventually.'

'Still got that necklace I bought for you? The hummingbird?'

Vicky's hand reached for her throat automatically. 'Yeah, it's at home, you know...' She looked away.

The awkward silence descended again, but this time it was broken by the man from across the bar sidling up to Vicky.

'Hey.'

'Hey yourself,' she replied.

'Can I buy you a drink?'

'Sure, a pint of cider, thanks.'

'I'm Jimmy.'

'Vix.'

While he ordered, Anna hissed in Vicky's ear, 'What are you doing? It's supposed to be you and me catching up tonight.'

'What? He's buying me a drink, that's all. And you brought your boyfriend, didn't you?' Vicky hated the sound of her voice, all childish and thin. She had wanted Anna to think she was now grown up and sophisticated, just like Anna was after her countless life experiences at university, but instead she felt cheap and immature sitting in her big jeans beneath her helmet of preened hair, stiff with spray and mousse.

Jimmy handed her a fresh drink. 'This is Anna and David.'

'Hey,' they said in unison. With his baggy sweatshirt and loose jeans, Jimmy looked far more relaxed than buttoned-up David.

With little left to say to Anna, Vicky started talking to Jimmy and found she had plenty to say to him, from discussing football to laughing about the latest episode of *EastEnders* and movies they'd seen. Vicky spent a lot of time alone in movie theatres these days, watching anything and everything. She liked the dark anonymity of it.

'Have you seen *Judge Dredd* yet?' she asked him.

'Not yet. Is it good?'

'It's brilliant. You have to see it.'

'You see a lot of films then, Vix?' Anna interrupted.

'Yeah, I do. You?'

'Not really. I've never really understood what the point was. Remember that time you made me go and see *Dirty Dancing* three times? I used to hate it.'

'Then why did you go?'

'Because you had no one else to go with.'

Vicky narrowed her eyes and turned back to Jimmy. David shifted uncomfortably in his slip-on loafers.

More pints followed and Vicky started laughing raucously at Jimmy's jokes, even when they weren't funny, because she knew it was winding Anna up. The cider was filling her with aggression and she wanted Anna to see that she didn't need her in her life. She didn't need Anna to come back and save her because she was doing just fine without her.

Are you, though? Are you really?

When she came to climb off the bar stool some time later, she stumbled as the cider pushed her off-balance.

'Woah, someone's had too many pints,' Anna said.

'Fuck off, Anna,' Vicky replied.

They stared at each other for a moment, then Anna grabbed Vicky by the arm and pulled her towards the bathroom at the back of the pub.

The bright lights made Vicky squint as Anna turned on her. 'What the fuck is the matter with you? If you didn't want to see me, why did you say you would come out tonight?'

'I did want to see you, but not to have you parade your boyfriend in front of me. Ooh, look at me! I'm Anna and I have a posh boyfriend! I have a flat and a car and a rich daddy!'

'It's not like that. I wanted you to meet David because I want you to like him. I want us to be best friends again.' Anna's voice dropped an octave. 'Those people at uni weren't my real friends. They didn't get me like you do. They weren't down to earth, normal like you. I really missed you.'

'Down to earth? Is that another way of saying chavvy, is it? And why do you want to see me again anyway when you have such smart, clever, beautiful friends now? Because being around a loser like me makes you feel better about yourself?'

And that's when it struck her. Anna hadn't made any friends. There hadn't been hordes of people hanging on her every word, gagging to be in her social circle. Anna had been as lonely as Vicky had been – and as stubborn, keeping it to herself, putting a filter on her life.

When they had been at school, Vicky could see the envy on the faces of the girls around them, as though they were in awe of her, but they'd kept her at arm's length, probably from fear. Only Vicky had had the balls to be friends with her, to ignore her sharp edges and fiery tongue. However, at uni Anna had been out of her depth. There were plenty of girls who were smarter than her, prettier, more in control, so the power that Anna had wielded in the small pond of high school had dispersed like a puff of smoke. Once there was no Vicky around to belittle in order to make herself feel better, Anna was just as lost as the rest of them were.

'What's happened to you, Vicky? You're so angry. What the fuck have I done?'

Vicky stared hard at the familiar face in front of her, a face she knew better than her own, and wanted to tell her everything. Wanted to shout at her that if Anna had been there, it would never have happened. She would've stopped Dan and his mates treating Vicky like a slag, using her and tossing her aside like the dripping condoms they'd shed, telling everyone they knew that she was the kind of girl that slept with two men in one night. Laughing about it over beers, clapping each other on the back.

Come and get your good times here, boys.

Instead, Vicky felt all the fight drain out of her, like a popped blister, and she collapsed into herself as her shoulders slumped.

'Sorry,' she mumbled. 'I just… things haven't quite worked out the way I've wanted them to since Dad died.'

'You're not still stuck on him, are you?'

Vicky didn't want to cry, especially not in a dirty toilet surrounded by girls touching up already thick make-up and teasing up their fringes. She pulled up her sleeve and held her forearm out to Anna.

'Do you remember this?'

Anna looked down at the tattoo on her forearm where the shape of the cartoon face looked out at her.

'It was the doodle you drew around the bruises that time. Now it's there as a permanent reminder – of him, what we—'

'We are not talking about this.' Anna pulled Vicky's sleeve down abruptly. 'Let's get you some water and get out of here.'

'Need to pee first,' Vicky mumbled. She shuffled into a cubicle and loosened the tight button of her jeans, immediately feeling relief as her stomach spilled out.

Sitting on the toilet, she pulled her sleeve up again and gazed at the tattoo. The tattoo artist had thought it a strange design, but Vicky knew what it meant. A reminder that every action has a reaction. That she was a product of her mistakes. She hadn't shown Anna the hummingbird.

They returned to the bar where Jimmy and David were standing together, not speaking.

''Bout time. Thought you'd flushed yourself down. Hey, you fancy getting out of here? My place is just around the corner. We could go there where it's quieter…'

Vicky picked up what was left of her drink. 'Tempting.'

'Vicky! You are not going with him. If anything, you're coming home with me and David. We're staying at my mother's tonight. Come on, for old times' sake.'

David squirmed next to Anna, clearly not overjoyed at the idea of hanging out with Vicky for longer than he had to.

'Come on!' Anna grabbed Vicky's arm, but Vicky shrugged her off, choosing to do so with the hand that held the still quarter-full glass of cider. The cider sloshed up out of the glass as if in slow motion and hit Jimmy full in the face.

The room seemed to go silent around them, at least to Vicky's ringing ears, and then she heard Anna start to laugh, which set her off too.

Jimmy was scowling as cider dripped from his long fringe. 'Fuck's sake! It's not funny! You're a psycho, you know that?'

Anna and Vicky just laughed harder as he shoved past David and stormed off.

Vicky snorted, which set Anna off again. David just looked bemused.

'Come on, let's get out of here,' Anna said in between sniggers.

They caught a cab back to Anna's old childhood home. It looked eerily the same from the outside and not much had changed inside either. Still immaculate. Still very cream and beige in décor. Still eliciting the same feeling in Vicky that she was dragging in mud when she walked through the door.

There was no sign of Anna's mother, but it was close to midnight. They piled into the lounge and closed the partition doors behind them. David went to choose a CD while Anna poured them stiff vodkas from the cabinet in the corner.

'She still stocks a full bar,' Anna said.

Vicky reached into her bag and pulled out her box of cigarettes.

'I don't think she would like us smoking in here though,' David said pointedly.

'Since when have you bothered about what your mother thinks, Anna?' Vicky replied.

Anna threw a glance at David.

'Besides, I'm not smoking a cigarette.' Vicky pulled a small bag from the box and some cigarette papers.

'That's more my style!' Anna clapped her hands in joy.

'What about you, David?'

'He doesn't usually partake.' Anna looked mildly annoyed, which Vicky noted with interest.

'Maybe you'll make an exception tonight?'

'Not my thing, sorry, Vicky.'

'Oh, come on. Where's the harm? I don't have much on me anyway.'

He watched her roll the joint and light it, watched Anna take a deep drag and Vicky follow her, listened to them start to reminisce about places he hadn't been to and people he didn't know. Then he reached over and took the joint from Vicky's fingers.

'Go on then.'

Anna squealed in excitement. 'Yeah, we're the three amigos!'

Vicky just smiled quietly and took another drag of the joint.

Later that night, when David had passed out in an armchair and Vicky and Anna were sitting with their arms around each other, sipping from the same glass, Anna said to her, 'So what do you think of him?'

'He seems okay, I guess.'

'Just okay?'

'Well, he's a bit… straight. You know, serious. He could do with loosening up.' Vicky saw Anna's mouth tighten. 'But then it's not me that has to like him. I'm not going out with him, am I?' she added.

'No, you're just shagging strangers.'

Vicky let the retort go. 'Do you like him?'

Anna paused. 'Well, he's good-looking, comes from a wealthy, middle-class family and looks like he'll do well, maybe earn lots of money one day, so yeah, I like him.'

'But there's more to it than just money, surely?'

'Is there? When has love ever got anyone anywhere? It just makes you weak. No, David is the kind of man I will marry. He has prospects, he'll do as he's told and he adores me.'

Vicky hoped Anna was joking, but the matter-of-fact tone to her voice and the steel in her gaze made Vicky realise she was serious.

Then Anna looked at her intently and said, 'Besides, the only person I truly love is you, Vix. There'll never be anyone else for me but you. And there'll never be anyone for you but me. We've been through too much, stuff that no one else would understand or will ever find out about. Best friends forever. Until death do us part.'

8

David had a headache. Too much booze with Chloe last night. It had been lovely to see her, but the whiskey was taking its toll today and he was glad he was finally home.

He sat in his car in the driveway and looked at the house in front of him. Bricks, cement, tiles. It was just a pile of building materials artfully arranged into a shape, but it held in its belly so much more than that. Hopes, dreams, expectation, disappointment, sadness.

Anna had loved this house. She said it reminded her of her childhood home and he could see why. Except Anna had wanted her version to be full of life and vibrancy, unlike the magnolia shell that her own mother had created. Anna's mother had died a few years back, but the few times David had met her, she had never been a lively woman. Rather, she had come across as an empty vessel – pretty to look at but with little substance. Anna had done her best to be the opposite – full of fire and brimstone, never sitting still, keeping him on his toes.

David hadn't particularly liked this house. He preferred something with character. Nooks and crannies; alcoves and cornices. This was all sharp corners and rectangular rooms. No curves or bends.

Funny, he used to like his women like that too – until he met Anna, who was the epitome of straight lines and pointy edges.

Now when he looked at his house, he still saw Anna everywhere. From the miniature bay trees standing guard at the front door to the midnight blue painted front door. That paint had taken weeks to choose, with Anna agonising over paint samples like the fate of the world was at stake if she chose the wrong hue.

He should just sell this place. Get something more suited to him. The kids would be okay with it, as long as they were close enough to keep going to the same school. Definitely something to think about, especially since he felt his chest constrict every time he walked through the front door, as though he expected her to be standing there, all of it a sick joke, before she started telling him off for leaving his ties dangling over the banister or for not opening his pile of post before it toppled over under its own weight.

He sighed and lowered his chin to his chest.

He could just drive away now. Vicky was with the kids. They'd be okay. He could start the engine and drive somewhere, anywhere, just away from here.

Anna would tell him he was being a coward.

And she would be right.

Instead, he climbed out of the car with flat feet and a thumping head, grabbed his bag from the back seat and approached the front door of his wife's house.

He pushed it open and felt the blood drain from his face.

Standing with her back to him was Anna.

Her dark hair fell iron-straight to her shoulders. She was wearing one of her favourite lilac sundresses and her feet were bare, with licks of lilac polish on her toenails.

She turned towards him and he swayed on his feet, sure he was going to pass out in relief, shock, joy.

As she turned, he noticed a small tattoo above her ankle that he hadn't seen before. It looked like a miniature bird, a hummingbird maybe. And yet it was familiar.

Confusion clouded his thoughts. The voice saying hello to him didn't sound like Anna's clean, clipped tone.

'David? You okay?'

'Vicky?'

Vicky frowned at him. 'Yeah, who else would it be? You okay?'

'Too much whiskey last night, not feeling well,' he mumbled and used the motion of closing the front door to turn his back on the image of her and catch his breath. His chest hurt.

'I'll make you a coffee, shall I?'

'Thanks.' He listened to her feet pad away before he turned around again. His hand reached to cover his mouth, holding in the scream he could feel trying to claw its way out of his throat.

He loosened his tie and threw it over the banister in rebellion since apparently Anna wasn't here after all and couldn't shout at him. Now that the tightness in his chest was abating, he felt dangerously close to weeping. He sat heavily on the stairs and put his head in his hands.

Other noises now came to him as the shock wore off. The TV was on and the kids were bickering at each other over *Blue Peter*. The sound of the dishwasher being either loaded or emptied. The whirr of the tumble dryer in the utility room pushing the smell of fresh laundry into the air in puffs.

It was all so normal and so real. She wasn't here. She was still dead.

Then he felt angry. What the hell did Vicky think she was doing?

He pushed to his feet and bypassed the lounge altogether to head straight into the kitchen.

Vicky was busying herself with the coffee machine. It gurgled and spat thick, treacly liquid into a mug. She was frothing milk, humming to herself. She looked up and smiled.

'How was your day?'

His anger lost its impetus as quickly as it had inflamed. 'Okay, I guess.' He looked at her closely. 'You've had your hair done.'

She smiled in delight at the recognition. 'Yes, fancied a change. Do you like it?'

'It… it looks like Anna's.'

'Really? I guess the colour is similar to hers now and I had it straightened. I want to see if brunettes are taken more seriously after all. What do you think? Do I look sophisticated and smart?'

'You look like Anna.' His voice sounded strangled to him, but Vicky didn't seem to notice.

'Well, I'll take that as a compliment.'

'Is that her dress?'

Vicky looked down. 'Um, is it?' She paused. 'Actually, come to think of it, yes, it is. I borrowed it from her last summer and never got around to returning it. I'm just pleased I can finally fit into some of her clothes now. The last time that happened, we were in school.'

'I… er… I'm going to lie down for a bit.'

'Here, take your coffee.'

'No, thanks – you have it.' He turned away, then said over his shoulder, 'Sorry, but would you mind maybe taking the dress off? I don't… I…'

'Oh, right, sure.'

'Thanks.' Then he felt like a shit for saying it. Why should she? It's not like Anna was going to wear it again. The anger bubbled up again, but this time at Anna for not being here. 'Actually, no, leave it on. I'm being ridiculous.'

Then he headed to his room and closed the door firmly.

He lay on the bed, staring at the ceiling, trying to figure out who he was angry with and why. Vicky for being here? Anna for not?

She had looked so comfortable in Anna's dress, like it had been hers all along. Like she was meant to wear it – or had been waiting to. Something Chloe had said to him last night came back but with today's context as its lens. She'd said that Vicky had scored by moving in with him and his ready-made family. He hadn't thought anything of it last night, just the ramblings of someone whose nose was out of joint. It was no secret that Chloe disliked Vicky.

But seeing her today with her imitated hairstyle and wearing Anna's clothes, David felt the cogs in his brain rotate and align into the beginning of a thought. Not one he could put weight to or mould into something concrete, but just a slight shift in his head, enough for him to feel a niggle of unease and for a shudder to run over him.

He shook it off, blamed the whiskey for his paranoia and turned on his side before closing his eyes against the dull light filtering through the window.

Half an hour later, a light knock on the door woke him from a nap he didn't know he was enjoying. Harper stuck her head around the door.

'Hey, H. You okay?' He was groggy, disorientated.

'Hi Daddy.'

'Come over here and give your old dad a cuddle.' Yawning, he patted the bed next to him. She crawled up and curled into his body, a warm bundle of deliciousness, and he felt better for a moment.

'So what's up?'

'Vicky says dinner will be ready soon.'

'Right, well, we'd better go and eat it then. What is it tonight?'

Harper scrunched up her face in thought. 'I think she said some kind of curry.'

'Hmm, well, that sounds alright to me.'

He let her drag him from the bed and lead him downstairs by the hand. He was inexplicably nervous as he approached the kitchen again, mostly from fear that he would conjure up an image of Anna again. He didn't think his heart could take it a second time.

But she had changed out of the dress into jeans and when he actually looked properly, her hair was still lighter than Anna's. The T-shirt she was wearing meant her arms were bare and he noticed the small tattoo of a cartoon face on her forearm – Anna had never told him what it represented and he had never asked Vicky – and he exhaled in relief now that he knew he was not in the Twilight Zone.

'There you are. Feeling better?'

'Yeah, thanks. Sorry, migraine coming on.'

'It's fine, no problem. Dinner is nearly ready. Harper, could you help your brother set the table for me please?'

Later that evening, as the silence of the house settled around him, David sat in the armchair in the lounge bay window and stared out at the night. It was one of those nights where the sky looked like someone had tipped a sugar bowl across an inky tablecloth. Not a cloud in sight and even the moon was hiding from view.

'Beautiful night, isn't it?' Vicky's voice intruded into his thoughts and he turned his head to find her standing right beside him. He hadn't heard her approach.

She had a strange look on her face, but he couldn't identify it because most of her face was in shadow.

'Yeah, it is.'

'Migraine gone now?'

He swallowed, feeling uncomfortable, but needing to say what was on his mind. 'Can I be honest?'

'Sure.' She sat on the arm of his chair, uncomfortably close, her hands cradling a glass of water.

'When I walked through the door earlier, I thought… I thought you were Anna. You had your back to me and with your hair cut and the dress…' He shrugged. 'Then when you turned around and it wasn't her, I got angry. Stupid, right?'

'No, not at all!' She laid her hand on his knee. Her palm was warm. 'God, I'm so stupid. I just didn't think. I'm so sorry. I'm supposed to be making things easier for you and all I'm doing is making it harder.' She withdrew her hand and looked away, her lip trembling.

'No, no, it's me. I'm a mess. I keep wanting to blame someone for what happened, find a reason why, understand it and I can't.' His voice caught in his throat.

She looked at him with yearning eyes, the schoolgirl in her desperate to be liked. 'I understand, I really do. I can't get my head around it either. I keep expecting her to burst through the door, shouting the odds as she used to do. I'll try harder. I really don't want to upset you.'

'No, no, really, don't worry about it. God, I don't know what I'm doing. I don't have a manual on how to deal with being a widower,' he said. 'I feel like I'm just making one mistake after another.'

'I think we're both muddling through, but we're doing an okay job. The kids are happy and we haven't killed each other yet.' She chortled awkwardly and he wanted to flinch at her inappropriate choice of words. 'I think we have to let this evolve on its own, this situation, our arrangement. Let it take on its own shape and form, try not to force it into something it's not.'

He looked out of the window again, as much to not acknowledge the look of intensity on her face as anything else.

'You know what tomorrow is, don't you?' she said.

'Yeah. It'll be a tough day for the kids.'

'Yes, but we'll get them through it.'

He looked back at her, then reached out and took her hand in his. His other hand reached up and smoothed a lock of hair away from her cheek. 'I really do like your hair this way. Anna would've liked it too.'

Harper and Lewis were very quiet over breakfast.

David raised an eyebrow at Vicky as he ate his cereal, the silence heavy around the table.

'What's up, guys?'

Harper pushed her Cheerios around the bowl. 'Today is Mummy's birthday.'

David set his bowl aside. 'It is, you're right. But I think instead of being sad, we should try and have a fun day because I bet that's what she's doing. She's probably organised a massive tea party in heaven and invited a whole bunch of famous people, like David Bowie and George Michael.'

'Who?' Lewis asked, puzzled.

'Never mind. The point is she would want us to have fun.'

'Daddy is right,' Vicky said. 'I think I might have a little surprise for you when you get home from school, something to make us all feel better. What do you think? And maybe Daddy can be home earlier today too to join in? Besides, it's the last day of term before school's out for summer. We should be celebrating.'

'I can probably make it home by the time you two finish school. Sounds intriguing!'

When he got home later, he walked into a chocolate wonderland. The kitchen had been transformed by brightly coloured balloons, bowls of rainbow-coloured confectionery were dotted on every surface and dominating the dining room table was a large chocolate fountain that filled the air with the intoxicating smell of cocoa and sugar.

He wandered around the table gaping. There were party poppers and glittery sprinkles everywhere, tall bottles of cold fizzy pop and trays of nibbles.

Vicky had gone to a lot of trouble to throw what looked like the ultimate birthday party.

He heard her key in the door and went to greet them. He smiled at Vicky and mouthed 'thank you' at her above Harper and Lewis's heads.

Then they ate sausage rolls and vol au vents, recited bad jokes from a book that Vicky had bought, dipped fruit, marshmallows and cubes of cake into the continuously streaming chocolate, and played silly party games like musical chairs, pass the parcel and Twister.

By the time bedtime came around all too quickly, they all had tummy aches from too much chocolate and aching cheeks from laughing.

Later that evening as David and Vicky tidied away the detritus of the party, they shared a bottle of wine, then David opened a bottle of champagne and toasted Anna with a crackled voice. Once that bottle was empty too, they retired to the lounge on unsteady feet and opened an old bottle of Baileys, which had been one of Anna's favourites. The creamy, smooth liqueur coated David's tongue, making him think of Christmas and roaring fires. They never seemed to drink it at any other time of the year.

David and Vicky got to reminiscing about things they'd done with Anna, places they'd been, experiences they'd shared. Mostly, David talked and Vicky listened as the level on the bottle fell.

'She had a way of making you feel as though you were the most important person in the world, didn't she? But just as quickly she could dismiss you. She commanded the air around her, to the point where she had all of us at her beck and call.'

'She was certainly a bit of a mood barometer for all of us.' Vicky sighed. 'Exhausting sometimes though.'

'Yes, but I loved that I had to work hard for her, you know? I wanted to. She was like an expensive drug that I had to have in my blood. And now I feel like I'm in a terrible withdrawal phase.' He felt a dry sob creep up his throat.

'You and I used to have a laugh together though, didn't we? All those nights when I came over to see Anna and she was working late or whatever last year. We used to have really deep and interesting conversations, set the world to rights some nights, waiting for her to get home.' She took another sip of her drink. 'I missed that after she died too, that closeness we had. I'm pleased we're back in that place, the two of us.'

'Yeah, but it wasn't always like that. You didn't like me at all when you first met me.'

'That's not true!' Vicky said, her eyes sparkling. 'Okay, maybe not. Do you remember that first night?'

He laughed as he swiped at his eyes. 'Do I ever. The first time I smoked pot. I was so uptight back then. It was a weird night until then, wasn't it? But then you brought out that joint. God, we laughed like mad, I remember, then I felt sick and threw up in her mother's kitchen sink.' He chuckled again. 'Can I be honest?'

'Sure.'

'The next morning, I lied and told Anna's mother it was you who had thrown up.'

'David!'

'Well, I was still trying to impress.'

'She was used to my bad behaviour by then. She thought I was a terrible influence, especially after Murphy the cat.'

'The cat?'

She waved her hand dismissively. 'Yeah, Mrs Maxwell had this cat and… it died. Because of me.' She started to cry gently.

'Hey, hey, don't cry,' David said, pulling Vicky into a hug. 'It's a birthday party, remember?'

He held her tightly for a moment and could feel her push into his arms, heavier than Anna, less brittle. He pulled back and wiped at the tears glistening on her cheeks.

Then he kissed her, gently, like he wasn't sure what he was doing, then with more ferocity. Her lips were fuller than Anna's, the cheek he was stroking rounder and softer under his thumb.

He pulled back, a stricken look in his eyes.

'I'd better go to bed,' he said and lurched from the room.

Vicky remained behind, her expression blank and the tears drying into a crust on her cheek. She drained her glass of Baileys and poured another one. Then she stood and approached the fireplace, picked up a frame with a photo of Anna in it, taken on her wedding day. In the far corner of the picture, Vicky's silhouette was barely visible, staring up at Anna in wonder, but Anna was turned away, looking at David as though she had won the lottery.

Vicky set the frame back on the mantelpiece, looked at it one more time, then casually knocked it from its ledge onto the tiled fireplace below. The frame landed face up, the glass splintered and fractured across Anna's face.

31 December 1999

Vicky lay in bed with the duvet pulled up to her chin but the curtains open, looking out at the damp, foggy morning behind the glass.

New Year's Eve.

David and Anna's wedding day.

Only Anna would try to outshine the turn of the century with an occasion of her own.

She looked around the tastefully decorated room, one she had slept in probably more times than her own bedroom. The spare room at Mrs Maxwell's house had become her own over the years and she felt safe here, despite the fussy Cath Kidston décor. Mrs Maxwell still treated her like a ghost, but that was still better than the ghosts that lived in her head.

She turned her eyes back to the grey outside and felt a ripple of joy that the skies weren't perfectly crisp and blue as Anna had wanted. Sometimes Vicky thought Anna had the power to control the elements, like a modern-day sorceress, because things always seemed to go her way, even when the odds were stacked differently.

But it seemed that today Mother Nature was having none of it. Anna would be fuming. Vicky smiled into the duvet. For a moment she had an inkling of the erotic pleasure Anna seemed to enjoy when others around her failed.

Noises filtered through to her. A door opening, shuffling, a knock on her own door. The creak of wood as the door opened.

Anna's face scowled into the room, as grey as the morning sky outside.

'Have you seen this weather? It's supposed to be a nice day! Cold I can live with, but damp and foggy? What about the fireworks? And I'm going to freeze in my dress.'

'You have a fur jacket.'

'Only for later when we're outside watching the fireworks. Now I'll have to wear it to the ceremony too. It will ruin the effect of the dress.'

Vicky sat up and ran her hands through her bed hair. 'It'll be fine, Anna. The fog will burn off soon.'

'Are you going to get up then? I told you not to drink so much champagne last night. You should see the state of your eyes. And that hair will take time to sort as well.'

Vicky sighed. She had needed the champagne last night to put up with Anna's overbearing narcissism as she bossed her mother and David around, confirming and reconfirming details for the big day. Anna's mother had looked on the verge of tears a few times and had fallen into her usual bottle of vodka with enthusiasm last night. Anna had only just started speaking to her again after the candle fiasco. Apparently, Anna had mentioned the idea of having candles adorned with cupids on all of the tables and her mother had willingly obeyed, as she always did when it came to any of her daughter's demands. However, when the candles arrived, Anna proclaimed that they looked ridiculous and refused to admit that she had asked for them. Vicky had backed Anna up, despite having witnessed the original conversation and knowing full well that Anna had indeed asked for the cupids, and the look of disappointment on Mrs Maxwell's face had burned Vicky to her core.

But she did not want to get on Anna's bad side this close to the wedding. Vicky had had a taste of her wrath in morsels over the years and Anna could be a venomous adversary in a battle. Despite that, their friendship had strengthened again once Anna returned from uni, almost as if she'd never left. If only Vicky could blot out the years before… but she couldn't.

David had grown used to sharing his girlfriend's time with Vicky because that was how Anna wanted it. And what Anna wanted, Anna got. Everyone knew that.

As it was, Anna had refused to speak to her mother for the last few days, using Vicky as a go-between instead, even when her mother was sitting in the car with them as they headed to last-minute dress fittings, cake tastings and florist appointments. All of this had been incredibly awkward for Vicky, especially since Mrs Maxwell didn't like talking to her anyway. Finally, Anna had let the frost thaw last night, but typically still got payback by throwing snide comments at Mrs Maxwell, who took refuge in a vodka-induced mist, and then tormenting her mother with little things like hiding her vodka glass or pouring out the contents and sniggering at the confusion on Mrs Maxwell's face as she struggled to remember drinking it all.

Anna had stayed away from the champagne last night so that she was picture-perfect this morning. She had inherited her cool sense of control from her father, a man who always exuded calm and restraint, even when he had his various secretaries pinned to his office desk, it would seem.

Anna was the same. In all the years they had been friends, Vicky had never seen Anna lose control apart from that one day with Murphy the cat. Even when she was drunk, Anna seemed to hold herself in check. Vicky had never had to hold Anna's hair back while she threw up in the street or had to rescue her from a dangerous situation after a reckless decision backfired. It was always Anna coming to Vicky's rescue and the older they got, the greater the frequency with which Anna would remind Vicky of this.

'You're going to cover that up with foundation or something, right?' Anna said, nodding her head at Vicky's tattoo on her forearm.

Vicky looked down at the cartoon face, feeling the familiar tightening in her chest as she did.

'I… er… I hadn't thought about it.'

'Well, I don't want that man intruding on my wedding, do I? And I certainly don't need you getting all miserable about it if you get – sorry, *when* you get pissed today.' Her eyes were like shards of flint against her pale skin. 'Because we both know you'll get drunk again. You can't help yourself when there's a free bar.'

Vicky wasn't about to admit to Anna that she would be taking some headache pills for her current hangover as soon as she was alone. She looked out the window, but her thumb rubbed against the tattoo, as though trying to erase it from her skin.

'I won't get drunk, Anna. It's your big day. I promise.'

'Yeah, we'll see. Anyway, get up. We need to start making you look acceptable. Did you get those Spanx I told you about?'

Vicky flushed. 'They are so uncomfortable though. Feels like I can't breathe.'

'Then you shouldn't have eaten so much. I've been living on fucking lettuce for the last month.' She stretched her long, slender body to the ceiling, then placed her hands on her tiny waist. 'Come on! Get up!'

They sat at the breakfast table in silence, Vicky with her hair pulled into a messy ponytail and staring disinterestedly at the slices of melon on her plate, Mrs Maxwell nursing a large coffee and wearing ridiculously large sunglasses indoors like a misguided celebrity, and Anna with a facemask on, trying to feed herself fruit without cracking the glaze on her skin. At least it meant she couldn't bark orders at them.

The timer on the table next to them blared, and both Vicky and Mrs Maxwell jumped. Anna turned it off, pushed to her feet and stalked from the room. Vicky could feel the collective exhale as she did.

'Well, I'd better get in the shower,' Vicky said. Although she couldn't see Mrs Maxwell's eyes behind the dark lenses, she thought she saw her nod her head slightly.

Vicky stood under the hot water, trying not to get the spray on her hair, but relishing the scalding sensation against her skin. She needed to be on her best behaviour today and couldn't let herself get distracted. No booze, no piling her plate with food, especially since the dress Anna had chosen for her was rather unforgiving around her stomach. She had thought, not for the first time, that perhaps Anna had chosen it because beside her Anna would look all the more statuesque and lithe, but then she'd felt dreadful. Of course, sometimes Anna made it easy to think the worst of her.

Vicky could hear her name being called and sighed. Today was going to be a long day, but Anna deserved to be the centre of attention. If she ever got married, she would probably be Bridezilla too, right?

Two hours later and her hair was tamed and sprayed into a helmet of curls, her make-up had been expertly applied to hide the lingering hangover and she sat in a dressing gown watching as the experts preened and tarted around Anna.

'David really likes you, you know,' Anna said.

'He's a nice guy. We get on well. I like talking to him.'

'No, I think he *really* likes you.' Anna gave her a sideways glare.

'Don't be daft, we're friends.'

'I know that. And I know you would never do anything with David, but I think he has a bit of a crush on you.'

'You're being ridiculous, Anna.'

'I'm *serious*.' Her eyes sparked. Anna was in one of those moods, where she would say and do anything to get a reaction. Probably nerves. Vicky bit hard on the inside of her cheek to stop herself from rising to the bait. The atmosphere in the room was charged, like the ten minutes before a thunderstorm when you can feel the pressure building, taste the crackle of electricity in the air and hear the distant threatening rumbles.

'He always laughs at your jokes. He has so much more fun with you than with me, and we are so different. I think he likes that.'

'No, he sees me as your best friend and might find me funny, but he adores you. You know that.'

Anna stared hard at Vicky. 'As long as you don't have a crush on him.'

'What?'

'But you don't do that kind of thing, do you? You'd never sleep with one of my boyfriends.' The hairdresser working on Anna's hair flushed and looked over at Vicky, hungry for gossip.

Vicky went cold. 'What are you talking about? No, I wouldn't – and I certainly have never slept with David.'

Anna smiled and turned back to the mirror. 'Oh, I know that. I'm just winding you up. You're not his type. He likes his girls thin and tall.' The hairdresser raised her eyebrows, but carried on without a word.

Vicky swallowed, feeling acid rise in her throat. 'Who wants a cup of tea?' She got to her feet and headed towards the bedroom door.

'Oh, I meant to tell you, guess who I bumped into the other day?'

Vicky halted in the doorway, one hand on the handle. She felt like a mouse caught in a cat's paw, bruised from being toyed with endlessly. She hoped Anna would get to the point and put her out of her misery.

'I saw Dan! Do you remember Dan? My boyfriend before I went to uni?'

Ice crept up the back of Vicky's legs.

'He asked how you were. I didn't realise you two knew each other so well.'

'We don't really,' Vicky mumbled.

'But you went out that time? Just after I left?'

'Well, I kind of bumped into him at a club…'

'Actually, that was my doing. I mentioned to him before I left that if he ever happened to see you while I was away, he should take you out. I thought you'd be lonely with no other friends. He said you had a fun night that night, but you never mentioned it? I actually hoped you two could be a couple or something. I wouldn't have minded.' She was looking at Vicky with feigned innocence. 'Anyway, a cup of tea would be lovely, thanks. Tessa, would you like one?' she said to the hairdresser.

Vicky fled from the room, closing the door behind her. She sunk to her knees in the hallway, breathing deeply, hoping the nausea would pass.

Anna knew. That was the only reason she had brought it up. She didn't say things just for fun. He must've said something to her. But why didn't Anna just ask her outright? Maybe she just suspected they had slept together. She surely couldn't know what he had done? What his friend had done?

No, Anna was just nervous about today and taking it out on Vicky. She always did this. Whenever her life was tough or stressful, she distracted herself by taunting Vicky. This would pass. It always did.

Vicky continued to breathe deeply, feeling her heartrate slow. She stumbled to her feet and headed to the kitchen, focusing on the task of making tea and trying to block the unwelcome memories threatening to push into her head.

The ceremony itself was like candyfloss passed from hand to hand, eliciting contagious feelings of sugary sweet happiness and saccharine smiles from everyone. Anna looked radiant in her taffeta and lace dress. She carried a bouquet of stunningly simple winter flowers and her hair was a cloud of dark, glossy curls dotted with tiny white flowers and a glittering diamanté tiara. She held herself with a quiet authority, as though commanding the room to look at her, admire her, yearn to be her. Looking at the faces turned towards her as she glided up the aisle, the spell she was casting was hitting the mark. Vicky followed behind, the only bridesmaid, and felt obsolete. Invisible.

In contrast, David looked nervous, pulling on his collar at the altar as he waited for Anna, his eyes flicking around the church like a nervous tic. He stumbled over his vows, eliciting a frown from Anna but giggles from the congregation, and Vicky could hear his shiny new shoes creak with every step. He looked over at her during one of the hymns and he looked petrified. Her heart swelled with empathy for him then, knowing what it could be like once enrolled in the cult of Anna, and she winked at him before looking away. She thought she saw him smile out of the corner of her eye, but then Anna was handing over her bouquet to her and the moment passed.

As they stepped out of the church, the earlier grey skies had dissipated to leave the crisp, bright winter day that

Anna had hoped for. Mother Nature had indeed toed the line after all.

It bothered Vicky how annoyed she was feeling today. She should be happy for her best friend, but instead she felt aggravated and on edge, as though she'd been stripped of her armour and put into a flimsy dress that exposed all her weak points. As they stood on the steps of the church, with well-wishers fawning and cooing over Anna, Vicky took a step backwards into Anna's shadow and looked down at the tattoo on her forearm barely visible beneath the thin layer of foundation. But Vicky could still see it and knew it was there. It would always be there. He would always be there, looking over her shoulder, breathing in her ear.

Her thoughts were interrupted by a familiar, acrid voice. 'Vicky, you scrub up well.'

She looked up at Chloe, standing with her arms folded tightly across her chest. She looked beautifully understated in a simple floral dress with a little bolero jacket flung over her bare arms against the chill air. However, the hat perched on her head looked ridiculous, like a lilac satellite dish, and she had the look of someone who had caught a whiff of something unpleasant.

'Chloe, nice to see you,' Vicky replied, resisting the urge to ask if ET would need to use her hat to phone home later. She sucked down a giggle.

Chloe dismissed her witheringly and moved on to congratulate her brother and his new wife. Vicky stuck her two fingers up behind her back.

It felt like forever before the crowd thinned and it was time to move on to the reception. David introduced her to his best man, a podgy, rugged-faced man called George who had known David since their rugby-playing school days and was still his 'best mate' apparently. Vicky slid into one of the wedding cars next to George and rested her head back against the seat.

'Awfully intense, that,' he said in his plummy voice.

'Yeah, intense.'

'Lovely wedding though, just lovely.' He paused and gazed out of the window. 'Can't wait to get my hands on a pint of Doom Bar though.'

'I could do with one myself.' She looked across at him and they both started to laugh.

The ride to the reception venue was brief and she chatted casually with George, finding him not at all as stuck up and full of public schoolboy bravado as she had expected. When she climbed out of the car at the venue, she was feeling better about what lay ahead and was already entertaining the thought that perhaps George might be an interesting distraction later in the evening. She didn't normally go for posh boys, but when in Rome...

The manor house Anna had chosen was in the leafy greenery of Coombe Hill and lay nestled in stunning gardens at the end of a long, gravelled drive. Vicky had been to see it with Anna when they'd done some food and cake sampling, but felt as out of place in such a plush environment today as she had then.

Before George and Vicky could quench their thirst for a pint, they had to endure the cheek-numbing monotony of smiling endlessly for the photographer, who seemed intent on taking shots from every angle and in an infinite number of configurations. In one group shot, Vicky stood next to Mr Maxwell, whom she hadn't seen in years, and he complimented her on her dress, bringing a warm flush to her cheeks. She'd always found his intense masculinity rather overwhelming. He was so different to any other man she had ever met.

At one point the photographer suggested including Mr Maxwell's latest wife, a young slip of a girl not much older than Anna herself, but one look at Anna's face and the photographer quickly moved on. Meanwhile, Mrs Maxwell stood upright and regal in every photograph in which she was required, saying little and smiling absently. But Vicky could see the tremor in her hands as they clutched white-knuckled at her purse.

Looks like someone else could use a drink too.

Then a waiter appeared with a tray of champagne flutes and the entire group giggled in relief. Vicky drained her glass in three long gulps. Mrs Maxwell drained hers in one and immediately reached for a second.

David's family, on the other hand, proved to be a lively bunch, full of laughter, jokes, warm smiles and banter. All except for Chloe, that is. Vicky immediately warmed to his mother, Louisa, with her round face, large bosom and down-to-earth chat. She looked to Vicky like the kind of woman who wasn't afraid to roll up her sleeves and get on with it, with an outwardly 'keep calm and carry on' stoicism, and she clearly adored her son.

Not that Louisa or any of David's family paid Vicky much attention. The day was all about Anna. Vicky was invisible, just part of the entourage.

It was interesting to see Anna respond to Louisa's tactile displays of affection, allowing the older woman to hug her and hold onto her arm in between poses, but still trying to maintain an element of distance, as though humouring her on the surface while secretly enjoying the physical contact.

Vicky wanted to feel what a hug from Louisa Price was like. She imagined it would feel similar to what she remembered her own mother's hugs were like.

The feat of endurance that was the photography session now over, the troupe followed Anna and David into the ballroom to the delight and applause of the rest of the guests. Hoots and brays erupted from David's rugby friends, all delegated by Anna to tables as far away from the head table as possible. The head table itself was small by traditional standards as Anna hadn't wanted any of the parents sitting with her. There were four places set for Anna, David, Vicky and George. Mrs Maxwell sat with her family and friends, but far away from Anna's father, while David's family all sat on the other side of the room, everyone a safe distance apart to save on any potentially embarrassing gaffes.

George held her seat out for Vicky and she thanked him and settled in, placing her small clutch bag at her feet. There was nothing in the bag but a tenner (all she had left this month), fags, tissues and the key to her room upstairs in the manor house, an old-fashioned, stone-walled boudoir with frills, drapes and paintings of the English countryside on the thick walls. George took his position next to her and immediately called a waiter over and ordered a pint.

Vicky ordered a Diet Coke.

'Are you feeling okay?' Anna leaned in and said into her ear.

'Yes, why?'

'It's a party with free booze and you've ordered a Diet Coke.'

'Yes, but I want to behave today. It's your day after all. I'm your wingman.'

'Waiter, we'll have four shots of peach schnapps please,' Anna said loudly, grinning at Vicky wickedly. 'One won't hurt.'

'Ugh, Anna, I hate that stuff,' David said.

'You two are such killjoys. One won't hurt and it is *my* day after all.'

The shots arrived, Anna handed them around, then held her glass aloft. 'Here's to the best day with my favourite people – and George.'

'Hey!' he objected good-naturedly and they all clinked their glasses and sunk the shot.

Vicky winced at the sickly sweetness of it, then washed it down with a gulp of equally saccharine Diet Coke.

Anna then went on to order more shots as the dinner unfolded, but while David, Vicky and George were encouraged to drink them along with the large glasses of wine that the waiters were pouring, Anna seemed to manage to avoid drinking altogether. Every time she raised her glass, she would coincidentally see someone she hadn't spoken to and would disappear. Vicky didn't even know where she knew all these people from. Considering all the years they had known each other, none of these people had ever hung out with them.

The evening wore on, the dancing took over and Vicky remained where she was, eating course after course of food (and even helping herself to some of Anna's since she hadn't touched any of it), drinking more despite her earlier promises to lay off the booze and tapping her foot absently to the random mix of wedding music chosen by the over-spirited DJ.

She watched as David spun Anna around the dancefloor, noting how he never took his eyes off her, always with a nervous, edgy adoration, as though he were dancing with a wild cat that could strike out at him at any moment.

This thought was reverberating through her head along with the beat of the music, so she didn't notice Anna's father slide into George's empty seat next to her.

'Vicky! How are you? It's been a long time.'

She jumped at the sound of his voice near her ear. 'Mr Maxwell, hi.' Her cheeks flushed deeply, muscle memory of her teenage crush. His aftershave was so pungent, she could taste it.

'What are you doing these days? Something terribly clever with numbers, I bet? You were always so good with maths and I still credit you with getting Anna through her exams.'

Vicky felt burning shame creep up her head at her inadequacies. 'Unfortunately not, Mr Maxwell. I work for a small stationery company at the moment.'

'Oh please, none of this Mr Maxwell business. Call me Andrew. We've known each other long enough.' His breath smelled strongly of whiskey and the roasted parsnip soup from dinner and she could hear a tell-tale, alcoholic softening in his diction.

'Mrs Maxwell seems nice,' Vicky said to be polite.

'Which one?' and he brayed loudly at his own joke. 'Eliza is lovely, yes. Says she wants more children though. One is not enough.' He rolled his eyes.

'Each to their own. I'm not the maternal kind, I'm afraid.'

He winked at her. 'I knew I liked you for a reason.' Then he brayed again and Vicky recoiled somewhat.

'You know, I never understood you and my darling Anna. So different, the two of you. Anna is… well, Anna is Anna.' He looked out towards the dance floor where she stood with a group of young women around her, clearly commanding their attention as they hung on her every word. 'She's smart, beautiful, driven, knows what she wants from life – and you're so… well, it's all about having a good time with you, isn't it?'

'What do you mean?' The hair on her neck bristled as the DJ changed musical direction and Paul Weller began to blare from the speakers. This song still made her feel sick to her stomach.

Andrew leaned closer into her ear and his hand slid across the table cloth towards her.

'Well, you were always up for a good time when you two were teenagers, according to what Anna would tell me. Are you still like that? I must say, you've certainly grown up.' His eyes dropped to her chest straining against the tight bodice of the pale blue dress.

Vicky wasn't sure she was reading the signals correctly. Surely Andrew Maxwell wasn't coming on to her at his daughter's wedding?

'You're not an awkward little girl any more, are you, Vicky? Or can I call you Victoria? That's a more suitable name for a shapely woman like you.'

She felt his leg press against hers under the table and went numb.

He continued, his hand reaching for her thigh beneath the tablecloth. 'You know, we should—'

'Dad, everything okay?'

Andrew Maxwell shot back in his seat as Anna stood over them.

'Yes, darling. Just getting reacquainted with Vicky after all this time.' He coughed, then got to his feet. Vicky could still feel the warmth on her skin from where his hand had pressed against her thigh. 'Lovely to see you again. Maybe a dance later?'

He picked up his tumbler of whiskey and stumbled away.

Anna watched him go, then turned back to Vicky. 'You two looked cosy.'

Vicky looked into her wine glass. 'No, he was just asking what I was doing, you know, work and stuff.'

'Right.' She glared at Vicky. 'That's not what it looked like to me.'

Vicky said nothing as a feeling of timid outrage burned in her gut. What was it with men thinking she was worth nothing more than a quick shag? Did she have some sort of sign above her head?

Anna sat down heavily in the seat Andrew had vacated, her skirt billowing around her, and leaned into Vicky's ear, much the same as he had done, except her voice was icy.

'Look, just because today is all about me, doesn't mean you have to try and ruin things by flirting with my dad. That's just sick and twisted.'

Vicky looked at her in disgust. 'That's not what happened! He was coming on to me!'

'As if, Vix.' She scowled at Vicky, making her feel like shit on the bottom of her shoe with one withering glare. 'Just because your dad was a good for nothing turd. You've always had a thing for mine, haven't you? You used to stare at him all the time when you were at our house, like he was some sort of Greek god or something. Pull yourself together. You're embarrassing yourself. And remember, a secret is only a secret until someone tells. You don't want to make me cross.'

Then she got to her feet and stalked away on her spindly heels.

Vicky watched her go in shock, then picked up her wine glass and drained it in one.

The song still played loudly around her. A groundswell of nausea rose over her and she lurched to her feet and out of the room towards the cloakroom down the corridor. It was thankfully empty and she catapulted herself towards a cubicle, but was far short of her target as vomit rose from her stomach. She propelled puke all over the toilet, the floor and the stall walls. The air filled with the stench of peach schnapps and gravy. She wiped her hand over her mouth, then froze at the mess she had left.

Panic suspended her brain until all she could think was that Anna would kill her if she found out about this. She could try and clean it up, but there were only fancy cotton hand towels or toilet paper on offer and if anyone came in, she'd be mortified and once more labelled the chav of the party, the one who liked to party and get drunk, just solidifying what everyone always thought anyway.

She made a split-second decision and fled the scene of the crime before anyone saw her.

She stumbled through the nearest door and found herself outside on a terrace with the dark sky above her and the cool air caressing her burning cheeks. She leant against a stone pillar and breathed deeply, letting the night air replace the acidic smell lingering in her nose.

She jerked as a voice near to her said into the dark, 'Need some air too, huh?'

David walked out from behind the pillar, a cigarette burning to ash in one hand and a beer in the other.

She breathed out in relief. 'Hey.'

'You okay?'

'Yeah, just needed some air. Had a bit of an argument with Anna.'

'Oh? I thought she looked stony-faced about something.'

'You got another one of those?' Vicky said, indicating the cigarette.

'Yeah.' He pulled a packet from his inside jacket pocket and handed her one, then held a lighter to it. His face was unreadable in the flicker of the tiny flame.

'You having a good time?' she said after inhaling deeply.

'I guess,' he said, looking out at the night. He paused, took a drag, the orange glow of the cigarette illuminating his face for a second, then said, 'Anna is really on edge. Like nothing is good enough today. Everything I say is wrong. She had a go because I cocked up my vows. My tie is the wrong colour…' He looked down at his shoes. 'It's just… exhausting.'

Vicky pulled on her cigarette again, her head spinning from the rush of nicotine and the alcohol in her bloodstream. 'Well, at least she hasn't accused you of flirting with her dad.'

David frowned, pulling his skewed jaw even more to the side in bewilderment. 'What the fuck?'

'I know. Actually, between you and me, Mr Maxwell was coming on to me. Told me I'd grown up into a "shapely woman".' She could hear her words slurring and hadn't meant to blurt that out. He would never believe her, just like Anna hadn't.

David snorted. 'God, that man is such a player. I'm not surprised. He's had more affairs than I've had hot dinners. No wonder Anna's mother is the way she is.'

Vicky smiled in relief. They were silent for a moment, each puffing away.

'I was nervous this morning,' David said in a low, drunken voice. 'Sometimes I wonder if I've done the right thing.'

Vicky looked at him but said nothing. She felt like the pillar pressed to her back was swaying in the wind.

'Don't get me wrong, I love her insanely, but that's just it. It's insane a lot of the time. She is so volatile and passionate, then cold and controlling, all in the space of ten minutes. You never know what you're going to get.'

He stubbed out his cigarette beneath his polished shoe. 'Sometimes I think she should be more like you. Normal, funny, smart.' He looked across at her and she was thankful it was too dark for him to see the flush in her cheeks.

Before she knew what she was doing, she leaned over and kissed him full on the lips, almost crushing her mouth to his. She felt him freeze, then his lips softened and responded for a second before he pulled away abruptly.

'Shit, sorry,' Vicky mumbled. 'I don't know...'

'It's fine, forget it. It's been a funny day for all of us.'

'I'm such a fucking idiot,' she spat.

'No, you're not. Forget it happened, okay? This stays between me and you.'

He reached up and stroked her cheek tenderly, then disappeared back indoors.

More secrets.

Vicky turned and pressed her forehead to the cold stone pillar. She felt like everything was spiralling out of control around her. Images of Andrew Maxwell, Dan, her dad all swirled behind her eyelids and the only way she could think of stopping it was to turn the still smouldering cigarette into the palm of her hand until the pain obliterated all other thoughts.

Feeling more in control and marginally more sober, she threw the now extinguished cigarette butt onto the ground beneath her feet and headed back indoors.

The rest of the reception passed in a blur. Vicky drank some strong coffee and watched as Andrew Maxwell danced with a woman that Anna had introduced her to as someone from her office. He seemed particularly taken with her boobs, which were straining against her leopard print dress.

Then Anna came up to her with a plate of wedding cake outstretched towards her and said, 'I'm sorry. My dad's a shit. I shouldn't have said what I said. Look at him, he's practically salivating on Bethany's tits right now. Here, cake as a peace offering. I know how you love cake.'

Vicky smiled, relieved that the argument had fizzled out. 'Thanks.'

'Oh, and you'll never guess the carnage that someone has made of the ladies' loos! Someone has barfed all over them! Why? I mean, who would leave that mess without cleaning it up? I bet you it was my mother. She's legless again, no surprise there.'

Vicky feigned innocence. 'That's terrible.'

'I know, right?'

They stood side by side in silence for a moment.

'I've made the right decision, haven't I, Vix?'

Her eyes had come to rest on David.

'Of course you have. He's handsome, smart, likely to be earning a very good salary very soon. What's not to like?'

'Is loving the idea of him and what he represents – you know, loyalty, security, a home like I never had, but with all the trimmings that I like – is that enough? I know he would never cheat on me like my dad did to my mother.'

Vicky looked over at her quickly, but her face was pensive, lost in the moment. 'I guess it's better than nothing.'

Then Anna recovered. 'Don't mind me. I think I've just drunk too much. I shouldn't drink gin at my own wedding. I do love him, of course I do.'

Vicky knew Anna had hardly had anything to drink and was probably the most sober there, but said nothing.

'Come on, let's dance. I love this song. And we don't have much time left before the fireworks and the last dance.'

She dragged Vicky by the arm over to where David was shuffling to a Robbie Williams song on the dance floor with George and some of the rugby lads, now with their shirts unbuttoned and their ties knotted around their heads like bandanas. David looked over at Vicky and winked, then carried on dancing.

Dear Anna,

I bet you're spinning in your grave right now.

Yes, you saw correctly. David kissed me. And I liked it. I wanted more.

He's a surprisingly good kisser. You used to moan about how boring he was in bed, how he only had a few moves and was very repetitive, mechanical. Well, what little I got to experience tonight was quite impressive, I thought.

Sorry, hun. Not what you'll want to hear.

It's not the first time, you know. The first time we kissed was at your wedding. Terrible, I know, but he was so confused about you and your future together, and I was still reeling from your dad putting the moves on me. You didn't believe me when I said he came on to me, did you? Why would you though? Why would your sophisticated, charming dad have been interested in me? The chubby, drunk friend.

Because he was a letch and you knew that. You knew what he could be like because you'd watched him all those years while your mother turned a blind eye.

Well, I can tell you the truth now. Your dad did come on to me, but I was too drunk to react properly. Again. I'm pleased you came over, actually. Saved me that time, didn't you?

And yes, I kissed David all those years ago, but only because I thought he deserved better than the way you treated him. But nothing really changed in all the years you were married. You treated him with disdain most of the time, like he could do nothing right, and yet he always went back for more. I wonder what would've happened if I had told him about your doubts that night. Would you have stayed married? Would we be where we are now? Would the night of your accident have happened as it did or would you still be alive today?

We'll never know.

But I do know that the wheels were set in motion on the night of your wedding and they accelerated over the years until they came to a screeching halt one rainy night in the dark.

Oh, and by the way, it was me that threw up in the toilets at the reception. Not your mother. But that was your fault too, wasn't it? You were quietly undermining me, getting me shot after shot but not drinking them yourself, taunting me, toying with me, until I did what I always do. I lost control.

Well done. You were always such a worthy opponent.

But I won the ultimate battle. I have had the last laugh.

Strangely, I didn't find it all that funny in the end.

Vix x

9

David felt awkward after the kiss. He knew it wasn't the first time, but the previous one had sprung from a moment of madness at his wedding, alcohol-fuelled, stress-induced, whatever. This time he had instigated it and for a split second it had felt right. Until he realised that it wasn't. But it had been playing on his mind ever since.

Olympics fever had built to quite a crescendo, which was helping to distract both him and Vicky, so he had managed to keep a bit of space between them for the last few days, especially since the kids were now on school holidays and she had her hands full. But every now and then he'd catch her watching him with a strange intensity on her face or he'd turn around and she would be standing right behind him, as though purposefully putting herself in his way so that they would collide, brush against each other, touch.

A few nights ago over dinner, Harper had mentioned that the Olympic torch relay was coming through Bushy Park on Friday before setting off up the river on the Queen's barge.

'We've been learning all about the Olympics and the torch at school,' Harper said. 'Can we go and see it, Vix?'

'See what?'

'The torch,' Lewis said. 'Harper says it will be in the park.'

'Sure, why not? We can take a picnic lunch, watch the torch relay, then move onto Kingston Bridge to see the Gloriana pass by. Should be a lovely day – as long as it's not raining, of course.'

'Can you come, Daddy?' Harper asked.

Vicky looked over at him, but said nothing.

He felt like he had missed a lot lately. It was different when Anna had been at home with the kids and he was off at work. That was what was meant to happen, wasn't it? But now, with Vicky looking after them, he felt guilty a lot of the time, like he was letting someone else raise his children instead of taking more of an interest himself. But the truth was he didn't have the energy. It was easier to let her get on with it. The kids were doing fine, she was very good at talking about Anna with them, keeping her memory alive, even if she did things very differently. It meant that he didn't have to do those things, but he knew that made him a coward.

'I'm sure I can make a plan to take the day off. Sounds like fun.' He noticed Vicky's eyebrows disappear into her hairline and the small smile.

'But only if you promise to eat your cauliflower, Lewis.'

'Ah, Daddy...'

Friday was indeed a bright and sunny day, with cornflower blue skies and thin, wispy clouds. The kids were up early, excited along with the rest of the nation at the idea of the Olympics finally kicking off. There had been a steady crescendo of excitement in recent weeks, with no one really sure what to expect once it began. Team GB flags strung from lampposts and windows fluttered in the light breeze and the air was charged with anticipation.

David shuffled into the kitchen at 8 a.m. in his gown and slippers, his hair on end and sleep still fogging up his eyes.

'Daddy, you need to get dressed!' Harper shouted. She was wearing every item she owned that was red, white or blue, it would seem, and was sitting in a chair at the kitchen table while Vicky painted her face with the Olympic logo, her tongue protruding from her lips in concentration as she copied from a picture on her phone.

Lewis was running around the kitchen table in laps like an athlete, his face already painted.

'Slow down, Lewis, you'll hurt yourself.'

'I'm doing the torch relay, Daddy!' And he set off again, dangerously close to banging into the corners of the table with every lap.

'We've got loads of time, haven't we?' David said, desperately needing coffee. He had struggled to sleep properly ever since the accident, but it had worsened lately as his mind replayed a nightmarish kaleidoscope of images behind his eyes as soon as he closed them – of Anna, Vicky, foxes running in front of cars, even one last night of Anna turning into a fox before Vicky ran her over in her car. After that, he'd sat awake, feeling foolish and distraught in equal measures, until he eventually fell back to sleep at 4 a.m. just after he heard the milkman deposit the fresh milk bottles on their front doorstep. Some nights alcohol helped to numb him enough to pass out for a few hours, but the continuous broken sleep was taking its toll, making him jumpy and agitated.

'No, we want to get there early to that we can get to the front and see everyone,' Harper insisted.

'Harps, stop moving! This is starting to look less like the Olympic logo and more like undecipherable hieroglyphics,' Vicky was saying. 'Right, that's done. Where's the hairbrush?' She got to her feet and left the kitchen as David sunk into a chair and put his head in his hands.

Suddenly he thought he could feel Vicky watching him from the doorway, her eyes tripping over his skin, but when he spun around, she wasn't there.

God, he needed that coffee. Why had he agreed to go with them?

He pushed to his feet and headed to the coffee machine just as his phone vibrated in his dressing gown pocket as a text message was delivered.

Hoping it was work saying he would have to come in after all, David pulled it out and read the message on the screen.

You think you knew your wife, but you didn't. She was evil and she deserved what she got.

David went cold from the roots of his hair.

Lewis was still running around him. 'What's a unsiph hi-ho-glyphic? AGGGHHH!' Lewis screamed as he lost focus and collided with the corner of the table. He immediately crumpled into a sobbing heap on the floor just as Vicky returned to the kitchen, a hairbrush clutched in her hand.

'I told you to slow down, Lewis!' David shouted, to which Lewis cried even harder. He looked from Vicky to the phone and back to Vicky.

'David, go and get dressed. I'll deal with all of this,' she said calmly.

He blinked at her, then stalked from the room, the phone still clutched in his hand.

He stopped in the hallway and read the message again, confusion and anger rippling through him.

Why would someone send that? Was it a prank? A sick joke? He'd heard of people tormenting victims' families. Was that what this was?

He couldn't get his head around it, didn't want to, so deleted the message with a brisk swipe.

If he couldn't see it, it never existed.

Half an hour later, Vicky, Harper and Lewis sat at the bottom of the stairs, their shoes on and their faces propped up in their hands, waiting for David to come down so that they could go. He stood at the top of the stairs, looking down on the heads below and forced a smile. The tightness in his chest that he'd been grappling with ever since he'd read the text had relaxed a little, but he could still feel his teeth clenching as he tried to stay in control.

The kids were doing okay. It would be okay. He would be okay.

It was like a mantra he had to repeat to himself.

'Right, I'm ready! Let's go!' he announced.

He descended the stairs to cheers and whoops and they headed out into the morning sunshine.

They cycled to the park in convoy, with David shouting at Harper and Lewis to 'stay to the side' and 'slow down', while Vicky cycled on Anna's upright vintage bicycle down the middle of the quiet streets, her knees sticking out as though they didn't belong to her and her skirt billowing in the breeze like a parachute. The bike had a basket on the front and she'd stashed the picnic lunch into it, but the long baguette poking out the top made her resemble Mary Poppins after one too many gins, especially the way she was weaving all over the road.

As they neared the main road through the park along which the torch relay would travel, they could already see crowds of people lining the route.

'Told you we needed to be early,' Vicky said.

The atmosphere was reminiscent of a jolly summer fair, with resonant laughter, shouting children and dogs barking. Even the royal deer had turned up to show their support as they lay in the shade on the grass.

They parked their bikes against a tree and David struggled to get a bike lock through all of the wheels as the other three ran off to find a good vantage point.

Vicky seemed to know all sorts of people, who greeted her warmly. 'How do you know all these people?' he whispered as he caught up with her.

'From school pick-up really, hanging around in the playground. It's sometimes nice to chat to the other mothers.'

'Anna didn't know that many.'

'Small talk was never her thing though, was it? And she was never there. The au pair did it for her.'

The anticipation of the spectators rose in tandem with the temperature and before long the relay was winding its way along the road amid a cacophony of clapping. The kids had manoeuvred their way to the very front and were within touching distance of the torch as Vicky snapped photos of them on her phone.

'Stand together so that I can get one of the three of you,' David said and Vicky hugged the kids to her and smiled contentedly. She looked beautiful with the sun above her, lighting up her face.

A voice behind him said, 'Here, let me take one of all of you. It's a nice memory to have with your wife.' David turned to see a man smiling and holding out his hand. David was about to correct him, but then found he didn't want to.

'Thanks.'

He moved around behind Harper and Vicky smiled up at him as she pressed against his side. David smiled into the camera just as he felt Vicky's hand press into his waist and squeeze it.

The photo opportunity taken, they moved apart again and went to gather up their bikes and find a spot for their picnic before making their way over to Kingston Bridge for the riverboat procession.

Vicky laid out a small blanket and the kids ran around them with a ball as they relaxed. David stretched out on his back, his arms behind his head, peering up at the cloud shapes floating above him. He could feel his jaw slowly unclenching as the atmosphere relaxed him. In fact, right now, in this moment, he felt more casual than he had in months, even before Anna's accident.

He voiced as much to Vicky. 'Well, that's Olympics fever for you,' she said.

'Yeah.'

'And maybe it's more than that. Maybe you're accepting what has happened and ready to start taking steps to move past it.'

He turned on his side and propped himself up on one elbow. 'I don't know.'

'David, it's not a bad thing. It's not that you're forgetting, certainly not. But at some point it won't be a gnawing, empty ache every time you think of her. And that's okay. You're allowed to be happy. It doesn't make you a terrible person.' She reached out and laid her hand on his bare arm. The hairs on his skin shot up in response.

'I don't know if I'm there quite yet.' He thought about the sleeplessness, the paranoia, the text message from that morning.

'No, but you will reach a point when you can remember the good stuff without feeling pain over the bad stuff. I really hope I'm one of the reasons for that. You deserve to be happy. And so do I.' She paused to stuff a cocktail sausage in her mouth. 'Things were quite stressed between you two before the accident, weren't they?'

David frowned. 'What makes you say that? Did she say something to you?'

'No, no, I just…' She looked over at the kids making daisy chains in the grass. 'I just got that feeling from her, that's all. Reading between the lines, you know?'

'Yeah, well, living with Anna was a challenge of its own most days. But I did feel like she was more distant. Not unhappy as such, but… I don't know. I asked her about it, but she always said she was fine.'

'I think, between you and me, she found motherhood quite boring, monotonous. Not that she didn't love her kids, because she did, but she craved something else, you know? She loved to be the centre of attention and of course, once kids come along, you get shoved to the bottom of the pile. I'm not sure that ever sat well with her.'

David lay back again. 'Yeah, I know.' He was thoughtful for a moment. 'It's a shame you never had kids of your own. You would've been a great mum.'

'Well, the stars never aligned for me and I can't see it happening now. So I guess I'll just have to be a mother to these two instead.'

David looked over at her face, but the sun was behind her so that he couldn't make out her expression against the blinding white light.

Despite the warmth of the day, he shivered, as though someone had tickled the back of his neck with icy fingers.

Luck was on their side as they made their way along the river. With the amount of people trying to secure tables and viewing points at the numerous bars and cafés lining the water's edge, they were incredibly fortuitous to walk past a table just as a couple got up to leave. Vicky launched herself at the open seats and plonked herself down before anyone else could wrestle it from her.

The kids deposited their bike helmets on the table and headed towards the river's edge to sit with their feet dangling over, along with lots of other children.

'Be careful, guys!' David called.

'They'll be fine. Relax – go and order us some drinks. Make mine a gin and tonic – double,' Vicky urged, letting her fingers linger on his arm.

He threw another look at Harper and Lewis, then weaved through the bodies to the bar.

It was packed inside, with people ordering frantically before the boat passed. The volume in the room had been turned to maximum and the noise started to grate on David's ears. Some of the people around him had clearly been in the pub since opening and had reached the loudly raucous stage, and the warm day was making itself evident in underarm sweat stains and glistening brows, accompanied by the sickly sweet smell of body odour as people reached around him to grab their drinks.

He finally managed to get served and negotiated his way outside as best he could with a pint, a G&T and two orange juices in his hands. He approached their table and saw a woman sitting in his chair, her back to him, talking animatedly to Vicky.

He put the drinks down on the table and the woman looked up. 'Oh, sorry, I've stolen your chair.' She leapt to her feet. 'Isn't this just a fabulous occasion?' Her eyes were as wide as her smile. A small, stocky woman with a short, mousy bob and pink cheeks from too much sun, she didn't wait for an answer but gabbled away like a turkey, her cheeks wobbling animatedly. David picked up a hint of the Midlands in her voice. 'The sense of community brings tears to my eyes! This is just what the country needs right now, isn't it? And the weather! What a summer this will be! Do you have tickets to any events? We've managed to get beach volleyball – such fun! Oh, how rude – I haven't introduced myself, have I? I'm Janet. I met your wife in the playground at school. Lewis and my son, Harry, are in the same class. Well, we've only just moved to the area actually, so we don't know that many people, but Vicky has been so welcoming to us.'

She stopped after running out of breath and Vicky took the opportunity to step in. 'This is David.'

But then Janet was off again. 'I must say, your wife is just such a lovely and giving person. I watch her with your children and she is just a joy to watch. They have such fun and I can see that they are the apple of her eye. You must be so proud of your family. And they look just like her, don't they?'

David paled and felt as though someone had flung a bucket of cold water over his face.

'She's—' A splash and then a scream from the water's edge interrupted him. 'Daddy!'

He launched to his feet and looked over to where Harper and Lewis had been sitting and where only Harper was visible now.

He knocked a chair over in his haste to get to them, ignoring the angry rebuke from the table behind, and rushed over to where Harper was peering over the edge.

The world seemed to slow down, with everyone moving in slow motion around him.

He was almost too afraid to look over the edge in case he saw his son's lifeless body being swept down river. But he did look – and saw nothing. Harper was weeping and pointing. 'What is it? Harper?'

'My hairband! It fell in the river!'

'What the f—'

'Get it, Daddy! Get it!'

'Harper, where is Lewis?' he said between gritted teeth.

'He's there,' she said in between sobs. She pointed behind him and he turned to see Lewis sitting in the chair that Janet had vacated, sipping calmly on his orange juice.

'Right, come away from the water's edge. It's not safe. And no, I cannot get your hairband. We'll find you another one somewhere else.'

His heart was still banging in his chest, painful against his ribs.

He fell into one of the empty chairs at their table and wiped a hand over his forehead. Vicky didn't seem concerned.

'Did you not hear her scream?'

'Harper? Oh, yeah, but I knew it would be nothing. She can be prone to histrionics sometimes. Gets it from her mother, I think.'

David felt the panic morph into irritation and then aggravation at her easy-going attitude.

'Lewis could've fallen in!'

'I doubt that.' She sucked from the straw in her G&T. 'Oh, sorry about Janet. She has verbal diarrhoea on the best of days. I've never managed to get a word in edgeways to correct her about not being their mum. I hope you don't mind, but sometimes it's just easier that way.'

He did mind, but he clamped his mouth shut as he didn't trust himself to speak yet. His neck was cold and clammy, and a headache was settling in behind his eyes. He put the pint glass to his lips, but the beer slid down his throat with razorblades, so he set it down again.

The river procession was a blur after that, seen in snatches between waving hands and flying flags. Vicky had another couple of gins and chatted gaily to people around her, but David couldn't bring himself to drink any more beer. He craved strong coffee and peace and quiet, away from the shouting and hilarity as the spectators fell into their summer drinks, bald heads and bare arms growing pinker by the hour.

The drama of the lost hairband long forgotten, Harper and Lewis had made friends with some kids of similar ages sat with their parents at the next table and David felt like a scrooge for wanting to go home. This was their summer holiday after all. He hadn't made any plans to go away anywhere this year because he knew he would find that too strange and impossibly sad. The single dad at some resort, left to sit at the Social Table every evening because he was on his own. No, it was too soon for all of that.

So he stuck it out for them, watched with mild disdain as the adults grew steadily drunker and the children more obnoxious as the afternoon wore on, listening to Vicky chattering away in her reedy voice and demolish a plate of chips smothered with ketchup, ordered because she was apparently ravenous. He was relieved when Harper said she was tired and wanted to go home. They walked their bikes over the bridge and then clambered back on them to cycle home. Vicky looked even more unsteady as the gin pushed her balance out of kilter. It was a slow ride, with much whinging from the kids as exhaustion from the sun and the excitement hit them.

Once the kids were in bed, Vicky was pushing to pour more drinks and watch the opening ceremony, but David cried off with a headache and said he would get an early night. He gathered up his small pile of post that had greeted them on the mat when they got home and headed upstairs with concrete legs and annoyance buzzing around his head like a niggling mosquito.

He changed into pyjama bottoms – something he had only started wearing once Vicky had moved in to save them both from any embarrassing moments. He propped himself on the bed, turned the TV on and watched the opening ceremony with one eye while opening the letters that had arrived. Some junk mail from the local Indian restaurant with a special Olympics offer – he had the overwhelming sense that he would grow tired of Olympics fever before too long – the credit card bill and a handwritten letter addressed to him but without a return address on the back.

He was distracted for a while as someone who appeared to be the Queen was seen parachuting out of a helicopter alongside James Bond and he chuckled despite his bad mood. When songs from The Who and the Rolling Stones started blasting out through the stadium, he turned the volume down and his attention back to the envelopes on the duvet beside him.

He didn't expect the credit card bill to be heavy. Anna had been the only one to use it much. He was more conservative and preferred to spend only what he knew he could afford to pay off every month. They'd had some heated arguments over the years about her capacity to be extravagant, a habit learned from years of watching her father throw money at her mother to keep her distracted from his extracurricular activities, no doubt.

He ran his finger under the flap of the envelope and felt a sting as it cut into his skin, leaving a wafer-thin line of blood. He pulled out the pages and frowned as he saw the total on the covering page. There were two more pages attached, one connected to the transactions from his card, showing one tank of petrol and congestion zone charges for last month; the second page was for Anna's linked credit card. That cold feeling of icy fingers up his neck crept over him again. The list of transactions numbered around twenty and were all for clothing brands, cosmetics and high-end department stores – all dated after Anna's death.

He put down the pages and stared unseeing as Emile Sandé started singing 'Abide with Me' on the TV screen in a haunting lilt. It provided an unnecessary soundtrack to his unease.

There must be a mistake. Even if she'd bought all of this stuff just before her accident, it would've been on last month's bill. This had all been bought since then.

Vicky.

He had said that she should treat this as her own home, but he hadn't given her Anna's credit card. He paid her by bank transfer and gave her extra cash for food and whatever the kids needed. She must've found the credit card somewhere and started using it.

Then mortification swept over him.

Oh god, what was he going to say to her?

He hated confrontations.

But then what had Chloe said?

Sounds like quite a cushy setup to me.

Was she playing him? Taking liberties?

No. He'd seen her with the kids and knew she loved them. Maybe she had intended to pay him back once she got the bill and had forgotten to mention it. He should give her the benefit of the doubt.

As the athletes began to pour into the stadium, he turned off the TV and lay back against the pillows. He could just make out the sounds of the ceremony filtering up through the floorboards from the lounge. Should he go and speak to her now?

No, he couldn't bear it. His body felt compressed with exhaustion, like something heavy was sitting on his torso. He leaned over and gathered the pages together and shoved them back into the envelope. His eyes fell on the one other letter waiting for him.

He opened the envelope more carefully this time to avoid more paper cuts. Inside was a letter handwritten on thick white paper. He picked up the envelope again and saw no postage stamp. It must've been delivered by hand.

David,

I'm sorry for the loss you and your children have had to endure.

No child should have to live beyond their parent, no matter who that parent is.

For that I am sorry, but for Anna I am not.

You didn't know her. You didn't know your wife well at all.

She was very good at taking things that didn't belong to her.

It was only a matter of time before someone hit back.

Everything happens for a reason, David.

There was no signature.

David sat bolt upright and read it again, disbelief coursing through him. What kind of sick person would send a letter like this? He read it a third time, the disbelief turning to anger. It must be from the person who sent the text message. It was too much of a coincidence. They clearly wanted to tell him something about Anna, possibly about her accident?

He needed to show this to the police. Was the writer saying she had been killed on purpose? That it wasn't an accident after all?

He flung the letter on the bed, as though the poison it contained was contagious. It fell on top of the credit card bill. His mind lurched.

Taking things that didn't belong…?

Did Vicky have something to do with this? She was starting to look like she had scored from their arrangement. From Anna's death. But why would she pen a letter like that if she was indeed on a good wicket with him? That didn't make sense. And she hadn't sent the text, unless she had another mobile phone somewhere.

His mind twisted and somersaulted, ideas banging against his skull to be heard.

No, Vicky didn't write this or the text. Why would she? But a voice in his head told him to be careful.

He folded the letter back into the envelope and placed it on the bedside table. He'd show the letter to the police, maybe mention the credit card bill too, before he said anything to Vicky. If only he hadn't deleted the text message.

He knew sleep would be even more elusive now. He felt cold to his very bones, although the room was warm and airless. He turned the TV back on and watched on autopilot as athletes preened like proud peacocks around the track.

★

David sat bolt upright in bed.

The light of the television illuminated the dark room, an advert for online bingo hoping to lure the insomniacs of Britain into a web of addiction.

It wasn't the television that had woken him though. He was sure of that much.

Definitely a noise. Like the creak of a floorboard or the nudge of a door. He looked across at his bedroom door, but it was closed, as it had been earlier.

He grabbed the remote and turned off the TV, then flung himself back onto the pillow, feeling heavy and drained after being yanked from what had been a thin sleep anyway. He rubbed at his eyes, then listened again, still wondering what had woken him. Maybe Vicky had been up for the toilet or something. Or one of the kids.

Everything was quiet now, the kind of silence that you only experience at night, dense, oppressive. He turned onto his side, his back to the door, and hugged his arms around Anna's pillow, breathing into the cotton, wishing it smelt more of her than of fabric softener.

His eyes fell on her bedside table and he stiffened as he saw the book sitting there. It was the novel that Anna had been reading before she died. The one he had started but Vicky had then taken herself to read.

He was sure it hadn't been there when he went to bed earlier. In fact, he'd put that horrible letter down on the table before he'd fallen asleep. But now he could just make out the corner of the envelope poking out from under the book.

Which meant Vicky had come into his room when he was asleep and put it back.

The idea made him feel weirdly violated, knowing she had looked down on him sleeping, at his most vulnerable, and he had been completely unaware. Perhaps it was her leaving the room that had woken him.

But why creep in, knowing he might be asleep? The book would've waited until tomorrow. But the TV was on, so she might've assumed he was still awake. He shivered and burrowed further under the covers, pulling the pillow tighter as though it could comfort him. Something sharp jabbed into his arm and he felt around under the pillow with his fingers.

He pulled something small and metal out and peered at it in the semi-darkness. It was a gold earring in the shape of a hummingbird. He knew it well. Anna had worn those earrings every day since Vicky had given them to her on their wedding day. She had lost one a few weeks before her accident and had been distraught.

But how was it still here in their bed? The sheets had been changed a number of times since she'd last slept here. Unless it had been caught in the actual pillow, but that was unlikely surely?

Perhaps Vicky had found it? But why put it in his bed? Under her pillow? Like a childish sacrificial gift to the tooth fairy?

So many questions and not enough answers.

The strangeness he was already feeling jumped up a gear as he turned the earring over in his fingers. He reached out with a goose-bumped arm and laid it carefully on her bedside table on top of the book.

He had the sudden inexplicable feeling that someone was now standing over his bed, behind him, peering down on him malevolently, and he flung himself onto his back, fear pricking at his skin. But there was no one there. Just shadows dancing across the ceiling in the hazy moonlight filtering through a gap in the curtains. Just his imagination playing silly buggers with him. He was driving himself mad with paranoia and exhaustion.

Even so, he turned on his side to face the door and saw out the night with one eye open, sleep no longer an option.

May 2005

Vicky sat in the back seat of the taxi next to Matt, her legs crossed awkwardly so that she could lean back a bit to avoid her belly protruding over the waistband of her tight black jeans. The jeans were fine when she stood up, but as soon as she sat down, everything pushed up and out. Matt's hand rested lightly in hers and she was worried her palm was sweaty.

She felt quite drunk. She had met Matt in a bar in Esher last week. Anna was supposed to have come to meet her, but hadn't turned up. She had wanted a girls' night out, the first one they'd managed since Anna's baby was born in February, but as it was, Harper had thrown up everywhere just as Anna was leaving and she hadn't wanted to leave her with a babysitter. By then, Vicky was already on her way to the bar, so had decided to stay for a drink on her own. Better that than yet another evening on her own in her empty flat.

Matt had been having drinks with work colleagues and they'd started chatting, then flirting. She'd given him her number and he'd finally called to ask her out tonight.

They'd met for a drink first, then he'd offered to cook dinner for her at his place. By then, she'd had a few drinks and had agreed eagerly. She was starving and he seemed nice. An estate agent and much more of a pretty boy than she was usually attracted to with his quiffed dark hair and slim-fit shirt.

The radio in the taxi was playing an old Heart ballad, the singer professing, 'All I wanna do is make love to you,' and Vicky wanted to giggle at the absurdity of it. Matt stared out of the window unfazed.

The taxi pulled up outside a nondescript terraced house and Matt handed over cash, thanked the driver and clamoured out. He didn't open her door for her, just reached into his coat and grabbed a set of keys without looking back.

She mumbled her thanks to the driver and got out of the car, a little irked at Matt's lack of manners. Come to think of it, he'd said very little to her since they'd left the bar.

She followed him into the hallway and saw the house was split into maisonettes, with his on the first floor. A mountain bike was attached to the wall and she had to shuffle past its muddy tyre to get to the stairs, which were carpeted in an astonishingly loud green that looked like it hadn't seen a vacuum cleaner in a while.

She could feel herself sobering up rapidly. She hesitated, then followed him upstairs.

The maisonette itself was a little cleaner than the hallway but minimalist, with just a sofa, a large TV and a small galley kitchen on offer. Down a short hallway, she could see two more doors closed to prying eyes.

'Drink?' she heard Matt say over her shoulder. She turned to see him standing right behind her.

'Um, yeah, thanks.'

He peeled her coat from her and tossed it onto the couch. 'Make yourself comfortable.' The way he said it made her feel uneasy.

'So, what's on the menu?' she said brightly as he disappeared into the kitchen.

'Huh?'

'Dinner? You said you would cook something?'

'Oh, yeah, well, I'm not much of a cook. Let's just stick to booze.'

Her stomach rumbled on cue – she hadn't eaten all evening.

'Should we order something in instead then?'

He returned with two glasses of wine, gulping from one of them.

'We don't need food. Let's just have a good time.' Putting the glasses down on a cluttered coffee table, he grabbed her by the arm and pulled her onto the couch next to him. Before she could even breathe, he had pressed his mouth to hers and was shoving an expectant tongue between her clamped lips.

'Um, wait…' she tried to say as his hands started roaming under her crop top.

'Relax, let's have a laugh. Why else are you here?'

She could feel her heart starting to pound as the reality of the situation hit her. This wasn't right. It was like Dan all over again.

No. No. NO.

She shoved hard at his chest and he shot back, looking wounded. Then his expression changed to a smirk. 'Oh, I get it. You wanna play games. Okay, that's alright with me. We can play games.'

He came at her again and she leapt from the couch, grabbed her handbag and rushed down the corridor and through the nearest doorway. Closing the door behind her, she saw she was in the bathroom. She hastily locked the door and rested against it, panting.

She looked around her, panicked, then rummaged in her bag for her phone.

It was answered after only one ring. 'I swear this child is full of vomit. Where is it all coming from? It's disgusting.'

'Anna, you have to help me.'

'Vix? You okay? What have you done now?'

'I'm in a man's flat and he's all over me and... I'm scared. Please, help me.'

'Where are you?' Anna's voice was suddenly very serious.

'I'm in his flat in Esher somewhere. I've locked myself in the bathroom.'

'Okay, good. Stay there. Can you remember anything about where his place is?'

Vicky thought hard and repeated the address Matt had given the taxi driver.

'Okay, do not come out of that bathroom until I say so.'

Vicky started to cry – from fear, embarrassment, disappointment and relief. She sat down heavily on the toilet lid and put her face in her hands.

'Hey! Open up!' Vicky jumped as Matt banged his fists on the door. 'What the fuck are you doing?'

'Go away!' Vicky shouted feebly.

'You're in my bathroom, you mad bitch!'

'Leave me alone!'

'Jesus, whatever.' She heard footsteps retreating and exhaled the nervous breath she was holding.

The bathroom smelled of mildew and damp and she felt nausea swirl in her stomach.

Minutes passed and she remained on the loo seat, crying quietly at the shit show that was her life, breathing deeply to try and calm herself, and berating herself for getting into this kind of mess again.

She had to start getting her life in order.

Just as she was about to emerge from the bathroom and attempt to fight her way out of the flat, she heard a doorbell ring, muttering and then footsteps tramping down the stairs.

She heard a door bang back against a wall and a furious voice power through the flat to demand, 'Where is she? Where's my best friend? If you've laid one hand on her, you'll be swallowing your own balls!'

Vicky unlocked the bathroom door and rushed into the lounge just as Anna appeared. She stood with her hands on her hips and her cheeks flushed, all pointy fingers and sharp syllables. At first glance, Vicky thought she was wearing a cape, but it was actually a papoose in which a gurgling Harper was strapped, her little fists clenched and pumping the air in quiet solidarity.

'Jesus, who's this mad bitch?' Matt said from behind Anna.

Vicky rushed at Anna and pulled her into a hug. 'Careful, watch Harper. Right, let's get out of this shithole.'

Vicky grabbed her coat and pushed past Matt, not wanting to look at him, with Anna and Harper close on her heels.

'Wait a minute, what about all those drinks I bought you?'

Anna stopped in her tracks and turned back towards him. 'What? Drinks? Is that what you wanted? Payback for a few drinks? So you thought rape would be the best way of getting what you think is owed to you?'

'Woah, hey, I never raped anyone. I never touched her.'

'That's funny, 'cos she phoned me from where she was locked in your bathroom because you were all over her.'

'You're both mad.'

Anna went right up in his face, until Harper was so close to him, she was pulling on his shirt button. 'Yes, we are. And if I hear that you have tried to get in touch with my friend ever again, I will shout rape as loud as I can and you will end up in prison playing husband and wife with a big bald bloke called Gary. Your word against both of ours – do I make myself clear?'

Matt backed away, his hands held up in surrender.

Anna glared at him one last time, then swept from the room, pulling Vicky along with her.

Once in the street, Vicky managed to say, 'Oh my god, thank you so much, Anna. You were like a caped superhero! Brilliant! I'm so sorry I called you, but I didn't know who else to call. I have no one else to call.' Vicky was jabbering in relief. 'You properly frightened him. It was brilliant.'

'Yeah, okay, Vix, it's fine. I know what you're like. You'll never change. But I'm here to pick up the pieces. That's what best friends are for, right? And besides, you owe me. And I'll make sure you pay me back one day.'

February 2006

Vicky stood on the doorstep of Anna's impressive double-fronted house, wondering if the house envy she felt every time she came here would ever abate. Her arms were full of presents she couldn't afford to buy, but it was her goddaughter's first birthday party and she just had to spoil her.

She had a headache and knew her eyes were bloodshot – the bloke she was with last night had been keen to party into the early hours.

Taking a deep breath, she reached up with shaky fingers to ring the bell, but the door opened before she could. David rushed out and nearly knocked her over, his arms full of brightly coloured balloons.

'Shit, sorry Vix. Didn't see you there.'

She laughed. 'Got enough balloons?'

He rolled his eyes. 'It's not like Harper will remember any of this, but Anna is on one of her missions.'

'Eek, okay, I'll tread carefully.'

'Go on in, she's in the kitchen with the caterer.'

Vicky meandered past him and headed through the house to the kitchen where she could hear Anna barking orders.

'Don't leave the crusts on the sandwiches. They won't get eaten. Careful of the cake!'

Vicky stood in the doorway and took it all in. A harassed pair of women, dressed in aprons, were juggling trays of food while Anna arranged roses in a crystal vase on the table.

'Hey, birthday mum!' Vicky said brightly.

'Oh, thank god you're here! David is driving me mad and I need a glass of fizz before I lose the will to live.'

Vicky dropped her pile of presents on the table and pulled a bottle of prosecco from her bag. 'Your wish is my command!'

'Oh, don't put those there. That looks so awful. There's a table set up in the lounge for presents.'

'Okay. Get some glasses then.'

Vicky dumped the presents and returned to the kitchen where Anna had finished faffing with the flowers and was now sitting scowling at the caterers.

'Bloody useless,' she said in a loud stage whisper. 'I could've done a better job myself.'

'Why didn't you then?' Vicky said.

'Fuck off, Vix.' Then she smiled. 'Right, booze. Let's drink to me being a boring housewife, shall we?'

Vicky grabbed the bottle and popped the cork just as David appeared in the doorway. 'Starting already, girls?'

'Yes, David, we are.' Her voice dripped ice. 'This is a party after all.'

'Okay, okay!' He held his hands up in surrender and backed out of the room.

'Everything okay?' Vicky asked quietly.

'Later. I'll tell you later. Cheers!' She clinked her glass to Vicky's hard enough for some of the bubbles to spill over the rim.

Halfway down the bottle, the doorbell started to ring with guests arriving for the party. People that Vicky didn't know streamed into the house, their arms full of babies and presents. The air was potent with women's perfume, forcibly cheerful banter and a subtle undertone of dirty nappies. Her head pounding, Vicky kept to the side of the room and watched with curiosity as the guests placed their babies on the rug in the lounge that was covered in various toys to keep the little humans engaged, while the caterers, now without their aprons, passed around trays of snacks and David rushed in and out with drinks. He had the look of a man out of his depth.

Dads stood to the side, talking football and slugging from bottles of beer, while the women fawned over the babies, wiping tiny dribbles or inexplicably lifting the babies and sniffing their bottoms. Vicky found it all mesmerising and so alien to the world she still inhabited of one-night stands and microwave dinners.

The women were impeccably dressed in varying hues of beige and blue, their tiny hips clad in skinny jeans and their sleepless nights hidden beneath expensive foundation. In contrast, Vicky felt like she stuck out a mile in her baggy jeans, Metallica T-shirt and the leopard print Doc Marten boots she'd been wearing for years. She'd pulled her hair into a bushy ponytail and still had the shadow of last night's make-up under her eyes.

She looked around for Anna, who fitted in perfectly with these people, with her tiny jeans, blouse that skimmed her still pert boobs and hair as dark and glossy as ever. Even motherhood agreed with Anna. No sign of a flabby baby belly or any extra pounds still lingering. But then, she had joined a health club as soon as Harper was born and spent most mornings in the gym while Harper went to the crèche.

A woman came to sit on a spare chair next to Vicky. The baby in her arms was niggling, seconds away from a full-blown tantrum. The woman loosened some buttons, reached into her blouse and pulled a boob from her bra like a ripe melon. Vicky had time to notice the deep veins and taut skin before realising she was staring in fascination as the baby latched on hungrily. Vicky looked away in embarrassment.

'Which one is yours?'

'Sorry?' Vicky said.

'Which baby?' the woman said, indicating the playgroup assembled on the floor.

'Oh, none of them. I'm Harper's godmother.'

'Ah, I thought you looked too... nervous to be one of us. You can tell the mothers in the room – we all look like we're ten seconds away from falling asleep on our feet.' She laughed, but her face looked the opposite of tired as she gazed down at her baby's head. She looked utterly at peace. Vicky wondered what that kind of love must feel like. It was a love she couldn't fathom – and certainly not one she remembered ever experiencing herself.

Vicky looked away again, the slurping sounds coming from the baby making her feel nauseous.

After a moment, the woman shifted and popped her boob away before lifting the baby to her shoulder and patting it hard on the back. 'I'm feeding on demand. It's exhausting,' she said, as though Vicky was interested. The baby let out a loud burp, then followed through with a spurt of milky sick that shot over the woman's shoulder and splashed onto Vicky's T-shirt.

'Oh, I'm so sorry, she has a touch of reflux. Of course, you're in the wrong place if you want to stay clear of vomit today. Ha!' The woman laughed jovially.

Vicky smiled thinly and got to her feet, the smell of milky vomit clinging to her nostrils.

She headed towards the downstairs bathroom, but found the door locked. A voice said gaily, 'Sorry! Changing a nappy!'

Vicky headed up the stairs and saw another body leaning over the changing mat in the other bathroom too.

Anna's bedroom door was closed, so Vicky figured it would be safe to use her en suite instead.

She turned the handle and bundled into the room, holding the neck of the T-shirt away from her nose as the smell grew too much.

She pulled up short.

Anna was sitting on the bed with a man Vicky didn't know. He had his hands weaved into her hair and it looked like he was trying to swallow her whole.

'Anna.'

Anna jumped away from him and had the good grace to blush. The man leapt to his feet. 'Oh, er…'

Anna smiled wickedly. 'Oh, it's you. Vicky, this is Colin. Colin, my best mate Vix.'

'I, er, I just wanted to use the bathroom. The others are full and…' She pointed at the white gloop on her black T-shirt.

Colin coughed loudly. 'Right, well, I'd better...' He pointed to the door and retreated without looking at either of them.

'What the fuck, Anna?'

Anna rolled her eyes. 'Oh, come on, it's just a bit of fun. I'm just, you know, playing with him.' She sighed. 'He's been eyeing me up for weeks, gets all flustered when I speak to him. It's sweet. So I thought I'd make his day, give him a little party bag, if you will. It was just a kiss. I wasn't going to shag him or anything.'

'But David is downstairs!'

'So? So is Colin's wife.' She grinned again. 'Did you see his little face? He was like the cat that got the cream.'

'God, what are you like?'

She sighed like a bored teenager as Vicky flumped onto the bed next to her. 'I'm bored, Vix! Motherhood is dull. God, it's like watching paint dry most days. Bloody *Teletubbies* and Dora the fucking Explorer all day, vomit on me constantly.' She indicated the stain on Vicky's shoulder. 'Shit everywhere.' She stuck out her bottom lip. 'I just wanted to have a bit of fun.'

Vicky shook her head. 'You don't know how lucky you are sometimes, you know. I would kill to have your life.'

'Whatever, Vix. You're single, can sleep with whoever you want, go out when you want. I can't.'

'Yeah, but you have a husband who adores you, a big house and a beautiful child.'

Her sulk deepened. 'Stop trying to make me feel bad. It was just a kiss.' Then she glared at Vix. 'Do not tell David! Or anyone!'

Vicky narrowed her eyes. 'Have you done this before?'

'No.' Vicky wasn't sure if she could believe her. She had the look on her face she used to get when she was planning to nick money out of her mother's purse or pull a prank on a girl at school that she didn't like.

'Anna!'

'I haven't! But promise me you won't say anything.'

Vicky sighed. 'I won't.'

'Because I've kept secrets for you, don't forget. Big ones. Truths that you don't want coming out.'

Vicky felt an icy draught blow over her skin. 'Fine. No need to remind me.' They glared at each other for a moment. 'You know, you could always go back to work. That would help with the boredom,' Vicky said eventually. 'And it might actually keep you out of trouble, because that's where you're headed if you keep up with this.'

'Alright Mum! Actually, I've been thinking about it lately. There's a PR agency in town looking for an events co-ordinator.' She looked thoughtful, her lips pursed in contemplation. Vicky could understand why Colin had wanted to kiss them. Then Anna snapped out of her reverie and said, 'God, go and clean your shirt, Vix. You stink.'

Then she left the room, leaving Vicky sitting on the bed, goose bumps running up her arms.

A few hours later and the party was winding down, with only a handful of people left. Three babies lay sleeping in pushchairs lining the hallway. Colin and his wife sat in the lounge with David, while Anna stood talking to the woman whose baby had vomited on Vicky.

Harper had been put to bed for the evening and Vicky was working her way through another bottle of prosecco while seated next to a woman called Amanda who was nanny to one of the baby boys sleeping in his pushchair. Amanda was flying solo at the party, the baby's parents having dispatched her to attend so that they could have the afternoon off.

'They're probably at home shagging or something while I'm here.' Amanda was very drunk. She leaned over and refilled her glass from the bottle next to Vicky. Vicky felt drunk herself and found Amanda hilarious with her stories about being a nanny to a very wealthy family. She had just told Vicky about how she had been told to dust and clean above the fridge the other day, only for her to knock a filthy vibrator off the top of the fridge with her feather duster. It had apparently poked her in the eye on the way down. Vicky's cheeks were still aching from laughing.

'Don't get me wrong, I love Caspian to bits, but being a nanny is hard work. No time to yourself, working most evenings so that they can go out, I only get one day off on the weekend, so my social life has gone to shit.' She slurred her words and spittle landed on Vicky's cheek.

Vicky drained her glass and poured another as she looked over at Colin. He was staring longingly at Anna while his wife gesticulated and talked with rounded vowels to David. Anna was taking no notice of Colin now, her disinterest scathing.

Colin and his wife got up to leave at the same time as the mother of the vomit baby. Colin flushed as he said goodbye to Vicky, his guilt plain to see. Vicky watched as Anna politely kissed the air next to his cheek and dismissed him without a second glance. No one would've thought that a few hours ago she had had her tongue rammed down his throat.

Now only Amanda remained. David busied himself with tidying up around them, coughing and yawning loudly in Amanda's direction, but she didn't take the hint. Instead, she poured more fizz into her glass and leaned over towards the stereo to turn the music up. 'This is a great party.'

Vicky was thrilled at the look of annoyance that swept across Anna's face.

Amanda got to her feet and started dancing around the room and Vicky got up to join her. She pranced and gyrated to the music, then stumbled as her foot landed on a plastic toy on the carpet. She heard it shatter under her foot.

'Vix, you've had enough. Time for bed, yeah?' Anna said with a scowl.

'But I can't leave poor Mandy on her own.'

'Oh, don't worry, David has called a taxi for Amanda.'

'Great, I—' Then Amanda lurched from the room into the downstairs loo and the sound of retching filled the air, along with crying as Caspian woke up in his pushchair.

'Fuck's sake!' Anna said loudly.

Vicky decided that this was a good time to retreat. 'Can I crash here, Anna? I think I should go to bed. I'll help you tidy up tomorrow.'

'Sure,' Anna said, stony-faced.

Vicky leaned her head into the downstairs loo to see Amanda slumped on the floor in front of the vomit-splashed toilet bowl. 'Nice to meet you, Amanda,' she said, but got only a groan in return.

She staggered upstairs and into the spare room, where she had slept countless times before. She threw off her jeans, wrestled out of her bra and climbed between the clean sheets in her knickers and the still rank T-shirt.

Her eyes closed almost immediately, a headache already setting in behind her eyes.

Not long after, Vicky woke to the feeling of someone sitting on the mattress next to her. Panic gripped her throat, the sensation of the mattress moving of its own volition bringing long-buried memories hurtling into her brain.

'Here you go, Vix. I've brought you a glass of water,' Anna's voice said and Vicky exhaled.

'Listen, sorry about before. I shouldn't have... you know... with Colin. It was stupid. And I shouldn't have said what I did. You know your secret is safe with me,' Anna whispered while stroking Vicky's hair with her hand.

Then the mattress shifted again as she got up and left the room.

Vicky lay for a long time staring into the dark, her fists clenching the sheet by her sides.

10

Excited shrieks pulled David from a restless sleep the next morning. He must've passed out at some point in the early hours. The last time he had looked at the clock, it had been 4.15 a.m. He turned his head slowly. The earring still sat on the bedside table on top of the book, the envelope still poking from underneath.

It hadn't been a dream then.

A cold sweat coated his skin like grease and he had a dull headache pulsing behind his eyes, as though the myriad of theories he had concocted before he fell asleep had been trying to punch their way from the inside out.

He was lying on his side, halfway down the mattress, still facing the door, his legs tangled in the duvet and one arm trapped under his head. His arm tingled with pins and needles. He lifted his head and wiped the crusty drool from where it had dried on his chin.

The sun was already warming the room. His brain throbbed as he sat up and listened again to the noise that had woken him.

Laughter and shrieks from downstairs. The kids were obviously up to something.

For a second, he considered lying back down and putting his head under the pillow. Then his eyes fell on the earring again. He needed to start taking more notice of what was going on around him.

Anna's dressing table sat in the bay window of the bedroom, the same one she had had as a child. Pretty, shaped like a heart, with drapes around the drawers and a multitude of potions and lotions scattered across the glass surface. His eyes roamed over the hairbrush, perfumes and trinket boxes.

'Tell me what happened, Anna. Tell me the truth. I feel like I'm going mad,' he said into the empty room. His eyes prickled.

At the back of the dressing table, hiding to the side of the large mirror, was an A4 photo frame with a collage of various photos from Anna's past. Everything from school days to university to their wedding, all made into a mosaic of memories. Another gift from Vicky. David had seen it a thousand times over the years, but had never actually looked at it.

He got up on tired legs and went over to the dressing table. Scooping up the frame, he smiled as he saw photos of Harper and Lewis as babies, and himself leaning in for a kiss on their wedding day. Then he looked closer at the other photos. They were all of Anna and Vicky, but not standing arm in arm and smiling equally into the camera.

Most showed Anna smiling and Vicky gazing up at her, as though captivated.

He hadn't noticed that before. He knew they were close, closer than sisters really, and he had always known that Anna was the dominant player in their friendship, but seeing them like this, he realised how Vicky had followed Anna's lead, emulating her as best she could, not quite getting it right most of the time but desperately fighting to share a bit of her spotlight.

The thought bothered him – but why?

He didn't have time to think it through any further because a loud crash thundered through the house from downstairs.

He threw on a T-shirt over his pyjama bottoms and rushed downstairs.

The kitchen looked like a children's arts and crafts centre, with paint pots standing open, paintbrushes lying in pools of water, brightly coloured paper littered across the table and glitter sparkling on every surface and the floor.

Vicky was on her hands and knees cleaning up shards of porcelain. She looked up as he rushed in.

'Careful where you stand,' she said with a huge grin.

'What the hell was that?'

'Sorry if we woke you. Just a little accident with a vase.'

'What's going on?'

'It's the cycle race today.'

'What?'

'The road race in the Olympics. It's due to come past Hampton Court later and the kids wanted to go and cheer them on. We're making banners.' She looked so proud. 'Don't worry. We'll clean this up, won't we, kids?'

Harper and Lewis were currently throwing glitter at each other across the table.

'Harper! Lewis! Stop that right now!' he said loudly.

They froze, their eyes wide and the smiles freezing on their lips.

'Start cleaning this mess up immediately,' David growled.

'They're just having fun,' Vicky said quietly as she continued brushing up the broken vase.

'That's not having fun. That's being destructive.' He glared at Vicky, then turned back to the kids. 'I will be back down after my shower and I want this kitchen spick and span again.'

He stomped up the stairs, fury nipping at his heels. Anna would never have let them get into that state.

He knew he was mostly mad at Vicky – about the credit card bill, the lingering discomfort at knowing she had been in his room, his suspicious thoughts that circled and niggled – but he liked the anger. It made him feel alive and lately he had been too flat, too disinterested. That was part of the problem.

He needed to start taking part again, beginning with keeping a closer eye on what Vicky was up to.

Fifteen minutes later, he walked back into the kitchen feeling moderately calmer after a shower. The kids were still tidying and sweeping, their faces glistening as glitter stuck to their skin, but the kitchen was much tidier already.

'That's looking much better, thank you,' he said.

He went to make himself a coffee and felt Vicky come up behind him.

'Sorry, that got out of hand.'

'It's fine, my fault as I've kind of left you to it lately.'

'I don't mind. I'm loving it and we both know you weren't coping, so I'm happy to help. I have to say thank you actually.'

'For what?'

'For letting me do this. It's like I've found my calling. I love looking after these two and I haven't felt this good in years. It's like I've woken up from a coma or something.' She was smiling widely. Then the smile faltered and she added, 'Of course, it's also keeping me… distracted from… you know, the grief.' She suddenly painted a look of anguish on her face and rested a hand on his arm.

He bristled. He wasn't in the mood for what felt like amateur dramatics this morning. He carried on making his coffee, his back to her. She dropped her hand.

'Anyway, I said I would take them over to Hampton Court to watch the cycle race. Would you like to join us?' she continued hurriedly.

He turned towards her and said with conviction. 'Well, actually, I was thinking that I might like to take them myself. I haven't done anything with them on my own in ages. This is a good opportunity.'

Vicky's face fell, like a light had gone out. 'Oh. Right.'

'And you get a day off from running around after them.'

'Trying to get rid of me, are you?' She smiled thinly.

'No, why would I?' He looked at her with narrowed eyes.

She said nothing for a moment, then tucked her hair behind her ear and said, 'Okay, well, I'll… um…' She pointed upstairs, then left the room, her head bowed.

He felt guilt prick at him then. Despite his sudden suspicions, she was helping and he had asked her to move in, after all. And she was right – he hadn't been coping. Who knew though? Maybe if she hadn't moved in, he would've sorted himself out sooner, picked up the baton and run with it rather than passing it on to her like a coward. He took his coffee and headed into the lounge, grabbing his iPad from the kitchen counter on the way.

Taking a sip, his bare foot kicked something left in the lounge doorway, causing him to spill some of his coffee and burn his lip at the same time.

He winced and looked to see one of Vicky's shoes lying abandoned in the doorway. Its partner was flung just inside the door where she had kicked them off when she got home last night.

He breathed into his annoyance and kicked the shoes out of the way.

Sitting heavily, David set his coffee down on the side table and went to enter the security PIN on his iPad, but had to wipe glitter from it first. The screen filled with a kid's gaming site before a message flashed up that he was out of battery.

'Damn!' The kids knew not to use his iPad for games. Yet another rule ignored. He flung it down on the table and picked up his coffee, needing it more than ever.

Harper and Lewis appeared around the doorway gingerly, as though approaching a caged lion, and his anger dissipated somewhat.

'We've finished, Daddy. Can we still go to the cycling?' Harper asked.

'Yes, I'm going to take you.'

'I thought Vicky was taking us?' Lewis said.

'Not this time, buddy. Just us. Should be fun.' Then he gestured for them to come closer and wrapped his arms around them when they were within reaching distance.

'So let's get ready to go. We'll pick up some sandwiches and stuff at M&S on the way.'

'And Percy Pigs?' Lewis asked with delight.

David laughed. 'And Percy Pigs!'

David could hear Vicky in the kitchen as he got everyone ready, brushing hair and locating matching shoes.

He went to find her. 'So have a nice day then.'

'Thanks, but I might see you there after all. Some friends from my old job are going, so I've arranged to meet up with them. I've made a picnic and everything. It is a once in a lifetime occasion after all.' She smiled, but it had an edge of rebellion to it.

'Oh, right, well, we might see you there then. We're ready, so...' He turned to go.

'Um, but there's enough in the picnic bag for all of us if you want to arrange to meet somewhere later?'

'Oh, no need. I said we'd go to M&S.'

'We're getting Percy Pigs!' Lewis cried from the hallway.

'Oh, okay. Well, have fun. I know I will!'

'Thanks,' David muttered and shuffled the kids out the door before they could insist that she join them.

As they walked away from the house, he had the uncomfortable certainty that eyes were following him down the street. He turned back quickly and looked up at the house, but couldn't see her at the lounge window. Movement in his bedroom window dragged his eyes upwards, but he couldn't be sure if there was a person behind the shutters or if it was just shadows.

The atmosphere was as electric as it had been the day before, with thousands of excited faces lining the streets along the cycle route. Flags waved, hands clapped and voices cheered loudly in between mouthfuls of crisps and bites of egg and cress sandwiches.

David's spirits soared as he took it all in and he was pleased he'd decided to come. He found them a spot close to the palace grounds where they could see the cyclists coming and he relished in the joy of seeing Harper and Lewis's expectant faces. Just being here and away from Vicky and the house, with its memories of Anna and echoing suspicions, made him feel like he could breathe again. The sun was doing a good job of coercing everyone into a jubilant mood and it was contagious.

Before long, the excitement level geared up as the cyclists appeared in the distance, racing down the street fuelled by testosterone and Lucozade. David cheered along with the crowd, but all at once felt the hairs on his arms stand to attention with the sense that someone was watching him. He looked over his shoulder, but everyone was pressing in close behind him. He shook it off and focused on the action as the peloton hurtled towards them.

Harper and Lewis began to clap and cheer too, waving their arms in the air, but some of the fizz had escaped from David's mood. The sense of being watched was developing into an absurd sense of being stalked, like weakened prey. Absurd but real at the same time. The air around him had changed and was now charged with imminent threat. He spun around, but there were too many faces. None stood out with any clarity.

He turned back to the action, despite his lingering unease, determined not to let it ruin this for him. Whoever it was, it was probably harmless, nothing sinister. Lewis tapped David on the arm and asked if he could sit on his shoulders. As he crouched down, he scanned the crowd surreptitiously one more time and thought he saw one unsmiling face standing about three people back. A woman perhaps, not cheering, clapping or waving; just standing, her arms by her sides, conspicuous by her stillness, her long skirt flapping gently in the breeze, but her face was obscured behind a fat lady with sweat staining her T-shirt and bingo wings flapping enthusiastically as she waved her flag.

David frowned as he lifted Lewis onto his shoulders.

Lewis bounced and wriggled excitedly. 'Sit still, Lewis,' David snapped.

The cyclists drew closer and Lewis wriggled even more. David gripped tightly onto his ankles to pin him in place. The crown started roaring, 'Wiggins! Cavendish! Cavendish!' as their sporting heroes shot past in the lead group. The cold air of their slipstream washed over the spectators. David tried to twist around again to peer behind him, just as Lewis gave a particularly jubilant fist pump. David felt Lewis's weight thrust backwards and his grip on Lewis's ankles failed.

As if in slow motion, he sensed Lewis falling backwards from his shoulders. David turned to try and catch him in mid-air, but collided with someone behind him. They reached out their arms as, with a shriek, Lewis fell and was caught safely before he hit the ground. David looked up to see Vicky standing behind him.

'Got you!'

'Vicky!'

She put Lewis safely on his feet. 'Good job I was here. You nearly fell, Lewis!' She looked at David with a strange expression.

'What are you doing here? Where are your friends?'

'Oh, they're over there.' She waved her arm vaguely. 'I saw you in the crowd and thought I'd come and say hello. Besides, they're all going on to a boozy lunch and I made that picnic, so...'

David knew with certainty that it had been her watching him. The realisation was like cold water trickling down his spine.

'How long have you been standing there?'

'Only a few seconds really. I was trying to weave through the people, but there are so many bodies everywhere. I was over there by the trees and couldn't see anything.'

'With your friends?'

'Yes, they're all still over there.' She pointed to the right of where he was standing, meaning if she was telling the truth, it couldn't have been her staring at him. 'Then I thought I saw you and came over this way. Glad I did as you literally threw yourself at me!' She smiled down at Lewis and stroked his hair tenderly.

David swept his eyes over the crowd again, but the feeling of being watched had gone as quickly as it had arrived.

Vicky was lying. She had to be. But why?

David couldn't enjoy the rest of the day.

The feeling of ants crawling across his skin persisted, his paranoia making him anxious. Vicky laughed and played with the kids as normal, but David felt on edge, his mind ruminating over the letter even more and jumping to conclusions about her possible motive for spending time with them. She was always there, whenever he turned around, watching him, putting her hand on his arm, suffocating him.

And to hear that she was living her best life now? So soon after losing her best friend? He found that difficult to swallow.

Had she orchestrated this all along? Had her main aim been to make him feel that he couldn't cope so that she could move in? Was she finally getting to live the life she had envied from afar when it had been Anna living it? Or was it as simple as loving David from afar for all these years and now sensing her moment had come to act on her feelings? Was she that pathetic?

Vicky stayed with them once the riders were gone and the crowd dispersed. She carried the picnic hamper of food on her shoulder and insisted on sharing it, despite that fact that David had bought food on the way.

As they say cross-legged on the picnic blanket, with the kids telling Vicky all about the cyclists and the friends they had seen already today, David found he couldn't face eating the sausage rolls and scotch eggs she had packed. Instead, he stubbornly nibbled on one of the M&S sandwiches he had bought despite his paranoia having swallowed his appetite whole.

Harper and Lewis weren't being so discerning. They ate their way through all of Vicky's offerings but left the posh M&S wraps and crisps he'd selected. The Percy Pigs were demolished though. He felt a sense of resentment and betrayal towards his offspring as he watched Vicky show them how to pack their white bread ham sandwiches with prawn cocktail crisps and wash them down with Ribena, but drew comfort from knowing that Anna would've scolded them for their cheap tastes. She'd been a loyal Waitrose shopper for years and was known to scoff openly at the Wotsit generation.

He had to look away when Vicky chewed up her crisp sandwich, then turned to the children and opened her mouth wide to show them the masticated food inside, strings of saliva hanging disgustingly between her teeth, as the children roared with laughter, then copied her.

Even her barking laugh, a sound he had enjoyed in recent weeks because of how it filled every corner of the empty house and distracted him from noticing how cavernous it had become without Anna, was now starting to set his teeth on edge, as though Vicky were running her bitten nails down a blackboard. It was loud and brash, occasionally accompanied by a snort, and totally at odds with the gentle chortle that Anna would emit when amused. Her tendency to drop letters from words in her cheap, south London twang grated on him too.

When he could stomach it no more, he started to pack up the debris lying around and told the kids to get ready to go. They moaned and groaned, begging to stay longer, but a tension headache had set in behind his eyes and one more snort of hilarity from Vicky threatened to split his head in two.

Through gritted teeth, he said, 'You're welcome to come back with us now, or you can stay… whatever.'

'I will walk back with you, if that's okay?' she said, delighted, and began shoving the half-eaten dips and leftovers into the hamper. He wanted to tell her to wrap it all up properly, save it for another day, but bit his tongue again. He imagined his tongue swelling in his mouth like a slug, cutting off his throat until he slowly suffocated, and the idea wasn't altogether unwelcome. He swallowed thickly.

'Sure.'

He hid from her for the rest of the day, left them playing a board game and ignored Harper's pleas to join them. He couldn't still his mind. Every time he looked at her now, it was through a duplicitous filter.

So he hid like a coward.

He lay on his bed, stared at the thin crack that wove its way across the ceiling like a cobweb, turned on the news on the TV but didn't listen to the words coming from the presenter's mouth, watched out of the bedroom window as Clive over the road mowed his lawn shirtless, his big gut hanging over the waistband of his shorts and his arms the alarming bright red of those caught out by the sudden increase in temperature, in sharp contrast to the translucence of the rest of his torso.

Later, he knew he would have to reveal himself because he had promised the kids sausages and burgers on the barbecue, but he avoided any involved conversations. He was aware that he was answering in monosyllables and hiding behind his children with their constant chatter and requests to kick the ball around, bring them drinks, tie their laces and cut up their sausages. He remembered how Anna would often do the same thing when she wanted to avoid someone. She would tell him that children were the best invisibility cloaks money could buy because you could hover behind them and never need to have a conversation with someone. Just let them command all the attention.

By the time their bedtime rolled around, he had said barely two words to Vicky except for, 'Pass the ketchup, please.'

Before she could take over, he said pointedly and rather loudly to Harper and Lewis, 'I'll take you up to bed tonight. I feel like a story myself – how about *Unfortunately the Milk…?* I haven't read that in ages.'

'Yay!' chimed Lewis.

He avoided looking at Vicky as he herded them upstairs, then ran them a bath, played submarines in the warm water and helped Lewis into his pyjamas. She remained downstairs when he tucked them both into Lewis's bed. He sat between them, relishing the feeling of their warm bodies pressed into him, realising how much he had missed such simple displays of affection as a hug or a child gripping tightly to his arm in excitement at hearing him tell them a story. They smelled comforting and warm, an innocent mix of soap and apple shampoo, and he hugged them tighter to him. David felt a pull in his stomach at how distant he knew he had been from them since Anna had died and Vicky had moved in.

Once the story was over, he asked Harper to climb into her own bed and he lay down next to Lewis for a final cuddle before turning out the light.

As he reached for the light switch, Lewis rolled over and, his eyes wide and hazy, said, 'Daddy, should I call Vicky Mummy from now on?'

David froze with his arm outstretched and felt the bottom drop out of his stomach.

He left the light on and returned to sit on Lewis's bed. 'No, why would you ask that?' he said in as even a voice as he could muster, considering the tightness in his throat. 'Has she asked you to?'

'No, it's just that she's looking after us now. And I can't remember what Mummy sounds like any more.' He started to cry quietly and David gathered him up in his arms.

'Ah, Lewis, no. Vicky is just helping Daddy out while he has to work because I thought it would be nicer for you to have someone you know here. But Mummy will always be with you. She can never be replaced. And even if you can't quite remember what her voice sounded like or what her hair smelled like, or even how she smiled, she will be in your heart forever.' He felt silent tears track down his own cheeks. 'I know it's hard when someone leaves us, but it is our job to keep them alive here.' He pointed at his chest. 'I tell you what, should I get you a photo of Mummy all of your own to put next to your bed so that you can look at her beautiful face whenever you want?'

Lewis gulped and nodded while swiping at his nose.

'And can I tell you a little secret?' David continued in a stage whisper.

Lewis nodded again.

'Sometimes when I feel like I'm forgetting little details about Mummy, I talk to her out loud, tell her little things I think she would like to hear, as though she is sitting next to me, and it all comes flooding back. All her little mannerisms, the way she tucked her hair behind her ears and stuck out the tip of her tongue when she was thinking hard, the way the end of her nose tilted up, how she always had perfectly painted toenails in all sorts of pretty colours. Do you remember?'

Lewis was nodding more enthusiastically now, smiling through his tears.

David gave him another long hug, then tucked him back into his duvet. 'Okay?'

'Yeah,' Lewis replied, his eyes heavy.

'Good night, soldier.' David took one last look at his tiny body trapped beneath the dinosaur duvet, then turned out the light.

He spent an extra few minutes hugging Harper close too, feeling like he didn't want to leave them, didn't want to go back downstairs and have the conversation that was needed with Vicky. But after Lewis's tearful words, he knew he had to tell Vicky to go. His stomach burned with an acidic fusion of blistering anger at himself for letting Vicky become so entwined in their family when he should've been taking up the responsibility himself, aching grief and longing for his wife, and niggling irritation and resentment directed at Vicky.

He descended the stairs with leaden legs to find Vicky in the kitchen pouring red wine into two large glasses. She looked up, but he avoided her eyes.

She handed him one of the glasses, then sat at the kitchen table and said, 'So do you want to tell me what's going on?'

'What do you mean?'

'You're avoiding me. Have I done something wrong? Is it about today?'

'Why were you there?' He felt anger bubbling in his chest, like a simmering pot with the lid still on.

'I told you. I met up with old work friends, then saw you guys and didn't fancy a boozy lunch. I'm sorry if spending time with you three is more fun these days. I know it's pathetic.'

'Oh please, I know you don't have any other friends. Anna was your only friend and now she's gone.' His words were brittle and meant to hurt.

'You don't know anything about me, about my life outside of this house. I did have a life away from Anna, you know!' She kicked off her shoes and left them on the floor, where he knew they would still be tomorrow.

The anger began to spit, the lid lifting a little.

'Next time I'll stay away. I know when I'm not wanted,' she said, her voice petulant. She stared out of the kitchen doors into the still sunny garden, despite the clock nearing 8:30.

'There won't be a next time,' David said in a low voice, then took a large glug of his wine.

Her head whipped around. 'What?'

'I think it's best if you move out. It's too confusing for the kids.'

'What makes you think that? They've been doing fine since I moved in. They're happy; they're laughing again. You said so yourself!' She got to her feet, her hand reaching towards him, but he took a step backwards. 'Please, don't do this.'

'I have to! Lewis just asked me if he should call you Mummy. What do I do with that?'

'I'll talk to him. He's only little. He doesn't understand.'

'I've already spoken to him,' he snapped back. She dropped her hand as though scalded by the anger simmering under his words.

She turned her back to him, looked out into the garden, the wine glass clasped in white knuckles.

'I don't think I can cope without you guys. You're right, I don't have anyone else. With Anna gone, no family, no boyfriend – what do I have?' She turned back to him, her eyes beseeching. 'Please, David, we can come to some sort of arrangement. Maybe I don't get involved with the kids on the weekend or I take them to school and back, and you can take over from when you get home from work and I'll make myself scarce? I'll do anything.'

He exhaled heavily and slumped into a chair. 'Do you want to tell me about the credit card bill? Anna's credit card that you've been using?'

Her eyes flicked to the right, then back, almost imperceptibly. 'Harper and Lewis needed new clothes, shoes, that kind of thing, and I thought it would be easier that way rather than asking you for money all the time. I should've asked you first though.'

'That would make sense if the bill didn't include shops like Oasis and Accessorize. I can't imagine there are many kids' clothes in those stores?'

She ran her hands through her hair. 'I'll pay you back,' she said quietly. 'It's just that… I've never been able to afford stuff like that, the stuff Anna wore once and threw away.' She smiled cynically. 'She always had such beautiful taste, but I couldn't fit in her cast-offs and couldn't afford to buy my own. It's no excuse, I know, but I just wanted to feel what it was like to wear clothes like she did, to feel as confident as she did. Stupid, I know. And you didn't like me wearing her stuff.'

'Clothes won't make you into Anna,' he said coldly. 'She was an amazing woman. Smart, beautiful, headstrong, independent.'

'And I'm not any of those things, right?' she replied, her voice suddenly thin with anger. 'Clothes don't maketh the man – isn't that what they say? Oh yeah, she was a real gem, was our Anna.'

David narrowed his eyes, but Vicky continued before he could reply. 'She had everyone wrapped around her finger, didn't she? Me too, of course, from the day we met. She could bewitch anyone, but you most of all. I used to watch her from the outside and wish I had her life because I knew it would matter more to me than it ever did to her.'

'Her kids were everything to her,' he growled.

'Oh, she loved them, sure – but she was not the person you thought she was.'

He felt the numbness rush over him. 'You wrote that letter.'

'What letter?' She frowned, thrown by the change in conversation.

'The letter telling me I didn't know my own wife, implying that there was more to her death. Why? Why would you write something like that?'

'David, I don't know what you're talking about. I'll admit to the credit card, but I haven't written any letters to you. I live with you, so why would I? I could just talk to you in person!'

He knew she was making sense, just voicing his own niggling doubts about suspecting her, but still the anger

267

pulsed through him like a bass beat. He watched her carefully, trying to determine a hint that she may be lying, but she looked baffled more than anything.

'Well, someone is trying to tell me something!' he shouted, spittle flying from his lips in exasperation. He turned his back on her, his fists clenched. 'Damn it, Vicky, I feel like I'm going mad. People telling me that I didn't know my own wife… I knew her! I loved her!'

She was quiet for a moment, then said, 'You knew a version of her, David. The version she let you see. But she could be a lot of things other than a wife and mother. And often it wasn't pretty.'

He spun around to face her. 'You're lying! You just want what she had – the lifestyle, the family, all of it. You were jealous of her and now you're just trying to colour my memory of her so that you can take her place.'

She paled then. 'No, I… I admit I lived my life in her shadow, always wishing I could be like her, but then these last few years… no, I didn't want to be like her at all. She could be cruel, manipulative, cold. She did things just for fun without thinking about who she would hurt in the process.'

He advanced on her. 'What are you on about? I would know if she was any of those things!'

'It's true! I don't want to hurt you, but—'

'Then stop it! All of it!' He raised his hand and slapped her hard. The noise reverberated around the room, freezing everything in its path.

'Oh my god.' His face crumpled and he dropped his hand.

Vicky said nothing, but she took a step backwards, her hand held up to her rapidly reddening cheek.

'I'm so sorry, I'm so sorry...' he repeated, stricken.

'I know,' she replied. 'It's my fault. I should never have said what I did.'

'I don't know what to say. Please forgive me, Vix. I'm drowning. I don't know what to even think any more. I don't recognise myself any more. The man I'm turning into. That letter...' He shook his head in despair. 'It feels like someone is tormenting me.'

She took a step towards him. 'David, it's fine. You're upset and I shouldn't have said those things. It's all too raw still.'

'I feel like I'm picking at a scab and it keeps opening and bleeding, then scabbing over again. But I can't seem to leave it alone.' He started to weep.

She reached out, then pulled him into a tentative hug. He resisted at first, then she felt like all the weight rushed out of his body as he leaned into her. She held him as his breathing slowed. He could feel her heart beating hard in her chest, alive and vital, unlike Anna's, and all he wanted was real, physical contact again. He pulled back a little and looked at her carefully, his eyes sweeping over the angry red skin on her face, then he kissed her gently at first, then harder, the torment and anguish pushing him towards her.

Later, he lay in the darkened bedroom, trapped under the weight of Vicky's head on his arm, staring at nothing, feeling empty. Vicky was asleep, her breath wisping over his chest. His arm was numb beneath her and he wanted to pull it loose, but didn't want to wake her, couldn't face her just yet. His hand lay open on the pillow, pins and needles pricking the ends of his fingers, his palm cold.

If this was Anna, he'd be holding onto her, hugging her naked body close to him, not daring to move in case she pulled away before he'd got his fill of her. Anna didn't like to be held in bed and would move to the other side of the mattress as soon as she could afterwards. In their early relationship when they were still discovering each other, he had found it strange that someone so vital and alive one minute could be so distant once the lust had cooled. Then he grew to accept it, knowing that he had a grace period of about five minutes after sex when she would allow him to hold her tight.

Vicky was different. Eager to please, she had snuggled into the crook of his arm immediately afterwards, entwined her fingers in his and had wanted to talk in quiet tones. Was it okay? How was he feeling? Did he enjoy it? He had been monosyllabic in response and eventually she had drifted off to sleep while he felt the weight of his betrayal settle on his chest, pinning him to the now soiled sheets, still damp from their sweat.

Who the hell am I?

He felt bilious as he thought about how different it had been with Vicky. Halfway through he had started to notice how physically different they were. Anna was all points and sharp corners, from her jutting hip bones to her rippling ribcage. It was like he could feel every muscle moving beneath his hands. In contrast, Vicky was spongey and rounded, her body moulding around him instead of holding its own.

A lone tear tracked slowly down his cheek, weighted with despair and regret.

This fucked everything up.

The darkness pressed down on him and he started to feel claustrophobia clawing at his lungs, oppressing the air. He had to get out of here.

He pulled his arm free from the deadweight of her head and edged out from under the covers, resisting the urge to flee so as not to wake her. At least they'd ended up in Vicky's room, so that he could escape. But this brought him little comfort as he padded naked across the landing, his clothes bundled in his arms like an adulterer caught red-handed.

He flung his clothes down on his bedroom floor, went straight into the en suite bathroom and turned the shower on as hot as it would go. Stepping straight under the spray while the water was still ice cold, he felt his breath hitch. He closed his eyes and twisted and turned as the water slowly warmed until it reached a blistering temperature. He could imagine it scalding his skin, leaving bulbous blisters in its wake. Only what he deserved. When he could handle it no longer, he turned the temperature down to lukewarm and let the shower spray hit him full in the face, washing away his unseen tears.

Anna would say that he was a typical man, using what was in his trousers to distract him from his real problems. He had said that Vicky was after what Anna had had and now he had handed himself to Vicky on a platter, given her exactly what she wanted.

But he never thought he would raise his hand to a woman. Where had that come from? That disgust he couldn't wash away.

He turned off the water and wrapped himself in a towel. Wiping the steam from the mirror above the basin, he peered at the misty face looking back at him. He'd let Anna down. Now he needed to put it right. Anger at himself roiled and morphed into anger at Vicky again.

How could she taunt him like that? Say those things? Anna's best friend? Then use him like this? She'd always been a bit of a slag. He'd fallen for it and she'd got what she wanted.

His hands clenched the basin like claws. He felt like beating his head against the glass of the mirror until it shattered.

Outside in the dark night, a fox called out, the noise eerie and pained, as though it were in excruciating agony. Had that been the sound Anna had made that night when her car had tumbled and rolled, flinging her around inside like a ragdoll? Was that the noise the fox had made as her car connected with it? Had there even been a fox?

He moved away from the sink and over to the bedroom window. Pulling aside the curtain, he stared out into the quiet street, hoping to see the fox wailing into the dark, limping maybe or maimed in some way. Would that make him feel better?

But there was nothing to see. Just shadows swaying in the streetlights. Over the road, movement caught his eye. It looked like a person standing behind a tree, keeping out of sight, watching him back. But the more he looked, the more he thought it was just the night projecting back at him, the breeze pushing the branches, making them wave and beckon eerily.

Nothing to see here.

He let the curtain drop back into place. He still couldn't picture Anna's death in his head. He'd tried, but it was too simplistic. He had to believe that it had been as a result of something more meaningful, or even sinister, than a fox. She deserved something weightier.

And if there was more to Anna's accident, as the anonymous letter suggested, it was his job to find out the truth. He had to. He owed it to her. Especially now.

And Vicky? Well, if she was involved somehow, she would pay.

He'd make sure of it.

Dear Anna,

It's funny. I always thought that I'd be happier if I had your life. Your house, your looks, your family.

Well, now I have those things and I can't say I'm brimming over with delight.

You never seemed happy with it all either. I used to hate you for that. How you could be so ungrateful, so dissatisfied with your lot when from where I was standing, looking in on your picture-perfect life, you had it all.

I slept with your husband last night.

I didn't mean to do it. It just happened.

I actually laughed out loud as I wrote those words. How many times did you use that one to justify your actions over the years? That bloke at Harper's first birthday. The guy you picked up when we went out for your thirtieth birthday. You shagged him in the back seat of David's Range Rover while I sat inside the pub on my own, waiting patiently for you. That was classy. You considered it a birthday treat from what I remember, something else David didn't need to know about and I covered up for you. Did I tell you he phoned while you had your legs wrapped around another man? I told him you were in the loo.

But that was our deal, wasn't it? You cover for me; I cover for you. Except it was a lot more one-sided than that the older we got. You made me pay for that one moment when we were kids, kept bringing it up, like a bad song on repeat, until it became second nature for me to do everything you asked of me, even if I didn't agree with it or felt bad for those you were hurting.

Then you took it too far.

I tried to tell David that last night. Tried to get him to see just a little of the grubbiness you carried with you, but he wouldn't hear of it.

Did he ever hit you? I can't imagine he did, because it wouldn't have been you in a coffin now if he had.

So here we are. I'm living in your beautiful house, raising your children and fucking your husband.

I've lost weight too. I'm not as skinny as you were, but cutting back on the takeaways and booze has worked wonders and I can actually fit into some of your clothes. Not that I'm allowed to wear them yet, but baby steps.

I've even cut and coloured my hair like yours. I thought David might like that, make the transition from you to me a little easier for him.

I haven't been downstairs yet. It's Sunday morning and everything is still quiet. David isn't here with me. He was gone when I woke up. I guess he needs time to come to terms with what happened. And it would be very confusing for the kids to see him emerge from *my bedroom. I'm sure it will be a bit awkward over breakfast at first, but I'll help him realise that this is a good thing.*

I'll make pancakes. His favourite.

He probably just feels guilty. Understandable, really. Moving on is confusing.

You used to say it wound you up when he wanted to hold your hand, hug you, stroke your hair. It made you feel like his pet dog. I'll let him hug me. He can be as tactile as he wants with me. He won't need to raise his hand ever again. I'll be the perfect wife.

We are the same but different, you and I. Different versions of the same story.

But I'm still here and you're not. I'm going to get my happy ending.

I just want someone to love me the way you were loved.

Vix x

February 2011

Vicky sat staring at the grey winter sky. A steady drizzle was falling, coating everything in a thin film of grime and making Feltham even more miserable than usual. She had a pile of invoices on her desk, but couldn't bring herself to look at them. She felt like putting her head on them and screaming into the laminated wood.

Looking through the glass office partition at Gavin, her boss, confirmed that he was also losing the will to live. He was staring vacantly into space, the life draining out of him with every tick of the clock as the day wore on before he headed home to a microwave meal for one and a can in front of the telly. Gavin had lost any vivacity he had when his wife of twenty-seven years, Sandra, had run off with a life insurance salesman. When he told Vicky about it after one too many pints at last year's office Christmas party, he had laughed bitterly and said, 'You can't make this shit up.'

And he was right. No one would make this shit up. The daily monotony of it was crippling. The sense that life was passing them by sobered them all while they sat in an asbestos-riddled office in grey Feltham, with Tracey answering the phone in her thirty-a-day gravelly voice for orders that only trickled in and Steve, the balding office flirt with halitosis, doing the books and probably fiddling them. He'd send them a postcard from Barbados long before Gavin figured out what he was up to.

Vicky had started as a PA to Gavin years ago and was now supposed to also fill the role of marketing assistant, social media consultant and logistics facilitator, but she had a feeling that none of them would have jobs of any description soon if Gavin didn't start pulling his finger out and get some new orders in. The internet had sucked the life out of the business and most companies preferred to buy their stationery from Amazon or a discounted online shop than from a short, moustached man in a grey suit with Campbell's cream of chicken soup dripped down his brown tie.

Vicky's mobile suddenly burst into life next to her. She jumped, then reached for it as it danced across the table under the volition of its own vibrations.

'Hey Anna,' she said wearily.

'Work that good, huh? You should be here. We're off to the pub. We've just landed a new account and Sebastian wants to celebrate.' Vicky's hackles rose at the mention of Anna's boss. She had met him once when she had been dragged to an industry do as Anna's plus one when David was ill and she had found him to be a smarmy, posh git with ridiculously lustrous hair and a smooth face that must be expensive to maintain. She also suspected he wore guy liner and mascara. 'I could still put in a good word for you with

Sebastian if you want?' Anna continued, her voice bubbling and giddy. 'He's so funny to work for.'

Vicky rolled her eyes. Anna had wanted her to go for a PA job at Sebastian's agency, but loyalty to Gavin and a physical revulsion to men like Sebastian meant she had swerved the suggestion and stayed put at Stationery Central instead.

'Anyway, I'm calling because I need a favour.' Her voice was low and echoed down the line.

'Are you in the loo?'

'Yes, I needed to talk in private, but I need to be quick. Listen, Sebastian wants to take me away tomorrow night, just me and him. He says it's a bonus for the hard work I put in on the pitch. Anyway, I need you to cover for me with David.'

'Hold up, why don't you just tell David you're going away on business?'

'Because I don't think Sebastian has business in mind.' She giggled. 'It's only me and him and… don't tell anyone, but we've been messing about a bit. You know, after hours… not shagging yet, but… stuff.'

'Jesus, Anna! Isn't he married as well? With a kid?'

'Yes, but his wife is pathetic. She doesn't do anything all day except look after their kid,' she spat.

'What am I supposed to say to David? I don't—'

'You don't have to say anything! I'm going to tell him I'm staying at yours because you've been dumped again and you want me to come over for drinks, then we're doing some retail therapy on Saturday. He'll believe that easily.'

'Yeah, no stretch to the imagination, that one.'

'Then if he ever asks you how our night was, you know to cover for me. I'll be back on Saturday afternoon and I'll make sure to buy some sexy lingerie in my lunch break tomorrow – I'll wear it for Sebastian and then pack it back in the bags for when I get home on Saturday. Maybe I'll wear it for David then too, just to make him forget to ask you how your broken heart is.'

Vicky scrunched up her face in disgust. Sometimes she was amazed at how easily lying came to Anna. And how little she valued other people's feelings.

'You have to, Vix,' she pleaded. 'Sebastian is amazing and if I don't accept, it might count against me when it comes to a promotion. Please? Think of my career progression.'

Vicky knew Anna was not doing this to get ahead in business. She was doing it because she wanted to. That was her sole motivation for everything.

'Doesn't Lewis have his big football match on Saturday morning? He's been looking forward to it all week.'

'Yes, but David can take him. He won't notice I'm not there.'

'He noticed last time. He was in tears when I turned up instead of you.'

'And he got over it! It was character building. Look, are you going to help me or not?'

'I don't know, Anna. I mean, David—'

'Do I really need to remind you about our deal? Remember, you have my back and I have yours. That's what we've always done. If that were to stop now…'

Sometimes Vicky found herself wondering what would actually happen if she stood up to Anna one day, whether Anna would ever have the guts to follow through on her vague threats. But that would mean losing a friend and for all her faults, Anna was her only friend. She sighed. 'Fine. I'll cover if it comes to it, but you're playing with fire here, Anna. If David ever does find out, you'll lose everything, you know that. All for a bit of a thrill. And not just him; Sebastian's wife too.'

'Are you threatening me?' The menace in Anna's voice heated the line between them.

'No, Anna, I usually leave that to you. I'm just telling you to be careful. I don't want to see you – or David and the kids – hurt, that's all,' Vicky replied.

There was a pause, then with the giddiness back in her voice, Anna said, 'Ooh, get you, all sassy! I'd better go. Thanks Vix – love you!'

Anna hung up before Vicky could say anything else. She swallowed hard at the bile in her throat as she dropped her phone onto the desk. She loved Anna like a sister, couldn't imagine not being her best friend, but some days that friendship was tested, pushed, poked and prodded.

She wondered what it would take for it to finally break.

And whether they would both survive the fall-out.

I I

David had struggled to sleep after he left Vicky's room. He tossed and turned, the sheets garrotting his legs, drifting in and out of consciousness, images of Anna burning into the back of his eyelids.

He gave up at 5 a.m. and got up, made a strong coffee and knocked back two headache pills to stave off the pressure behind his forehead. He felt like he had been fighting an army of demons all night and he was sure his face reflected the battle with puffy eyes and deep lines on his brow.

He sat in the kitchen, nursing the coffee and staring out at the garden as the sun rose. The garden was looking dishevelled. Long grass, weeds in the beds, bushes that needed pruning and shaping. Anna had organised that stuff, paid a local company to sort it or pruned the roses herself. She would rather do that than sit with a coffee like he was doing. She wasn't one for being still. She used to say that if she sat still for too long, her brain would start coming up with ideas that would get her into trouble, so she kept herself busy to keep her innocent. Vicky preferred sitting still, feet up, TV on.

Vicky. The two of them had become entwined in his head. Thinking about one led to thoughts about the other.

No, enough thinking about that. Think about the garden. Where could he find the number of the gardening company she had used? Throw money at the problem.

Throw money at the problem.

The idea came to him like a flash. That's what he needed to do. But first, he needed to find out what happened that night and how Vicky was involved.

A plan of action started to emerge through the fog in his head, which in turn lifted his mood. Knowing he could do something helped. But he needed to get away from her today. Space might bring clarity. He knew Vicky liked a lie-in on a Sunday. She wasn't a fan of an early morning run or yoga session like Anna had enjoyed. The kids would be up soon, so he could bundle them into the car and go and visit his mother for the day.

It was still early, but his mother was an early riser.

'Hi Mum.'

'Well, this is a nice surprise.' Her voice was warm down the phone line, like hot buttered toast.

'Listen, are you busy today?'

'Chloe is coming over with her lot and I'm doing a roast, maybe watch some Olympics on the TV. Why? Would you like to join us? You are more than welcome, of course.'

'Yes, please. Sorry, I know I've been scarce lately. I just needed to get on with things.'

'It's fine – and we just wanted to give you some space. Yes, please, bring the kids – and Vicky if you want.' Her voice was tight as she said that, but good manners always prevailed with his mother.

'I think she has plans. Can I come over now?'

'Well, yes, if you want. I'm just pottering around.' She paused. 'Are you okay, love?'

'Yes, just… looking forward to spending some time with my family, that's all. Okay, we'll leave in about half an hour. Thanks Mum.'

'Drive safely.'

He cut the call, knocked back the rest of his now lukewarm coffee and went to wake the kids. He needed to get out before Vicky woke up.

As he sat in front of the Olympics coverage in his mother's family room, the French doors open to the garden where Lewis and Harper ran around in their swimming costumes playing with water pistols with their cousins, he knew he'd made the right decision to get some space today – somewhere where Vicky couldn't follow them.

Sure, he'd run away with his tail between his legs, not wanting to see her, ashamed of what they had done the night before, ashamed of himself for turning into the kind of man he'd always despised, the one who threw his weight and his dick around. But for now, for today, he was okay with being a coward.

He had his bare feet propped up on the coffee table and was chatting comfortably to Greg, Chloe's husband, as Clare Balding bantered with Chris Hoy in the London Olympics television studio.

His phone buzzed on the table and he reached for it. It was a text from Vicky.

> Hey, where is everybody? I'm making pancakes! Will you be back soon? Vx

He felt a twinge of guilt. The kids had thought sneaking out without waking her was a fun game, like ninjas, but it had been necessary in case she'd invited herself to come along. She'd been known to do that over the years. He replied briefly.

> Gone to my mum's for the day. Will be back late and will take the kids straight up to bed. Don't wait up.

Anna's voice in his head scolded him. He waited, the phone clutched in his hand, his eyes staring at the screen, but there was no reply. He put it on the arm of his chair and breathed out.

Okay, message delivered. He turned his attention back to the sport in front of him.

His phone buzzed again.

'You're popular,' Greg said.

'Just Vicky,' David replied, noting Greg's raised eyebrows in response.

He opened the message. It was a photo.

He stopped breathing.

The photo was of a woman, naked, lying with her legs open. You couldn't see her face as the photo stopped at her neck, but someone had taken a selfie of themselves reclining on a bed. He peered at the duvet cover showing between the woman's legs. It was his duvet cover. His bed.

'Bloody hell,' he muttered, jumping to his feet.

'Everything okay?' Greg asked.

'I... er... yes, it's nothing.'

He went to reply just as another message popped up beneath the image.

This was what your wife got up to when you weren't around. You need to know you're better off without her.

He looked closer at the number above the message and could see now that it wasn't from Vicky's mobile as he'd assumed.

This was from someone else. He used his fingers to zoom into the image, feeling filthy as they brushed over the woman's naked torso. It could be Anna's body, but it was hard to tell from the angle. If it was Vicky, he would be able to recognise the tattoos, but her arms and legs weren't visible enough, nor was her face or hair.

He was sweating, the idea that Vicky was lying naked on his bed taking selfies right now almost as nauseating as the idea that this was Anna. And if Anna had taken it, who had she sent it to? Because she'd never sent it to him.

No, it couldn't be of Anna. This must be Vicky getting back at him. Maybe she had another phone. He'd wondered about that the other day. An old work one maybe. Lots of people did. She was just getting back at him for doing a runner this morning.

That had to be it.

He turned his phone off completely and wiped the clamminess from his forehead.

Chloe was standing in the doorway watching him. 'Everything okay?'

He avoided her eyes. 'Yip, fine.'

She narrowed her eyes. 'Can you come and help me in the kitchen for a minute please?'

Greg looked between the two of them, then studiously turned his attention back to the television. David followed her on shaking legs.

'I don't need another lecture, Chlo,' he said as she turned on him in the kitchen.

'I'm just worried. You look like shit.'

'Wow, tell it like it is.'

'Seriously, David, are you okay? I mean, under the circumstances, of course you're not, but you don't normally turn up unannounced like this. Not that we mind, but I can't remember the last time you came for Sunday lunch with Mum without booking it in your diary weeks in advance. And you look ashen.'

'That was because Anna… never mind.' He shook his head. 'I just needed some space – to think.' He felt like his insides had turned into a writhing nest of snakes, twisting and curling, desperate to get out but with no escape. And with every passing hour, his brain concocted yet another theory as to what had happened on the night of the accident and how it was connected to Vicky. Now the photo. He was scared that if he didn't talk to someone, the snakes would bite.

He took a deep breath and sank down onto a wooden chair at the kitchen table. 'I know you don't like Vicky – and you've said why before – but be honest. Is it just that you think her beneath you or is there more to it?'

'In what way?' Chloe sat down at the table too, frowning.

'Has she ever given you reason to... mistrust her?'

'Well, no, not exactly.' Chloe looked down at her clasped hands. 'I think it was more about the connection between her and Anna. It seemed a strange friendship to me. Toxic in a way.'

'They met at school though.'

'I know, but they were so different. And Vicky always seemed in awe of her, but almost like... what do they call that syndrome when a hostage falls in love with their captor?'

'Stockholm Syndrome?'

'Yeah, that's it.'

'I don't understand what you mean. You think Vicky was in love with Anna?'

Chloe looked thoughtful, then shook her head, sat forward and took David's hand in hers. 'David, I love you, but you were always a bit blind when it came to Anna. She could be a right bitch when she wanted to.' David recoiled, but Chloe carried on, still gripping his hand. 'You know it's true, really. She was an ice queen and she had you wrapped around her finger. Having said that, I loved her like a sister. But when I saw Vicky and her together, I always felt... uneasy. Anna used to be really mean to her. She'd put her down all the time, boss her around – sure, they had a lot of fun together, but Anna was in charge and Vicky just followed her around like an abused puppy. At first, I wanted Vicky to stand up to Anna, just once to put her in her place. Then I realised that Vicky *wanted* it that way. She needed Anna because she had no one else and she didn't have the backbone to stand up for herself. Vicky is weak and needy, and she fed off Anna. And for Anna, I guess having Vicky around stroked her ego. But now, with Anna gone, Vicky has no one. So, yeah, I'm worried she's going to feed off you instead.'

'So you're saying you hate her because she's weak?'

'No, I think it was as useful for Vicky to have Anna as it was for Anna to have Vicky. They were two parts of the same whole. I disliked Vicky because she stood in the way of you ever being truly happy with Anna. There were never two of you in your marriage; there were three. And she's still there now, taking advantage of you now that Anna is no longer standing in her way. She has an opportunity to have it all and you're happily taking her under your wing, giving her the keys to Anna's castle.'

David thought it over. 'Do you think…'

'What?'

David chewed on his lip. 'Do you think she would've hurt Anna?'

'Why? Do you suspect she had something to do with Anna's accident?' Chloe's tone was brittle.

'I don't know. I got a really strange letter through the door the other day – anonymous, but saying that I didn't know my wife and implying that there was more to her accident than just maybe avoiding a fox in the road. Like someone was there, had seen it. And there's been other stuff too… enough to make me feel a bit… unsure.'

'Wow, okay. But I don't get it. Vicky wouldn't send a letter like that. She's got everything she's ever wanted now – Anna's life, basically. All she needs to complete it is you.'

David coloured.

Chloe shook her head. 'Oh god, David! Really? It's like that, is it?'

'No, it's not like anything. It just…'

'Happened, yeah, I've heard that before.'

'It only happened once. It won't happen again.'

'Is that why you're here? You're avoiding her? Or have you two done this before? Oh god, don't tell me you did before Anna…'

'No!' he shouted.

Chloe threw up her hands. 'Okay! Just checking!' She shook her head again and David felt her disappointment settle on him like a heavy coat in summer, stifling and weighty. 'Look, what you do with her is your choice, but I think you've made a big mistake. She doesn't deserve to be used, no matter what has happened, and she probably won't let this go quietly, but in answer to your question, if Vicky hadn't loved Anna, she would never have put up with her shit for so many years. They were inseparable. So no, I don't think she would have hurt her.'

'But what if Anna pushed her too far and she snapped or something? I mean, they weren't even talking before the accident, but Vicky won't say why.'

'Then the letter suggests that someone else knows something, maybe about their argument or the accident that night, and you need to find out who it is, then find out what they know.'

'Vicky is living in my house. She's looking after my kids. I just want to put some distance between us because all I can think is: *What if she killed my wife?*'

'And I think you need to take a step back and breathe. For what it's worth, I don't think she did, but the only way to put your mind at rest is to find out the truth. You owe it to Anna.'

She was right, but the photo, the earring, the texts, the letter... It felt like someone was standing over him as he dangled from a ledge, watching as his fingers slipped one by one, waiting for him to fall, but not knowing who had pushed him over or why.

Everything kept coming back to Vicky.

Why was that?

David stayed at his mother's house until well after the kids' bedtime, letting them fall asleep in the car on the way home. He'd rather the discomfort of carrying them straight up to bed than having to see Vicky.

He pulled into the driveway at close to midnight after a slow drive home and sat for a moment, the engine off, staring up at the house. It was all in darkness except for a light in the hallway. He'd kept his phone off for the rest of the day and it was tucked, blissfully silent, into his pocket.

He climbed out of the car with heavy legs and opened the front door before leaning in and lifting the deadweight that was a sleeping Lewis onto his shoulder. He carried him into the house and started to climb the stairs carefully.

Vicky appeared in the doorway of the lounge, the room dark behind her. She went to speak, but he gave her an icy glare, shook his head and carried on walking. After tucking Lewis into his bed, David retraced his steps. Vicky had gone.

He then lifted Harper from the back seat of the car. She moaned in her sleep, but then snuggled into his shoulder.

She was getting too big for him to carry her comfortably, her legs so long now and almost reaching the floor as they dangled, but David struggled on and managed to get her upstairs and into bed without waking her or putting his back out. He tucked her in, kissed her sleep-creased forehead and tiptoed down the stairs to lock the car.

He felt like an intruder in his own home, creeping around, hoping not to alert Vicky to his movements. Let her think he was still settling the kids.

He didn't see her again that evening, for which he was thankful. Instead, he undressed quietly in his own room, climbed under the covers, then thought twice and got up to lock his bedroom door. Only then did he feel safe enough to fall into a thick sleep.

He hadn't been asleep long when he was awoken by the sound of the bedroom door handle creaking as it turned. He sat bolt upright and watched the round knob twist and turn. David listened carefully in case it was one of the kids, but his heart was thumping loudly in his chest. Lewis and Harper would surely call out if they found the door locked. No, this wasn't the kids.

After a moment, the door handle stilled. He listened for a bit longer, not aware that he was holding his breath, then he threw himself back onto the pillow and exhaled. His sleep was paper-thin for the rest of the night.

He rose early the next morning, dressed for work and headed out to his car before anyone else in the house was up. The day was warming up slowly, the morning sun weak but optimistic.

He climbed into the driver's seat of his car, then noticed a piece of paper held down by one of the wiper blades. Leaning out, he pulled it free, then closed the door behind him, anxious to drive away before Vicky woke up.

He quickly unfolded the paper and read the words that leaked off the page in blotchy blue ink.

Did you like the photo?
She never told you, did she? She promised me she would tell you. Now you get your cosy memories of a woman you didn't know and I get a painful daily existence. It's not fair. Anna ruined my life and I can never forgive her. You deserve to know what she did.
Ask Vicky.

The edge of the note was rough, as though someone had torn it from a notepad hastily. The words were scribbled in between the lines and the ink was smudged with what looked like drips.

David frowned, unsure what it meant. One more piece in a puzzle that somehow connected Vicky and Anna to some secret. A secret that someone was desperate to share. And whoever had written it had been here at some point in the early hours to pin it to his car. Outside his house while he was inside asleep.

No, he wasn't going to let this freak him out.

David crumbled up the paper and tossed it out of the window of the car into the paper recycling bin to the side of the driveway. It missed the mark and fell onto the gravel, where the light morning breeze picked it up and blew it under the bushes. He watched it on its journey, then swallowed down the unease in his throat.

He had to focus. He'd spent most of the early morning hours deciding what to do and he couldn't be swayed from his plan now, no matter what that note meant or implied.

He'd decided that he couldn't go on like this, like a trespasser in his own home, jumping at shadows. He needed to man up and take back control. And that was what he was going to do.

Stop being a coward, David.

He started the car and reversed out of the driveway a little too quickly.

He knew Vicky was taking the kids to see an outdoor performance of *Horrible Histories* at Hampton Court Palace today. He had booked the tickets for them a few weeks ago and the kids had been telling their granny about it yesterday, excitement levels riding high.

After an unproductive day at his desk, he left the office at 3 p.m. and headed home. Putting the key in the door, his pulse fluttered, even though he knew the house would be empty. Even so, a fine film of sweat broke out on his forehead as he pushed open the front door.

The house had the hollowed out, cavernous feeling of being uninhabited, but he called out anyway.

'Vicky! Kids? Anyone home?'

Hearing no reply, he threw his keys on the hall table and headed straight up to the spare room. He reckoned he had about an hour and a half before Vicky and the kids got home. He stood in the doorway and stared at the bed for a moment, images of the night he had spent with Vicky bombarding him. Her moans, loud in his ear; his feeling of disgust mingling with physical pleasure, like the ultimate guilty secret; his need to scrub it all away afterwards.

The photo in the text message.

He swallowed down his revulsion and looked around. The bed was made and the curtains were open, but it all looked dishevelled. The curtains had been flung back and had caught on a pile of clothes tossed on the floor, leaving them hanging crookedly. The duvet on the bed was crumpled and haphazard. Shoes lay abandoned, make-up was scattered across the chest of drawers, lids off, and empty chocolate wrappers littered the bedside table alongside open gossip magazines, empty mugs and dirty plates. He could smell something cheesy and spotted an empty pizza box on the floor, close to disappearing under the bed. It looked like Vicky had stayed where she was yesterday, imprisoning herself in her room with carbs for comfort.

He started to rummage through the clothes bursting from the drawers, but found nothing of interest, apart from noting the amount of new clothes with the tags still attached jumbled in with items of clothing he recognised as Anna's. He opened the wardrobe, but there was nothing untoward there either among the shoes, scarves and bags.

The bedside table held a pile of trashy romance novels with half-dressed men almost strangling underwear-clad women in their throes of passion. At the bottom of the pile was a newer book, larger in size. He pulled it out and saw little multi-coloured tags marking a number of pages. The book was entitled, *The Step-Parent's Parachute*. David flicked to one of the marked pages and saw Vicky had underlined some of the advice on how to gain approval and love from your new partner's children.

Cold crept up his spine. He closed the book and sat down heavily on the bed. His foot kicked against something under the bed and he looked down, expecting another pizza box. It was a shoe box, probably yet another purchase made on Anna's credit card.

But the box looked old, the image on the side faded but depicting a pair of black slip-on school shoes. He pulled out the box. It was dusty and felt heavy. He took off the lid and found the box stuffed full of letters. He flicked through some of the envelopes and saw with a clenched gut that the bottom letters were all in Anna's handwriting and addressed to Vicky, tied together in a thick red ribbon. They dated back to when Anna was at uni from the post stamps.

But the envelopes on top of the pile were addressed to Anna in Vicky's handwriting and looked newer. None of them had stamps on them.

He opened the top letter and began to read.

Dear Anna,

I've ruined everything.

You must be loving this, loving the fact that I've been rejected again. You used to lord it over me every time I was dumped. You'd say I was my own worst enemy because I didn't look after myself, was too needy with men, let them have what they wanted too easily. You liked to play power games and be in control, but I just wanted to be loved.

Well, after my blissful night with David last night, he has run away to his mother's house today and isn't answering my calls or texts. There may be a valid explanation, like his battery is flat or something, but I know he regrets what we did.

How could I have been so stupid? Things were going so well and I finally had a taste of the life I'd always wanted.

But I could never replace you, could I?

I can feel it all crumbling away in my hands. Of course, I could stop it. Come clean once and for all. About all of it. What we did, what you did.

I tried once before, didn't I? I told you we should tell David, that it wasn't fair on him and the children. And you threatened to go to the police about what we did all those years ago. I spent that week before you died waiting for the police to turn up and arrest me. But they didn't because you never called them, did you?

The glee in your voice when you left that message the night you died to tell me that you hadn't called the police – that hurt more than anything. You got so much joy out of toying with me. I'm not stupid. All these years we've been friends and I've accepted the abuse you subjected me to, the taunts and jibes, the manipulation, but I loved you and thought it was payback, retribution for what we did all those years ago. But this time was different. You took my biggest weakness and used it as a weapon. And you enjoyed it.

Well, it looks like you have had the last laugh after all. But you paid the ultimate price.

I just wish he would talk to me. We can make this work. I can make him happy.

I'm not you. I'm me. When will that be enough?

V x

12

The letter fell from David's fingers as he tried to process what he was reading.

How could he have let her into his home? Look after his children?

The pile of letters taunted him with the truths they contained. That Anna's best friend, her true soulmate, the person she had trusted over everyone else – and David had known from the early days of their relationship that that person would never be him but was indeed Vicky – had betrayed her in the most despicable way. He wasn't sure how, but the details weren't important.

There was no doubt in his mind that Vicky had been involved in Anna's death in revenge for threatening to expose whatever it was she did when they were younger. He didn't care what that was. All he cared about was making sure Vicky was punished now.

He had lost his wife, the mother of his children, almost his sanity, and so far she had gained the family she had always wanted, along with the security, comfort and material trappings that went along with it.

Before he could think straight, and before he even wanted to read any more of her words, he picked up his phone and dialled his mother's number.

'Mum, listen, don't ask any questions because I can't bring myself to explain just yet, but can you come and collect the kids for me? Let them stay with you for a few days?'

'Davey, is everything okay?'

'I can't…' His voice was reedy, the effort to speak draining it of any credence it may have had. 'Just please, can you come and get them? They'll be home from Hampton Court in about an hour, so if you leave now you'll be here when they arrive. I'll be here, but I don't want to see them or Vicky.'

'David, you're scaring me.'

'It's Vicky – I need to get her out of the house. She's…' He couldn't voice what he suspected, couldn't bring himself to say it. 'I think she's dangerous. I think she was involved in Anna's accident somehow.'

'Oh no, David! I always knew that girl was trouble. You should never have trusted her.'

'Mum, please.'

'Okay, yes, yes, I'll leave now.'

'But don't say anything to Vicky or the kids. Let me deal with this, okay?'

'Okay, that's fine.'

'Thanks Mum, see you in a bit.'

He hung up and took a deep breath before dialling Vicky's number.

'David, hi.' She sounded so happy to hear from him. He swallowed down the bile that rose in his throat. 'The show has just finished. They loved it – so gross but very funny.'

'I need you to come straight home please. We need to talk. My mother is coming to pick up the kids to stay with her for a few days so that we can have some space.'

'Oh! Okay, that's fine.' She sounded thrilled and he could picture her getting excited at the thought of him confessing his newly discovered love for her, suggesting they make their arrangement more permanent, maybe imagining him whisking her away on a romantic weekend. He felt a sickly thrill at knowing he was going to be strangling all of those hopes and inflicting just a fraction of the pain Anna probably felt as she lay dying in her car.

He hung up before she could say anything else.

He gathered up the box of letters where they lay at his feet and walked out of the room. He paused on the landing, suddenly unsure where to go, then headed into his own room, closing the door firmly behind him.

He sat on the edge of the bed, placed the box on the mattress next to him and waited.

After about half an hour had passed, he heard the front door open and his mother call out, 'David?', as she pulled her spare key from the lock.

He pushed to his feet, suddenly exhausted at the effort it took, and went to meet her. He stood at the top of the stairs and looked down at her, feeling like a kid again, in need of a hug from his mum and reassurance that everything would be okay. He could feel tears threatening, but fixed a stony mask on his face.

She stepped towards him, then said, 'I'll get their things together, shall I?' with a gentle smile.

He wanted to weep again but he'd done enough of that in the last few months. Instead, he sat on the top stair and waited while his mother fussed about.

Before long, he heard laughter and crunching feet running across the gravel driveway. He took a fortifying breath and stood, swaying a little on his feet before he grasped the banister. By the time Vicky's key was grating in the lock, he was standing at the bottom of the stairs, ready.

Harper and Lewis rushed in, their eyes lit up like Christmas trees. 'Daddy! You're home!'

'Hey guys, how was the play? Listen, some news for you,' he said before they could answer. 'Your granny is here and has invited you to come and stay with her for a few days. She's packing up your stuff now as she wants to get going before the rush hour traffic builds up, so why don't you go and help her?'

Lewis yelped in joy like a puppy. 'Is Vicky coming too?'

'No, Vicky will be staying here.'

'Okay,' Harper said before running off with Lewis.

Vicky was looking at him curiously, the cogs in her brain plainly trying to work out what had caused the atmosphere shift. He said nothing, didn't even look at her, just turned and followed the kids into the kitchen where his mother was going through the clean washing that hadn't been sorted and throwing shorts, T-shirts and underwear into a bag.

'That's fine, that should be plenty. I'll call you later,' David said, his finger tapping on the table and his brow knitted together.

She looked at him closely, then said, 'Right, you two. Go and grab your reading books and a cuddly toy, then we'll get off. We've got an epic baking session lined up for this afternoon, then maybe sausages on the barbecue for tea!'

'Yay!' They dashed past David, followed by his mother, who merely reached up and placed a warm hand on his cheek as she passed.

'Hi Louisa,' he heard Vicky say as she passed her, but his mother ignored her.

Vicky was frowning as she came into the kitchen and went to put on the kettle.

'Is she okay? Are you okay?' she asked over her shoulder.

'Let me just say goodbye to them, then we can talk. You might want to say goodbye too.'

'Sure, but it's only a couple of days, right?'

He said nothing in reply.

He looked away as they hugged Vicky tightly, then shuffled them out with a wave, before closing the door firmly, leaving him and Vicky standing in the hallway, his face in shadow.

'Wait here,' was all he said.

When he came back downstairs with the shoebox in his hands, she had moved into the lounge. Her flipflops lay on the carpet where she had kicked them off and she sat on the couch with her tea cradled in her hands and her feet tucked up underneath her, her eyes trained on the blue sky forcing itself through the window.

'Phew, I tell you what, kids are exhausting! That was loads of fun though, a great show and Lewis especially loved it because it was so gruesome in parts. All about the Tudors, which I remember loving when I was at school.' She was rambling. He could hear the nerves in her voice.

She finally looked up at him as he came to stand in front of her and paled as she noticed the box in his hands. 'You've been in my room.'

'I think you'll find it's *my* room.'

She shivered at the ice coating his words.

'I guess you've read them then.' It wasn't a question.

'I've read enough.'

'I can explain – it was—'

'I don't want you to explain. I want you to get your things together and get out. You have half an hour – and I'm being generous. I could've just dumped your stuff on the front step, but I didn't want to upset the children any more than the death of their mother already has – a death you clearly had a hand in.'

She shot to her feet. 'No! I didn't—'

'Save it, Vicky. I don't want to hear anything you have to say. You know, I was actually going to pay you off today – give you money to get you out, away from us, maybe a deposit on a new place or something. But now... finding these...' He shuffled the box in front of her stricken face. 'I'll be taking them straight to the police as evidence, but I'm honouring Anna's memory and misplaced love for you by giving you a head start to clear out before I do.'

She reached out a hand. 'But let me—'

'NO!' He shoved her away from him and she fell back onto the couch, banging her shin hard on the coffee table.

They say you see a red mist when you feel extreme anger, but all David saw was clarity. He noticed a pimple on her forehead like a red beacon, the dark, wiry hair poking from her chin, the unplucked eyebrows and grey hairs showing along her parting. His fury had turned her into a fairy-tale witch clad in red Converses.

'What are you going to do? Hit me again? I'm sure the police would love to hear about that.' This time it was her voice that was glacial.

He glared at her, but said nothing.

She laughed bitterly. 'You're just like all the other men I've known, aren't you? And here I thought you were different. Is that what Anna found out too? That you're just like all the rest? Is that why she wanted to get away from you? She did, you know. She didn't love you any more. She thought you were weak and insignificant. She *tolerated* you. But you couldn't see that, could you? You couldn't see her for what she really was. I was the only one who knew Anna inside and out. And some of it was ugly, putrid, festering.'

He felt his fists tighten and knew he could listen to no more. 'The clock is ticking, Vicky. You'll want to be far away from here when I do call the police,' he said, his voice flat. He marched from the room, the shoebox tucked under his arm like a treasure chest.

Once back in the safety of his room, he leaned against the closed door, his heart banging in his chest and the dark smog over his eyes pulsating in time. His eyes fell on the picture on Anna's dressing table of Anna in her wedding dress and Vicky in her pale blue bridesmaid dress. Anna was smiling into the camera, but Vicky was looking over at

Anna, a wide smile on her face and her hand holding up a glass of champagne.

He could hear Vicky climb the stairs on the other side of the door, her steps heavy and the sobs plain to hear, but the photograph taunted him. What he had always thought was a look of adoration in Vicky's eyes now looked more like envy and resentment at a woman who was always more beautiful, more captivating and more successful than she would ever be. The smog thickened and curdled into a dense fog as he kept one ear on Vicky, hoping she was packing a bag. His hands were clenched into fists and his knees were locked as he stood rigid behind the door.

Her words catapulted around his head until he wanted to scream. He'd finally seen Vicky for what she was: a covetous snake of a woman, consumed with jealousy at what Anna had and she did not.

Was that why they fell out? Did Anna finally realise the underlying truth to their friendship?

Then he thought about Anna trapped in her car that night. Thoughts he'd stopped himself from exploring until now. Did she cry out? In pain? Terror? Did she feel herself being tossed and turned as the car rolled? Or was she blissfully unaware, knocked unconscious? Did she know it was Vicky, her pain coming more from her betrayed heart than any physical injuries? Did it break her heart in two?

He felt more than heard the knock on the bedroom door. 'David? Please, I should never have said what I did. Let me explain.' Vicky's voice was that of a repentant child.

'Get out, Vicky. Now! You're not welcome here,' he growled.

There was a pause before he heard the landing floorboards creak, followed shortly afterwards by the front door closing. He put the shoebox on the bed, then went over to the bedroom window and stared down at the driveway. Vicky stood looking back at the house, a bag in her hand. As she turned to walk away, she looked up and her eyes met his. He stared, unmoved, until she walked away, her red Converses dragging in the gravel.

He headed downstairs, sat on the edge of the couch and put the shoebox in front of him on the coffee table. He needed to read the rest of the letters. But for a moment he couldn't. He needed to fortify himself. He found he couldn't get past the address on the envelope without the vice around his heart tightening until he couldn't breathe.

He reached for his mobile what felt like a thousand times, but couldn't bring himself to call the police either. He kept going over the same thoughts again and again. Would the police do anything? Was the evidence too circumstantial? Did that mean that she'd get away with it? And then what? He would have to live with knowing she was out there, breathing, living, laughing, while Anna was gone. Her life carrying on while Anna's was snuffed out in the roll of a car and a last blink of her beautiful grey eyes?

His breath hitched, a dry sob wrenching from his tight throat. He staggered to his feet, grabbed an open bottle of whiskey from the bookcase and poured himself a large measure that he knocked straight back. Then he refilled the glass, the warmth of the alcohol giving him the strength he lacked. Before long, the bottle sat empty next to the shoebox.

No. He couldn't let her get away with this. And he certainly couldn't live with himself knowing what he now knew.

He rushed from the room, grabbed his keys from the hall table and slammed the front door behind him.

The rush hour air was stifling as the summer heatwave continued. People milled around him with arms, legs and torsos exposed in barely-there T-shirts and shorts, the Olympic emblem and Team GB logo everywhere he looked. Smiles grew wider with every gold, silver and bronze added to the medal table, with new sporting heroes being crowned every day. David stumbled along the street, avoiding mothers with pushchairs and suited men on their way home. The smell of freshly mown grass, barbecues and burning wood filled the air. People would look back on this summer as one of the best they'd known, the most joyful, the most fun. David just wanted it all to be over.

He walked onto a train on autopilot and sat in the seat tucked in the furthest corner of the carriage. Most people had filed off the train and it was cavernous as it headed back to Waterloo to pick up the next round of commuters as rush hour ratcheted up. He didn't really have a plan. He was letting fury, grief and pain push him on through a whiskey haze. He wanted closure. An end to it all.

He pulled his mobile from his pocket and called Vicky, every word catching on his lips with barbs. 'Vicky, we need to talk.'

'David.' He could hear the tears in her voice.

'I'll meet you somewhere – I'm on a train. I think I need to hear your side of the story before I do anything.'

The relief was palpable down the line. 'Oh, David, thank you. Where? Where should I meet you?'

He checked his watch, thought about all those commuter trips he had taken home at this time of the day. 'Clapham Station in half an hour. I'll be on Platform 3 at the foot of the stairs.'

'I'll be there. And I—'

He hung up, not wanting to hear any more, but wanting to get this done. He needed her to be there to see, to look in his eyes and realise what her actions had done. What it had cost them all.

David sat in silence for the rest of the journey, feeling the warmth of the whiskey slowly evaporate into the heat of the stifling train carriage. Snatches of conversation drifted over him from the fellow passengers filtering in and out of the carriage, discussing their plans for the weekend now that work was done, which tickets they had secured for the Olympics, plans for get-togethers as Super Saturday approached.

He sat unmoved, numb.

As his train pulled into Clapham, he got to his feet and woodenly threaded through the bodies onto the heaving platform as the crowds built around him. He looked over at the platform opposite, where people were pressed tightly together waiting for the next train out of Waterloo. He headed in that direction, his mind blank.

His feet tramped up the stairs, over the concourse and back down the other side on autopilot, his hands clenched by his sides and his breath sweet and sour with whiskey. He pushed through the crowd, ignoring the frowns and tuts until he neared the yellow line, but far enough away from the stairs to see if she was approaching. He looked up at the platform number, then reached for his mobile once more.

He waited. She was always on time, he'd give her that. While Anna was always fashionably late, you could set your watch by Vicky, so he knew she would be here any minute.

A train hooted and barrelled past the platform behind him and he could feel his body buffeted with the force of it as it sped straight through without stopping. He checked his watch.

He looked over at the stairs and saw Vicky bouncing down, her hair now pulled into a high ponytail, making her look youthful and less like the wicked witch of before. For a moment, he doubted himself. Her eyes scanned the crowd and fell on him. He raised his hands, as if in surrender. She paused, then continued her descent, her eyes stuck to him. He felt his feet shuffle forward over the yellow line just as the conductor announced that the next train at Platform 3 would not be stopping.

Vicky was now pushing through the bodies just as he had done moments before. He took another small step forward, feeling the surge from behind as the space was filled as soon as it was vacated. He kept his eyes trained on her head pushing through to him. Out of the corner of his eye he could just make out the headlights of the train approaching in the distance.

She came to stand at his side, her eyes reaching out to him, the pain in them laid bare. He felt no sympathy for her. Seeing her in front of him like this, wearing one of Anna's favourite T-shirts, he felt ice-cold fury rise up again. He put his arm around her, as though he was going to hug her, just as the train charged towards them. He leaned into her ear, whispered, 'It's all your fault,' then in one swift movement he stepped back and pushed her forward.

December 1989

The cigarette burn was freshly branded into her skin, stinging under the plaster as her arm moved against the scratchy wool of her school jumper. She sat in the furthest corner of the school playground, her back pushed against the cold brick wall and her knees pulled up to her chest.

Anna rounded the corner, munching on a bag of salt and vinegar crisps. 'There you are,' she said as she sat down beside her and offered her the bag.

'No thanks,' Vicky muttered.

'Wow, something must be up. You never turn down food, which explains that…' she prodded the roll of skin around Vicky's waistband. Vicky shoved her hand away and bit back tears.

'O-kay. You going to tell me what's wrong?'

Vicky looked away.

Anna grabbed her arm. 'Hey, what's—' but stopped as Vicky winced in pain. 'He been hitting you again?'

'Worse this time,' Vicky mumbled.

'Worse?'

'He… he put his cigarette out on me yesterday because I forgot to put a load of washing on before I went to school and he had no clean vests.' Her voice was transparent, the pain clear.

'Fuck. Bastard.'

'I can deal with that though. It's just…'

'What?'

Vicky shuffled uncomfortably, wouldn't look Anna in the face. 'He's been looking at me funny.'

'What do you mean?'

'Like when I'm in a towel and stuff, you know…. leering at me, a bit like his disgusting friend Brian does. And he's been touching me – not inappropriately, not yet anyway, but it feels like he's working up to it or something. Something's changed in the way he's treating me and I don't think I can…' She broke down in heaving sobs.

'Hey, hey,' Anna said and wrapped her arms around her. 'Have you spoken to your nan?' she said into Vicky's hair. It smelled stale, like she hadn't washed it for a while.

'And say what? I think my dad is working up to raping me? Besides, she's working all hours trying to make ends meet. She's hardly there in between working her shifts and now helping at the care home as well.'

Anna was quiet for a moment, letting Vicky sob and snot into her chest. When she'd cried herself out, she sniffed loudly and sat back.

'I've got an idea.' Anna had that look in her eye that was usually saved for when she was seeking to cause trouble. 'He takes pills for his back, doesn't he?'

'Yes, but what's that got to do with anything?'

'Okay, hear me out before you say anything. I was thinking about it the other day. All you have to do is crush some of his pills into one of the beers he keeps asking you to fetch him. He'll knock the pills back and there you have it… it'll look like suicide. Easy peasy.'

'What the fuck, Anna?' Vicky recoiled in horror.

'What? Would you rather carry on living with him and find yourself raped and beaten until you can afford to move out? He's an evil bastard and frankly you're going easy on him by not stabbing him or smothering him in his sleep!'

'Shhh, keep your voice down.' Vicky looked around nervously.

'Look, this way, you can always say he was depressed and took too many pills. No one would suspect his teenage daughter, would they? He's been taking too many pills and drinking too much for years. Even your nan can vouch for that.' Her voice was very matter of fact, as though she was discussing her plans for Friday night. Vicky was amazed at how coolly she could discuss what was essentially murder.

'I don't know. I don't think I could do that. He's my dad.'

Anna shrugged. 'Your call. But don't come crying to me when he rapes you.' Her eyes were like chips of ice and Vicky shivered.

The bell rang. Anna climbed to her feet and held out a hand to pull Vicky up. 'And if you decide to do it, I've got your back. Your secret is safe with me.' She smiled wickedly.

Vicky let herself into the quiet house after school, threw down her bag and headed straight into the kitchen. She'd had no lunch again because she had no money – or appetite after her conversation with Anna – but found herself suddenly ravenous now that she was home. She made herself a cheese sandwich and put the kettle on, then heard a noise from the front room, like a grunt.

She froze. It was too early for either her nan or dad to be home just yet.

But he was. She could tell by the heavy breathing and change in the air that he was there and he was not in a good mood.

'Victoria!' he bellowed from the hallway. 'That you?'

'Yes,' she called quietly.

'I thought I could smell something. Get your pretty little arse in here.'

She sighed, the cheese sandwich forgotten, and walked tentatively into the front room.

'The least you can do after waking me up is make me a cuppa, you selfish cow,' he growled.

'Okay,' she said and retreated from the room.

She stood staring out of the kitchen window as the kettle boiled, her mood insipid. She smelt him come up behind her before she heard him, the stale stench of nicotine, sweat and beer drifting over her shoulder. He stood behind her watching her with lifeless eyes, the cigarette dangling from his fingers.

'You're starting to look a lot more like your ma now. Got her shape these days,' he said, his voice low.

Vicky said nothing, busied herself with getting a cup down from the cupboard. She turned to open the fridge, but he was right behind her. He took a long drag of the cigarette and she watched the end burn hot and orange, remembering how it had felt when he had stubbed it out on her forearm the day before, the smell as her skin had seared and blistered.

'Excuse me,' she said quietly.

'I just paid you a compliment. I said you're looking like a woman these days. Hope you're not acting like one.' He narrowed his eyes at her. 'Not letting those boys get anywhere near ya, are ya?'

'No, Dad,' she replied without looking at him. 'I need to get the milk.'

He ignored her and said, 'You've got quite the body on you now, child-bearing hips like your mother. She had great hips and a cracking set of legs. That means the boys will be sniffing around ya. Am I right?'

She shuffled on her feet, trying to get around him.

He grabbed at her arm, near to where the cigarette burn was still fresh and raw. She yelped and he scowled. The cigarette perched on the end of his lip, the ash dangling precariously from the tip.

'You're soft though. Get that from your mother too. If she'd been tougher, she'd probably still be here now. You need to learn a few hard lessons to toughen you up too.' His eyes ran over her, then over her chest under her jumper, and Vicky felt sick to her stomach.

'Fuck off, Dad. She'd still be here now if she hadn't had to live with you,' she said under her breath.

'What did you say?' The ash fell from the tip like dust. He plucked the cigarette from his mouth and scowled at her through the smoke cloud.

Vicky had a moment to think, then said it again anyway, this time louder. 'I said fuck off.' She glared at him, but her pulse hopped as the colour rose in his cheeks.

He grabbed her arm and twisted it painfully, his grip tight. 'How dare you,' he growled. 'I guess the lesson I taught you last night didn't sink in.' He yanked up the sleeve of her jumper and pressed the searing cigarette into her skin next to the burn already there, then again, leaving two angry red welts next to the one scabbing over.

Vicky cried out in pain. He shoved her away from him, sending her sprawling on the floor, then followed with a short, sharp kick in the ribs. She pulled her knees up as he flicked the now extinguished cigarette butt at her and said, 'Remember your place, little girl. Now, get your daddy a beer.' He yanked her to her feet and pressed his face to hers. His tongue darted out and licked her cheek. She shuddered and pulled her face away.

He smiled at her viciously and stalked from the room.

She could feel herself hyperventilating as she scrubbed at the skin where he had licked her, revulsion crawling over her like maggots. Anna's voice burst into her head.

It'll look like suicide.

Easy peasy.

Her arm throbbed and pulsed with cold heat, but her head was pulsating with red hot loathing. She lurched over to the fridge, her sight blurred by the tears clinging onto her lashes. She swiped at them with the back of her hand and pulled open the fridge door. The bottles of beer rattled in answer.

She grabbed one and slammed the door shut. Pulling open the drawer for the bottle opener, her eyes fell on the packet of painkillers sitting on the counter next to the kettle. With Anna's voice in her head urging her on, she opened the packet, pulled out the sleeves and popped the remaining pills onto the counter. Using the back of a teaspoon, she ground them up into powder, all of her anger channelled into her fingers. The beer bottle fizzed as she popped the lid off. Her hands were steady as she swept the powder into the neck of the bottle and used the handle of the spoon to stir the beer gently before reaching for a glass and pouring the beer into it, leaving the perfect head on top.

She dropped the bottle into the sink and walked slowly into the front room, the glass clasped in her hand like a seasoned waitress.

Her dad was reclined in his usual position in the LazyBoy chair, his feet up and his belly spilling over his trousers as he watched afternoon gameshows on the television, the volume turned up loud.

'Took your time,' he growled as she handed him the glass. He looked at it, then at her. 'The glass is a nice touch though.' She stepped back and watched as he drained half of the glass in one go. Then she reversed from the room, her heart banging in her chest, barely breathing.

Once back in the kitchen, she rinsed out the beer bottle in hot water, shoved it to the bottom of the rubbish bin and wiped the powder residue from the counter and floor with a wet cloth and cleaning spray. The cloth was then stashed in the washing machine along with the load of towels already in there. She set the machine to the hottest setting and turned it on.

Then she sat at the kitchen table and waited, staring into space.

After half an hour, her legs were numb. The television still shouted loudly, adverts and voices jarring and insistent. She got to her feet robotically.

Slowly, she approached the front room, not sure what to expect. She peered around the doorframe, but could only see his belly in the chair, not his face. She stepped closer and noticed his belly wasn't rising and falling. Then she noticed the glass lying on the carpet on its side.

She took another step closer. His face was turned away towards the television. As she drew closer, she saw that his skin had turned waxy, like a burnt-out candle. His mouth was open and a foul-smelling froth dribbled from his pale lips onto his chin. She rushed from the room and straight to the kitchen sink where she threw up a similar, frothy bile.

Wiping her mouth, she skirted around the kitchen table and past the lounge door without looking at him. Reaching for the phone, she called Anna's home number.

'Hi, Mrs Maxwell, it's Vicky here,' she said in a high, reedy voice bordering on hysteria. 'Is Anna there?'

A moment later, she heard Anna say melodically, 'Hey girlfriend.'

'I did it.'

The line was quiet.

'Did you hear me? What we talked about? I did it.'

'I never thought you've had the balls. Okay.' Her voice dropped an octave and Vicky had to strain to hear her. 'Call an ambulance, act like you've just found him, don't mention my name. We never had that conversation.'

Vicky started to sob.

'Vicky! Pull yourself together. Do you hear me?'

'Yes,' Vicky blurted out.

'Now do it. We'll talk later.'

'You won't tell, will you?'

'Your secret is safe with me, Vix.'

The police responding to the 999 call found a terrified and grief-stricken 15-year-old girl who had found her father dead in his chair when she got home from school. An alcoholic prone to bouts of depression, the death was ruled a suicide from an overdose of painkillers. There was no need to interview the girl for any longer than necessary, so clear was her distress at her discovery.

And there was no reason to suspect foul play.

Dear Anna,

It's all over. David found my letters and now thinks he knows everything.

I can't bear it.

He thinks I was jealous of you. I guess in a way he's right. I always wanted to be you, to have what you had. I spent so long when we were friends watching you, trying to imitate you, desperate to be like you, but I always fell short. Not pretty enough; not thin enough; not classy enough.

Then I started to realise that even with everything falling in your lap, you still weren't happy. I never understood why. If I had what you had, I'd be on top of the world. I'd do everything I could to keep hold of it all. You didn't see it that way.

You liked control most of all. I see that now. When we were young, you controlled everyone around you – me, your parents, especially your mum. And yet you detested her for how easy she bent to your will. Your dad too for a bit, but soon his wandering eye meant you didn't have as much power over him any more, so you stifled your relationship with him.

I like to think I was harder to control. I had moments when I fought back, but that made it more of a game for you. Ultimately, everything we did was choreographed by you in some way.

Even that night with Dan. Even on your wedding day when you told me it was your idea that he meet up with me. Of course, how were you to know that him and his friends would turn out to be rapists? I never told you the truth about that night, how I lost the hummingbird necklace. For a while I thought that if you hadn't gone away to uni, it would never have happened and I suppose part of me always hated you for that. Everything was different when you got back. You had David; I had another trauma to add to my list of damages.

But the truth is everything changed when I took your advice and killed my father.

I was never the same after that. I know your intentions were good. You could see where it was heading and you were protecting me, but with the usual Anna slant on it. You with the conductor's baton in your hand, flicking it this way and that until I did your bidding once more. And afterwards, there was no turning back. You had something concrete to hold over me, to dangle in front of my eyes if I ever got too big for my boots.

I've finally said it.

I killed my dad.

I gave him the pills, crushed them into his beer, all of them. And you were my willing accomplice. Hell, you *were the mastermind. The only other person who knew what I did.*

It actually feels liberating seeing those words written down.

So here I am. Alone again.

I can hear you telling me to stop being melodramatic, but it's true.

And now I have nothing to live for. David is probably calling the police as we speak and I don't think I can live with everyone thinking I killed you because I was jealous.

I guess our story has come to an end.

David will be okay. Harper and Lewis will be okay.

I was never okay.

I love you, Anna.

Vix xx

13

David sat in the early morning light that filtered weakly into the lounge. Dust particles danced in the rays cutting through the blinds. Little particles of people, both living and dead. How many of these particles were tiny specks of Anna still swirling around them, kissing them lightly before drifting away?

He heard the dull thud of the post hitting the doormat, but stayed where he was for a moment longer, the cup of coffee in his hands forming a skin on the surface as it cooled.

He knew he had to get up, call his mother, maybe even shower. He needed to pull himself together for when the police came knocking. And they would.

After he had seen Vicky tumble off the platform in front of the hurtling train, all pinwheeling arms and legs, he'd begun to shout.

'Help! Help! She's fallen! Somebody help her!'

He was certainly convincing. The trauma of the day had caught up with him and he couldn't stop himself from sobbing and wailing. Anyone looking at him would think it was shock, but he knew it as more than that. Relief, guilt, grief. He had given a statement to the police yesterday, saying she had stumbled and tripped in the rush-hour crowd, and the police had let him go since his monosyllabic responses suggested a man in deep shock, especially so soon after the death of his wife. Besides, the platform was so busy that it was likely to be ruled either an unfortunate accident or suicide. He hoped it wouldn't come back on him. For Harper and Lewis's sake, not because he was sorry for what he'd done.

But if the police went through the CCTV and noticed him leaning in and whispering in her ear before she fell, then he supposed he could blame it on a temporary moment of madness. Overwhelming grief for his wife. If he was sent down for it, then Harper and Lewis would be fine with his mother. There was almost a tangible relief at the thought that he wouldn't be held responsible for them any more. His mother would do a better job anyway. He'd turned out alright, hadn't he?

The irony made him laugh out loud into the empty room, the sound hanging in the air like a profanity.

He got to his feet, the effort to do so enervating. As he passed the front door on his way upstairs, the letter lying on the doormat seemed to scream out at him, demanding his attention.

It was Vicky's handwriting, addressed to him, but clearly hurriedly, the writing messy.

He looked at it like it was a grenade with the pin missing. His hands shook as he picked it up.

David,

You will have called the police by now. I expect them to turn up at any moment. I'm writing this from a bus stop. I can just see your house – my house for a while – in the distance. I have nowhere to go and one eye on the road, watching for the blue lights of the police cars. But before they find me, you deserve the truth.

All of it.

You think you know what happened, but you don't.

You never knew Anna like I did. I tried to tell you that. What she was capable of, how she liked to toy with all of us. She commanded everyone around her and the truth is I had grown tired of it. I couldn't watch her hurt you and the kids any more. As much as I loved her, I also hated her for how she was treating you.

I do believe she loved all of us in her own way, but that love was toxic.

I won't come back to the house again. I have one stamp in my purse and I've written one last letter to Anna, enclosed, and then there will be no more. Our story has ended. But I need you to know the truth about that night. You can choose what to do with it.

It started with her asking me to cover for her while she began an affair with her boss last year. I expected it to fizzle out quickly, like all the other affairs she'd had.

Yes, she'd had a few. Mostly one-night stands in bars or the odd snog with a married man (she thought of it as a public service, sending them back to their wives with a smile on their face); nothing of substance.

But this one lingered on. I guess because they were two peas in a pod. They both loved the dance involved *in manipulating people, the thrill of power, the buzz of doing something illicit.*

I begged her to tell you, to come clean because it wasn't fair on you and the kids, but she said that it added spice to your marriage, that without it she would be miserable and would take it out on you anyway. So I let it go on and I hated myself for it.

Then I met Sebastian's wife one day...

When David had finished reading both letters, he carried them over to the wood-burning stove, picked up a book of matches and watched them curl and burn until they scorched his fingers and crumpled into ash.

6 May 2012

'He's so sweet, treats me like a princess.'

'David treats you like a princess.'

Anna stuck out her bottom lip. 'He used to. Now it's all about the kids and work. He falls asleep in front of the television most nights. And when he's awake, we're arguing because he thinks I should be doing fewer hours at work. Do I look like a housewife? A stay at home mother? At the moment, work is where I'm happiest. They get me, you know?'

Vicky resisted the urge to roll her eyes.

'Anyway, the other night Sebastian took me to a really fancy place in Kensington. Champagne, good food, it was so romantic.'

'What did you tell David?'

'That I had a work function.' She shrugged, avoided Vicky's narrowed eyes.

Vicky put her wine glass down on the coffee table long enough to reach for the bag of crisps open in front of them.

'You shouldn't eat so many of those, Vix. You look like you've put on a bit lately.'

Vicky paused, one hand hovering in front of her mouth, crisp crumbs falling onto her sweatshirt.

'Thanks a lot, Anna.'

She shrugged again. 'Just being honest. That's what friends are for, right?' She sipped at her own wine and looked around her at Vicky's tiny lounge. 'You know, if you came and worked at the agency with me, you'd be able to afford a better place in no time. Somewhere that smells less… exotic.' She wrinkled her nose in disgust.

'You're just pissed off because you know I don't like you carrying on with Sebastian. Say all you like, but it's not fair on David.'

'For fuck's sake, Vix, *you* should marry David if you think it's so exciting.' She launched to her feet and paced towards the window overlooking the busy street below. 'It's so dull! Laundry, cooking, spelling homework, driving to endless ballet lessons and football matches.' She spun around to face Vicky. 'He enjoys it, but me? I can feel the life draining out of me, Vix! It's boring.'

She sounded like the Anna of old, the one who would suggest nicking something from a shop because it was exciting; the one who would play tricks on kids in their class just to get a rise out of them; the one who threw a word grenade, just to see the fallout when it exploded. Vicky had learned to dance around that girl, thankful that she often wasn't the victim in her crosshairs, riding it out and not reacting if she was.

'Besides, you didn't even like David when you first met him. Why are you his biggest fan all of a sudden?' Anna carried on.

'It's not all of a sudden. We've spent more time together while you've been off flirting or whatever with Sebastian. We actually have a lot in common. And I think he misses spending time with you. He's good for you and he adores you. Your kids are amazing too.'

'I know, right? Not sure how I got that right, to be honest.'

Vicky suspected that was more to do with David and the really good au pair they had hired rather than anything Anna had done. Anna hardly saw Harper and Lewis these days, now that her extracurricular timetable was taken up with Sebastian.

'Something else is going on here though.' Anna's eyes were thin lines of suspicion. 'You're not usually this… vocal.'

'It's nothing.' Vicky knew she sounded like a sulky teenager as she said it, but Anna had always brought this side out in her.

Anna sat down next to her again and stared at her hard. 'Don't give me that shit. I've known you long enough to know when you need to say something, so spit it out.' Her voice dripped venom.

Vicky looked into her glass and said quietly, 'I bumped into Sebastian's wife the other day. She was with their son.'

'So?'

'Did you know he's disabled? Their son? In a wheelchair?'

Anna looked away, her fingers fiddling with the cushion next to her. 'Yeah, so?'

Vicky shook her head. 'He's in a wheelchair, Anna! You told me she spends all her time looking after her kid, but you left that little nugget of information out! I saw her coming out of the chemist and I held the door open for her. She recognised me from that dinner you dragged me to last year when David was ill, remember? I was amazed she remembered me actually, but that night we spent a lot of it talking while you were on the dancefloor with Sebastian, grinding up against him. Anyway, she was so polite and chatted away to me in the street like I was an old friend, but all I could see was this little boy in the wheelchair, her leaning over him and wiping the spit from his chin while she talked, the bags under her eyes from tiredness, and I felt sick. She was going on about how busy Sebastian is at work and how he wasn't making it home much these days and how Luke – their son's name is Luke; did you know that? – how he comes alive when Sebastian is there. Where were you two that night? Some hotel room somewhere?' Vicky could hear the repulsion dripping off the end of the question.

'So what if we were? Why is she my problem? She doesn't work, stays at home with him all day, and when Seb gets home, she has a go at him because she's tired or whatever. She could get a nanny in or something…'

'For fuck's sake, Anna! Do you not hear yourself sometimes? This is a woman who is caring for her disabled son and her husband is screwing you instead of going home to help her. How do you not see how twisted that is? You have no concept of other people's feelings. You're a narcissist, Anna, blind to the damage you leave behind, the hurt you cause with a flutter of your eyelashes.'

'Oh, get off your high horse, Vix. You're just lonely and jealous,' Anna spat.

'No, I am miles away from jealous of you right now. I've turned a blind eye every other time, but this is too much.

It's gone on too long. David deserves better and so does Rachel. I have a good mind to tell them both what's really going on.'

'Oh, it's Rachel now, is it? Well, if you're so worried about her, find her so lovely to be around, then fuck off and be her friend then.' Now it was Anna who sounded like a petulant child. 'But just remember everything we've gone through—'

'Don't you dare bring up my dad again!' Vicky was surprised at the volume in her voice. The words rebounded off the narrow walls like an echo. 'I am sick of you holding that over me.'

Anna raised her eyebrows in surprise. 'You still shouldn't push me.'

'Do you know what? Tell the police! I don't care any more!' She got to her feet and stood, towering over Anna, her hands on her hips. 'I should've owned up to it back then because I've punished myself far worse than the police would have ever since. So do your worst, Anna! But you won't, will you? Because it was your idea. You're as much to blame as me.'

Anna got to her feet too. They stood eye to eye, the anger and hostility like a toxic bubble, years of resentment bubbling like lava from a reawakening volcano.

'It's my word against yours – and who would they believe? A smart, successful, married mother of two or a broke, lonely, fat chav like you?'

The slap cut through the toxic air. Vicky felt the sting on her palm and saw Anna's cheek redden instantly.

Anna put her hand up to her cheek and took a step back. Her voice was a low growl. 'You'll regret that.'

Then she grabbed her handbag and stalked from the flat, slamming the door hard behind her.

Vicky fell to her knees as sobs wrenched from her chest.

This was it. This was how it all ended.

You didn't take on Anna without paying the price. Vicky has seen enough evidence of that over the years. The likely outcome was that Anna would call the police just to be spiteful. She'd say that Vicky had confessed and that Anna couldn't live with the knowledge. She would come out squeaky clean and Vicky would finally face the punishment she'd been waiting for all these years.

With that thought came a bizarre feeling of relief though. A sense that she could finally be free – of her dad and Anna. She looked down at the hummingbird on her ankle and found she wasn't as scared as she thought she'd be.

She felt liberated instead.

Anna sat in her VW Beetle, the engine idling loudly. How dare Vicky confront her like that? They were supposed to be best friends, but Vicky had just stabbed her in the back.

After everything Anna had done for her.

Well, she would get what was coming to her.

Anna reached for her mobile and dialled 99… then stopped as her brain ticked over and a new plan began to emerge through the angry mist.

Calling the police was futile. They'd never act on something as circumstantial as this and there would be no evidence after all these years anyway.

No. She'd always enjoyed revenge more than justice. There was a better way. Let Vicky think she had called the police. She would torture herself without Anna having to lift a finger.

That'd teach her to mess with her.

How dare she blame Anna for the shit show she'd made of her own life? Let her spend a few days worrying about whether she'd been exposed. Before long, she'd come crawling back to Anna, begging forgiveness.

She pulled away from the kerb, feeling calmer, a smile teasing her lips.

13 May 2012 – 4 p.m.

Vicky was exhausted. She had picked up her phone what felt like a hundred times to call Anna to apologise, talk to her, put the argument behind them, but every time she'd tried, her fingers had refused to press the relevant buttons. It was like her body was telling her to stick to her guns, not let her win this time.

Instead, she'd gone to work on automatic, one eye on the door expecting it to be thrown open by the police. And every night she trudged home, relief at having survived another day but fearful of what the next twenty-four hours would bring. Once she'd even gone to the local police station in her lunch hour, ready to confess and put herself out of her misery. She'd stood on the steps, paralysed, until a policeman had come and asked her if she was okay. She'd walked away.

She had a headache. She scanned the shelves in the Boots chemist for painkillers. Something stronger than a paracetamol was necessary today, especially since she had decided to go over to Anna's house later and talk to her in person. She'd called in sick to work that morning, but had found that sitting in her claustrophobic flat was making her twitchy and threatened to push the headache into a migraine, so she'd driven into town with the thought of getting something for Anna to sweeten her up with later. If anything would lift Anna from a bad mood, it was a present.

She stepped back, away from the shelves that were blurring in front of her, and her leg collided with something. She turned and saw she'd kicked the tyre of a wheelchair.

Her breath caught as she recognised the child and then the woman standing behind her, reading the fine print on some flu medication. 'Rachel!'

'Vicky! Hi! We're making a habit of this! Actually, I've been meaning to call you ever since we swapped numbers last week, but poor Luke hasn't been well.'

Vicky smiled uncomfortably. This was the last person she wanted to see today.

'I'm sorry to hear that. What's wrong?'

'Oh, he has a nasty cold and it's keeping him awake, so it's keeping me awake.' She rattled the medication in her hand. 'I'm just trying to find something to give him. What about you? You look tired, are you okay?'

'Long week, migraine…' she shrugged.

'You work too hard. You should try and look after yourself more. I was saying the same thing to Sebastian this morning. He was talking about how he wouldn't be home again tonight and I just said to him that he would put himself into an early grave with all the hours he's putting in lately. It must be the same for Anna – they're working on a project together apparently.'

'Well, if that's what you want to call it.' The words had fallen out of her mouth without warning. Vicky clamped her teeth together to stop herself from saying anything else.

'Sorry?'

'No, nothing,' Vicky said. 'Well, I'll let you get on.'

'Wait, no, what did you mean?'

'I didn't mean anything, really. I'm just not feeling well and rambling. I'd better go. Hope Luke is better soon.'

Vicky fled from the shop before she could dig the hole even bigger, but she knew she'd said too much. That was clear from the look of realisation that had fallen over Rachel's face like a veil.

13 May 2012 – 7 p.m.

Vicky's mobile vibrated loudly across her bedside table, pulling her insistently from a deep sleep. She'd rushed home and flung herself onto her bed. Lying on her back, she'd looked around her at the only room in the flat that she'd ever decorated properly. For the first time in her life, she had a very feminine, beautiful bedroom, complete with rosebud wallpaper, a white, heart-shaped dressing table and scented candles. To an untrained eye, it was just a beautiful, calm space, but Vicky knew that she had styled it on Anna's bedroom from when they were children, with similar wallpaper, candles that smelled like the hallways and bathrooms of Mrs Maxwell's house, and the dressing table that bore a striking resemblance to Anna's that Vicky had found in a charity shop.

Anna had never commented on the décor, but Vicky knew she recognised the similarities. One more reason for Anna to find Vicky pathetic and needy.

She'd knocked back a couple of the painkillers she'd picked up in Boots and fell into a dreamless sleep.

That sleep was clinging to her now as she reached for her mobile. The number was withheld and her stomach clenched. Was this the call from the police she'd been waiting all week to receive?

She rubbed the sleep from her eyes, pulled herself to sitting and answered the call.

'Hello?'

'Vicky?'

The voice was at once recognisable and unknown, like song lyrics that were difficult to place.

'Yes? Who is this?'

'It's Rachel. I wanted you to know I understand what you were trying to tell me earlier.'

'I don't understand.'

'You wanted me to know – about them – but you couldn't tell me because she's your best friend. But I heard you. When I got home, I did a bit of searching around and I know what's been going on. I found her earring on the bedroom carpet. It must be hers – I don't have any earrings in the shape of hummingbirds.' A sob was audible down the line, followed by the loud blow of a nose. 'Just tell me one thing: how long has it been going on?'

'I'm sorry, Rachel, I don't know what you're talking about.' Vicky bit her lip, then peeled the skin back, feeling the sting as her teeth cut into the flesh.

'Please, just tell me how long. I have to know. I feel like such a fool. I feel like everyone knows but me.'

'Rachel, you're not a fool.'

'Oh, I am.' Her voice was layered with anguish. 'I trusted him. I thought he was building a future for us. For Luke.' At the mention of her son's name, her voice caught and Vicky could hear the tears soaking down the line. 'But he was playing me for a fool, using me as a nursemaid for Luke instead of respecting me as his wife.'

Vicky remained silent. She didn't know what to say.

'I'm going over there now – to her house. I know where she lives. I need to tell her husband.'

'No, don't do that, Rachel. Please.'

'Why not? He deserves to know too. He shouldn't be the last to find out.'

'And what good will that do? It will just ruin his life and their kids.'

'So? She's done that to us without thinking about how we will be broken by this! She deserves to lose everything.'

Vicky heard a click as Rachel hung up the phone. She called her straight back, but it went to voicemail.

Vicky launched to her feet, threw on her Converses and grabbed her car keys and handbag on her way out. If she went to Anna's house, she might get there before Rachel and persuade her not to tell David. Perhaps she could even convince Anna to tell him herself.

As she ran down the stairs to her car, she pulled out her mobile and called Anna for the first time in a week.

13 May 2012 – 7.35 p.m.

Anna's phone rang loudly as she turned off her computer at work. She was in a bad mood. Sebastian was supposed to have taken her for dinner tonight, but he'd given her a pile of work to do instead and buggered off with Bonny, the new receptionist.

What the fuck was that about?

She'd been watching him all week as he chatted to her. A blonde, petite, curvy girl half his age and with very few brain cells to rub together from what Anna could tell. Anna's toes had curled every time she'd heard her giggle at whatever he was saying as they stood over the photocopier.

She suspected his attention had wandered and she either had to work harder to get it back or needed to cut him loose. He was getting boring anyway and she was putting on weight with all the dinners he was forcing her to eat.

She looked at the screen on her phone. Vicky.

She ignored the call with a scowl. There was another one who had betrayed her lately. What was wrong with everyone?

Her stomach rumbled. She hadn't eaten all of her lunch because she had thought she would be going out with Sebastian. A half-eaten salmon and cream cheese sandwich sat on her desk from earlier. She pulled it towards her, then let an idea formulate.

Her trademark wicked smile crept across her lips.

She grabbed the sandwich and wandered through the empty desk partitions towards Sebastian's office at the back of the open-plan room. There was no one around, the threat of a tube strike making everyone rush out on time today. Anna had stayed behind, resenting the pile of last-minute tasks Sebastian had tossed at her.

His office door was open and unlocked. It was only ever closed for 'meetings' – often code for something else with him.

In the corner of the office sat a pile of brochures, manuals and flyers ready to be packed up and distributed at the gala presentation they had been planning for their most important client. The event was in two days' time and was part of the build-up to the Olympics – an evening celebrating past and present sporting stars and their achievements. Anna had fully expected to attend the event with Sebastian as they were not allowed to bring their own partners because of spatial limitations, but Sebastian had gone and invited Bonny to attend with him, apparently so she could see how these events worked so that she could perhaps start working on similar projects in the future.

Anna knew what he was really up to. That was how it started with him. Encouraging you in your work, taking you under his wing to mentor you, a bit of flattery about your proactive enthusiasm and then, before you knew it, he had you bent over his desk giving you a rise of sorts.

Okay, so she had wanted it as much as he had, but still. He was a twat.

She opened the packet containing the sandwich and peeled apart the two slices of bread to reveal the coral salmon inside. Then, with care and precision, she began to wipe the salmon and cheese filling in between the pages of the brochures and flyers, smearing the oily fish on as many pages as she could before shuffling them back into neat piles, as though nothing untoward had occurred.

She looked around the room, saw one of his ties hanging from the hook behind his office door and used it to wipe the fishy grease from her hands before hanging it back in its place.

She smiled to herself, took a step towards the door, then backtracked to his desk and pulled open the bottom drawer, which was full of papers, company cheque books, business cards and his appointments diary. Turning her back to it, she lifted her skirt and squatted over the open drawer. She wasn't wearing any underwear. She often didn't these days. He liked to know she was sitting at her desk at work like that. Thinking about it now, she couldn't believe how compliant of his weird requests she had been.

Another lesson learnt.

With a small sigh and a smile, she peed into the drawer, the acrid smell of urine filling the room as it splashed and trickled over the papers. Then, with a shake of her hips, she pulled her skirt back down to her knees and kicked the drawer shut with her stiletto heel.

Back at her own desk, she picked up her phone and saw another three missed calls from Vicky. This was the kind of thing she would normally tell Vicky. She felt a pang at that.

As she grabbed her bag and made a hasty retreat, she dialled Vicky's number. It went to voicemail.

'Hey Vix, it's me. Listen, you'll never guess what I just did. You'll kill yourself when you hear. Oh, I haven't called the police by the way. Anyway, call me.'

13 May 2012 – 7.55 p.m.

Vicky knew she had to try and stop Rachel, especially since Anna wasn't answering her calls, and now her mobile battery was flat. She drove over to Anna's house as fast as the lashing rain would allow. Her mind was gripped in turmoil – anger at Anna at putting her in this position; sympathy for Rachel as she tried to hold onto her crumbling marriage; fear at what Anna would do if she found out Vicky had inadvertently tipped Rachel off.

She pulled up at the traffic lights and sat patiently waiting, her fingers tapping on the steering wheel of her VW Polo. A dark-coloured 4x4 stood waiting in the lane next to her and she looked over at the driver, then felt her heart flip over.

It was Rachel.

She started shouting through the glass, but knew Rachel would never hear her through the rain. She pressed the button to lower the passenger window and was greeted with cold spray and wind that caught her voice and carried it away. The lights changed and Rachel pulled ahead. Vicky wound the window back up as the car behind her hooted impatiently. She pulled away with a lurch of the accelerator, then indicated and pulled in behind Rachel.

She flashed her lights and hooted, but Rachel accelerated away in her far more powerful car. Vicky pushed hard on the accelerator to catch up with Rachel and stuck to her bumper as she turned left off the main road and began to meander into the darker, more rural and wooded area beyond. Vicky knew it wasn't far from here to Anna's house and that she had very little time to catch Rachel's attention.

She began to lean on the horn and flashed her lights repeatedly and was relieved to see Rachel finally indicate and pull over a few streets away from Anna's house. Vicky pulled up behind her and climbed out of the car.

She ignored the rain lashing her face as she rushed over to the car.

Rachel looked out of the driver's window, confusion all over her face, then irritation as she recognised Vicky through the glass.

The window lowered slowly.

'Rachel!'

'What are you doing here, Vicky?'

Vicky could see she was crying.

'I just want to talk to you. This isn't how this should be handled. David doesn't deserve this.'

'And I do?'

'That's not what I'm saying.' The rain was pouring down her face, soaking her hair and running down the collar of her shirt. 'I just think…' Now that she was standing in front of Rachel, she didn't know what to say to her. 'Let me speak to David instead. Or to Anna – get her to tell him. I just think if it comes from you, it will break him.'

'Break him?' she shrieked. 'What do you think that bitch has done to me? To Luke?'

Vicky jumped back as Rachel threw open her car door and climbed out. Vicky had a moment to notice she was wearing house slippers.

'Do you know what it's like to find out that the man you put your trust in has been using you, lying to you? Do you know what it feels like to be used and tossed aside?'

Vicky thought back to that night all those years ago, to the feeling of horror and shock when her body was used against her will, to the self-hatred, repulsion and shame that had stayed with her ever since, to how she had let countless men do the same thing to her over and over ever since. 'Yes, I think I have an idea of what you are feeling. But that's not David's fault. He is as innocent in all this as you are. Imagine if it was David standing on your doorstep telling you that your husband was sleeping with his wife. Do you really want to be the one to deliver that message?'

Rachel looked away into the night. A car was approaching over Vicky's shoulder and the bright headlights illuminated the anguish on Rachel's rain and tear-soaked face.

'Let me speak to Anna. I'll get her to call off the affair and speak to David herself. You should go home and speak to Sebastian. He's the one you should be confronting.'

All the energy seemed to seep from Rachel's body in that moment and she sagged into herself. 'You're right. This is his doing as much as hers.' She looked up at Vicky again as another car headed towards them, the engine loud and rattling in the night. 'But promise me you'll speak to her. Promise me you can get her to end it.'

'I promise,' Vicky replied and grasped Rachel in a tight hug. They pulled apart as the car sped past, splashing them in the process. 'Now go home. You're soaked. And Luke really does not need you getting sick too.'

She stood for a moment and watched Rachel get into her car and drive away, before climbing into her own. She sat for a moment, relieved. She'd averted a disaster for now, but she was soaked, her teeth chattering with the cold.

Instead of carrying on to Anna's house, she decided to turn her car around and head home. She could speak to Anna later, when emotions weren't running so high. Plenty of time for that conversation.

13 May 2012 – 7.55 p.m.

It was dark, the rain hitting the windscreen vertically as Anna wound her way home. Once she was free of the city traffic and out into the emptier suburban roads, the way ahead was relatively clear and she pushed the Beetle hard. The streetlights began to peter out as she followed her route home through the back of Esher, the roads wooded and darker here. The car was quiet, just the rumble of the engine to keep her company as she thought back to her argument with Vicky. How had they got here?

She desperately wanted to tell her what she had done to Sebastian's office. Vix would find it hilarious. It was just the thing to get them over their argument. They'd never fallen out like this before and, although Vicky deserved what she got, Anna missed her, like a gaping wound that wouldn't heal.

There had been so much hatred in Vicky's eyes though. So much anger and resentment. Anna felt a physical lurch in her chest. Then she thought about the four missed calls after hearing nothing from Vicky for a week.

Shit. Had she done what she'd threatened and told David?

No, David would've called her or something by now.

The thought had just left her mind when she heard her mobile ring in her handbag. She leaned over, one eye still on the wet, inky night beyond the windscreen, and pulled her phone from her bag on the passenger seat.

David. Shit.

She moved her fingers to accept the call, but lost her grip on the handset and it fell into the footwell of the car. With one hand still on the steering wheel and half an eye on the road, she reached down to unclip her seatbelt, then leaned into the footwell, feeling around with her fingertips. She couldn't reach the phone and was about to lean even further when she saw a flash of brown and two beady eyes next to the road and sat up quickly. The fox disappeared into the night, but it had brought Anna's eyes back to the road and the lashing rain outside just as the road peeled sharply to the left. She flicked on her full beams.

She was close to home now. Only a few more dark and winding streets to go. She'd speak to David when she got home rather than risk life and limb now.

She could see the flicker of headlights coming towards her. She forced herself to lay off the accelerator a little as she approached the bend. Once around the corner, the road straightened out again. The approaching vehicle had its full beams on too. Anna flicked the lever on the side of the steering wheel to cut her headlights and expected the approaching car to do the same. It was travelling much faster than she was, not surprising considering the state of the Beetle's ageing engine.

The approaching car barrelled towards her and then shot past, the air buffeting the suspension of the Beetle as it did and causing a splurge of water to splash up onto the windscreen. As the wipers did their best to clear the sudden deluge and Anna began to breathe easier now that the car had passed, she caught a flash of something... someone standing on the other side of the road in the distance. She flicked on her high beams again and peered through the windscreen. It was two people, not one, standing in the pouring rain beside their cars.

Vicky and Rachel.

But what were they doing there? Together?

They hugged each other tightly as Anna's car careered past, anger seething through her as her foot pressed down instinctively on the accelerator.

What the fuck, Vicky?

She looked in her rearview mirror and saw them pull apart, then head off to their cars. Anna twisted in her seat to see if she could make out in which direction they were going – were they going to her house to speak to David together?

She couldn't quite see and twisted around further, yanking on the steering wheel in the process. The rear wheels responded and the car hurtled towards the ditch running along the edge of the tarmac. Panic gripped her. She pulled the steering wheel in the opposite direction and felt the tyres skid, losing traction and grip in the rain.

The left rear wheel of the car dropped into the ditch and the Beetle was thrust into a spin. As if a bystander, she felt her body, free of the restraint of the seatbelt, being buffeted from side to side as the car rolled and flipped. Her last thought as she was flung around like a ragdoll, the seatbelt flapping loose, was of Vicky.

Then the darkness from outside filled her head as the car battery was propelled from the back of the car into her skull.

Dear Anna,

This will be my last letter to you.

It's all over. I won't see David and the kids again. By this time tomorrow, I'll hopefully probably be far away from here. I've packed a bag and found my passport, and I'm going away.

I don't know where. We used to laugh about running away to Mexico, fugitives like Thelma and Louise. You were Thelma. Well, there's only Louise left, but I'm running away anyway.

I can't be here any more, surrounded by memories of you. David, Lewis and Harper deserve space to get on with their lives and I need to build a life of my own. Besides, he doesn't want me. He wants you.

So I'm going to cash in my savings and book a flight to somewhere, anywhere. See where life takes me. I've got nothing keeping me here any more.

I deserve it. After all these years of trying to live a half-life in your shadow, I deserve a shot at a life of my own.

There is one thing I want to admit to you before I go. That night with Dan, when you asked him to show me a good time, I was gang raped by him and his friend. There, I've said it.

I'm looking at the words on the page now and I feel… lighter.

I've tried so hard to blame you for it all this time, but the fact is that it was their fault and no one else's. They chose to use me like that and they will have had to live with it. I can't imagine they've lost too much sleep over it, but I have. And now I need to try and move on, heal myself, start living the kind of life I deserve to have.

I have my whole life left ahead of me – something that you don't have. And I want to live it. The one thing you never did was travel. It was as though the idea scared you because there was too much out there in the big, wide world that you wouldn't be able to control.

Well, I'll see it all for the both of us.

I love you. Despite everything, you were – and still are – my whole world. My family, my sister, my soulmate.

And I miss you.

It feels like someone has stolen the air I breathe every day, so that I'm slowly suffocating.

Maybe I'll be able to breathe again if I go away from here.

Then maybe one day I won't have to remind myself to breathe in and out.

You and me. Always and forever.

Vicky and Anna. xx

14

'Hurry up, kids. We need to get going!' David shouted up the stairs. 'Granny will be waiting for us and I'm starving. I want some of her famous Yorkshire puddings!'

He headed back into the lounge and grabbed his keys and wallet from the coffee table. He plumped a cushion, straightened a magazine, looked around him with satisfaction at the neat and orderly room. His reflection in the mirror above the fireplace caught his attention and he smoothed a stray hair away from his forehead.

He looked and felt better than he had in a long time. He'd been sleeping better – and without the need for whiskey – and he was starting to get on top of his life, putting a routine in place, getting himself organised and spending more time with his mother, who was happy to help.

His eyes fell on the picture on the mantelpiece of Anna in her wedding dress. The photograph was smaller than the original; David had cut it so that Vicky wasn't visible over her shoulder.

He looked away quickly and went to grab his mobile phone from the table. As he picked it up, the doorbell rang.

Sighing, he went to open it.

Standing on the front step, an expensive looking handbag in her hand and big sunglasses on her face, was a woman David didn't recognise. A big, dark red 4x4 was parked in the driveway behind his own car.

'Hi, can I help you?'

'David, I heard about Vicky's death. My name is Rachel Woods. We need to talk.'

ACKNOWLEDGEMENTS

I had a lot of fun writing this one and, as with all of the characters I have created, Anna and Vicky are close to my heart. They are flawed, but then aren't we all? While I explored their world and their relationship, I remembered all the friends who have come and gone in my own life. Some have been with me since childhood and others have only recently impacted my life, but it has been a life made richer because of the friendships I have formed over the years.

Thank you to all of my friends who have had my back on this journey.

To those who make me laugh and lend me their ears on dog walks and Friday nights over a glass or two.

To those who are far away and I only see once in a while, but it only takes a minute in each other's company before we are giggling like schoolkids again.

To those who are on the end of an email when I doubt myself and my writing abilities, ready with encouragement and support to keep me moving forward.

To those behind the scenes of the publishing world who champion my books and make me a better writer.

And to those who love me unconditionally and believe in me, even though I show them the best and worst of me on a daily basis.

Thank you. x

About the Author

Dawn's career has spanned PR, advertising and publishing. Now, she loves to write about the personalities hiding behind the masks, whether beautiful or ugly. Married, she lives in London with her two daughters and a British bulldog called Geoffrey.

Hello from Aria

We hope you enjoyed this book! Let us know, we'd love to hear from you.

We are Aria, a dynamic digital-first fiction imprint from award-winning independent publishers Head of Zeus. At heart, we're avid readers committed to publishing exactly the kind of books we love to read – from romance and sagas to crime, thrillers and historical adventures. Visit us online and discover a community of like-minded fiction fans!

We're also on the look out for tomorrow's superstar authors. So, if you're a budding writer looking for a publisher, we'd love to hear from you. You can submit your book online at ariafiction.com/we-want-read-your-book

You can find us at:
Email: aria@headofzeus.com
Website: www.ariafiction.com
Submissions: www.ariafiction.com/we-want-read-your-book
Facebook: @ariafiction
Twitter: @Aria_Fiction
Instagram: @ariafiction